OUR VICIOUS HEARTS

ARCHIVE OF FATE: BOOK 1

WHITNEY L. SPRADLING

Midnight Tide
PUBLISHING

Content Warning

This book contains adult themes that may not be appropriate for all audiences.

These themes include:
    graphic sexual scenes
    language
    alcohol and drug use
    death of a parent by suicide
    death of a sister by murder
    violence
    spirits/ghosts

Reading Order

The events of Our Vicious Hearts takes place after the Fates trilogy. However, you do not have to read Fates in order to read and enjoy Our Vicious Hearts.

Prologue

GHOST STORIES ARE ALWAYS JUST THAT. STORIES. Maybe there's a shred of truth to them. Something that compels the listener to believe. A shred of truth that invokes more fear. Something lurking behind you in the dark. But at the end of the day, most ghost stories are make believe.

At Lustros Magical University, however, those stories are more than fairytale. The cathedral on campus was built atop the ancient ruins of a church of some long ago abandoned religion. A religion where sacrifices and summonings were commonplace. Where magicals were killed and thrown from the cliffs into the raging sea below.

Here, you'll find ghosts that wander campus late at night, crying and lamenting the tragic ending of their story. The dead still claim Lustros Magical University as their home. Most of them ignore the living that have joined them on campus. But not all of them.

Walking campus at night, you risk running into something that isn't peaceful. Something that just might take notice of you that you want to stay far away from. A spirit malicious with evil intent.

Blood and death were once commonplace on this land. Now, lecture halls and libraries stand atop skeletons that are buried deep beneath the earth—where people pray they remain. The archaic practice of sacrifices has long since been abandoned, as magic no longer requires it.

But not everyone has forgotten the piercing of flesh with blades and the collection of blood in stone chalices. Some people remember the power death can bring, and where there is power, there is evil.

Aspen

SOMETHING ABOUT THE RAIN ALWAYS MAKES ME A little melancholy, despite how much I love it. And the melancholy always sends me down the roads of my past, wondering what I could have done differently in my 23 years of life. If I had turned left instead of right, would I be sitting here in this constant state of anxiety? If I had gone straight at that intersection, would I have the answer to the question that plagues me night and day?

And what about my future? What path should I travel down to find that answer? Do I want to find it?

I sigh and shake my head, my long black hair shifting with the movement. The books on my bed lay discarded in my absentminded thinking, and I run a finger over the pages of one. For some reason, I can't stay focused today. Every time I try to lose myself in a book, my attention gets drawn away.

My gaze lands on a picture sitting on my nightstand. A smile tugs up the corner of my lips as I grab it, remembering the chaos that ensued to get it. My mom sits on the porch steps, front and center, just like she is in our family, the glue that holds us all together. She's surrounded by her three mates—my dads. Between the four of them, they hold so much power in Lustros.

It's a magical world. Every kind of creature walks the surface, from vampires to fey, witches to shifters. Even a few extremely rare creatures, like my mom. But to me, the powerful people in the picture, they're my family. Their power and positions don't matter. Technically, I would be considered a vampire princess, even though I'm not a vampire. But my daddy Kai is the prince of the vampires—his dad is the king. My daddy Sterling is the alpha of the Iron Shadows pack. While I can't shift even a hair on my head, I still hold a position of power within the pack. And my daddy Cade is a rare violet mage. He uses his skills everyday to help heal people who can't afford healthcare.

However, Lustros is only magical for those who have power. Humans are looked down upon. Sneered at for their inferiority. My parents have been fighting for equality for humans for as long as my oldest brother has been alive. They've made a lot of progress, but these things take time.

Looking back at the picture, I smile at me and my brothers sitting in front of our parents. Adrian, the oldest, with his brown hair and amber eyes, and Rhory with his brown curls and icy blue eyes. And me. The baby, the only girl, the spoiled one. These people are my home. My safe haven. The only ones I can be myself around.

I put the frame back on the table, and glance out the window again. The rain patters softly against the glass, streaking down in big, wet droplets. The gentle tapping is rhythmic and soothing, and the fairy lights lining my ceiling and threaded through the potted plants cast my room in a soft white glow. There really is nothing more perfect than a rainy day in bed with books.

Except maybe a rainy day in bed with books and no annoying older brother relentlessly knocking on your door.

"Aspen, come on. Mom called us down for breakfast five minutes ago. She's going to be pissed if we make her wait any longer. She has a huge list of things we have to do today." The irritation in Rhory's voice is obvious despite it being muffled through the wooden door.

I ignore him and pick up my book to continue reading. It takes him another thirty seconds before he breaks.

"Seriously, Pen." He pushes open my door to finde me sprawled in my bed with my nose buried in another book, and he huffs. "Don't make me take those away from you. I don't want to deal with a pissy mom."

I glare at him, shoving my wavy hair over my shoulder. He's the only one allowed to call me Pen, and he takes full advantage of it because he knows I hate it, and he loves to tease me. "It's rude to burst into someone's room without being invited. And to threaten the books?" I place my hand over my heart in mock dismay. Well, slight mock dismay. It really is awful to threaten the books.

"Well, if you wouldn't have ignored me I wouldn't have had to." He crosses his arms over his chest, black tattoos peeking out from under his shirt sleeves. His brown curly hair glints in the lights from the ceiling as he leans forward and pierces me with his icy blue eyes. "Seriously, sis, come on. Mom is go—"

"What is taking you so long?" Another voice yells from downstairs. "I'm starving, and mom won't let us eat until we're all here!"

I raise one brow at Rho, and he grins. "All right, that was worth it," he says reluctantly.

Adrian, our oldest brother, is slow to anger, but when he does, he gets *angry*. All our lives, Rho and I have taken it upon ourselves to push Adrian to his limits, taking bets on how long it will take him to snap.

Rho pushes off the door frame and crosses the room to take the book from my hands. I protest, but he steps over my indignant squawk. "Worth it, but he's right. Let's go."

I sigh and stand from my bed, following Rho downstairs to the dining room. This cabin used to belong to Sterling. Before our mom got with our dads, it was only a small house, with one bedroom and one bathroom. After they essentially saved the world from mom's horrific ex-fiance's plans to build a genetically engineered army, they renovated the cabin into what it is now.

Neither me nor my brother's have lived away from home. At least, they didn't until they started grad school. But even through undergrad, we all lived here. My parents are truly amazing, and there's been no need to move out.

"Nice of you two to finally join us," Cade drawls as he sets a pot of coffee on the table.

"Someone," Rho says, hooking his thumb toward me, "wouldn't stop reading."

I don't bother saying anything. Growing up with three dads and two brothers, I'm used to the joking and know when to pick my battles. This isn't one of those times. Instead, I take a seat at the kitchen table and pour myself a cup of coffee.

Cade chuckles. "Quit picking on your sister. She hasn't had her caffeine yet, and I have no doubt she could take you if you piss her off."

"Highly unlikely," Rho snorts, raising his arms above his head and stretching, showing off his muscles.

Kai steps into the kitchen and smacks the back of Rho's head. "I've seen Aspen hand your ass to you, pup. Keep making her mad, and we can watch it happen again."

Rho glares at Kai and rubs the back of his head, but before he can respond, mom sets a plate stacked high with pancakes on the table.

"There will be no ass-handing happening today," she says with a pointed look at Rho. "We have too much to do to get you guys ready to go back to LMU."

LMU, or Lustros Magical University. It isn't a typical college, and not just because of the magic. LMU is basically a grad school for magicals. We've all already gone to college. I have a bachelor of science that I have no clue what to do with, but those of us that want further lessons in magic, or want to work in a career that's magic oriented, we attend magical grad schools, like LMU.

"Speaking of," Sterling says, sitting next to me. "You haven't heard from them yet, have you, Aspen?"

A piece of pancake gets stuck in my throat, and I have to take a gulp of coffee to get it down. I shake my head, refusing to look at anyone. The little bit of food I've eaten churns threateningly in my stomach. I don't say the words on my tongue because I've already said them before. Many times. And it only serves to piss everyone off. So, I keep my mouth shut and focus on my food, even though my appetite has evaporated.

I can sense Kai's attention on me, and he quickly changes the subject. With his empath abilities, he no doubt knows exactly how conflicted I am. The nerves and fear tangle with excitement and hope. The combination does nothing to ease the nausea slowly building in my gut.

I'm too lost in thought to hear what Kai says, but my mom's tinkling laugh draws me from the darkness. Not for the first time, I wish I was more like her—and not just in looks. Rho has her hair, all crazy brown curls. Adrian has her stunning amber eyes. I was lucky enough to get her high cheekbones, but that's it. My black wavy hair and gray eyes definitely come from my bio dad, Kai.

When I was younger, I never thought about which of my dads was my *actual* dad. I never had a need to. They all treated me the same. They all loved me equally. And in all honesty, I've always been just a tiny bit closer to Sterling. I blame it on how much he spoils me and the way he always knows exactly what kind of clothing to buy me.

But as I got older, I began to notice the similarities my brothers and I have to each of our dads. I look more like Kai. Rho has Sterling's icy blue eyes and shifter abilities. And Adrian could be Cade's twin with his violet magic.

I wish I had more of my mom's bravery and strength. Not a day goes by that I'm not amazed by her. The way she handles three mates. Her compassion and love for me and my brothers. The dedication she has to helping humans in need. It seems as if all of her good traits went to my brothers. Instead, I got the one thing from my mom I wish I hadn't gotten. The worst possible thing to inherit from her.

I finish my breakfast in silence, lost in my own thoughts.

When I stand to take my half-eaten pancakes to the sink, my mom stops me with a hand on my arm.

"There's some mail for you on the counter," she says with a warm smile.

I sift through the mail until I find the envelope with my name on it. When I see the logo from the sender, my heart stutters.

Lustros Magical University.

This is it. The contents of this little envelope will determine my fate. And I honestly don't know which direction I want it to go. My fingers tremble slightly as I tear the top. It's hard to believe just a few words on a couple scraps of parchment can cause me so much inner turmoil. Does the smaller sized envelope mean it's a rejection letter? Do I want it to be a rejection letter?

The soft chatter in the kitchen washes over me, but it's just a hum of background noise drowned out by the ringing in my ears and the echo of my racing heart in my head.

I hold my breath as I pull the slip of paper from the envelope and unfold it.

Dear Aspen Grey,

Congratulations, and welcome to Lustros Magical University.

My heart rate spikes alarmingly, and the rest of the words on the page blur. Distantly, I'm aware of my fingers gripping the page so tightly it's wrinkling in my hands, but as my vision darkens around the edges I can't bring myself to care. I was accepted into LMU. I should be thrilled. I *am* thrilled. But I'm more terrified than anything, and that fear gripping me so tightly in iron claws makes it hard to ignore the pressure on my chest squeezing, squeezing, squeezing.

Rho's voice filters through the blood rushing in my ears, but I don't register what he says. His fingers lift my chin so I'm looking at him. I blink to focus the image of him in front of me with his brows pulled low in concern.

"Hey, are you okay, Pen? You look like you've seen a ghost."

"I ..." I have to swallow to work moisture back into my mouth. "I was accepted." My voice is quiet, but the kitchen has gone silent as Rho's concern became obvious, and my words are heard by everyone.

Understanding flickers in his eyes, and he doesn't say anything because he knows. As one of the only people in my family who I feel really understands me, Rho gets how conflicting this is for me. The rest of my family cheers, though. Congratulations and excited whoops spill from everyone's lips as they surround me to pat me on the back or wrap me in a hug. It's a testament to how detached I am that their touches don't make my skin crawl.

Over their shoulders I see Kai staring at me from the doorway. Beside's Rho, he's the only one not trying to hug or congratulate me. Concern clouds his gray eyes as he studies me, no doubt using his empath abilities to read the raging storm of uncertainty inside me.

"Oh, Aspen, this is great!" Mom says, kissing my forehead. "And perfect timing. Now we can shop for all three of you today."

"We all knew you'd get in," Sterling says, patting my head. "With Kai being an alumnus and your brothers attending, you were a shoe-in."

Numbly, I nod my head in agreement because I don't know what else to say. Mom smiles and claps her hands in excitement, and the dread inside me grows. Everyone wants this for me. If I don't do it, they'll all be disappointed.

The crowd around me dissipates to finish their breakfast and get ready for the day. But Rho remains in front of me to make sure I'm okay.

"Pen?" he asks quietly so only I can hear him.

I shake my head. *I don't want to talk right now.* He squeezes my shoulder once before turning away. On autopilot, I flee to my room and flop face first onto my bed, burying my head in my pillow.

Sterling is wrong. Lustros Magical University has one very big reason to not accept me.

I have no magical powers.

Aspen

I DON'T KNOW HOW MUCH TIME PASSES AS I LAY IN silence with my body oddly numb yet wired at the same time. My thoughts rushing and sluggish, the combination leaves the beginnings of a headache at the base of my skull. I have no idea what to do.

A soft knock on my door draws a groan from my lips. I can't deal with the excitement. I can't fake the same joy everyone else feels at this moment.

"Aspen, can I come in?" Kai pokes his head into my room, and waits for me to grunt in response. He takes that as a yes and slips inside, closing the door behind him. The bed dips as he sits, and he gently runs his fingers through my hair like he has every time I've been upset since I was young. "Hey kiddo."

"Hi." The pillow muffles my words, and they seem so small as I speak them.

"Do you want to talk about it?"

"No."

"You know I don't try to read you kids, it's too much of an invasion of privacy. But you threw your emotions at me so hard down there I didn't have a choice." His fingers keep running through my hair, and the sensation eases some of my anxiety. One of the only kinds of touch I truly enjoy.

I sigh and roll over, scooting to sit at the head of the bed with my knees drawn to my chest. "I'm scared," I whisper, not looking at him. I don't want to see the disappointment in his eyes when he realizes my true reason for not wanting to go to LMU.

Kai nods. "About what? Why does going to LMU terrify you so much?"

I huff a laugh that's lacking in humor. "Where do I start? I won't know anyone. It's away from home. The campus is so intimidating. I don't know what I'd study. And ... and I know exactly how people will treat me. It will be the same as it was in high school and undergrad. I'll be the outcast. The one looked down upon because I have no magic..." My words trail off, and I pick at my comforter, still refusing to meet Kai's gaze.

"You don't have to go, Aspen. If you don't want to, no one is going to make you." His voice is gentle, a tone I've noticed he uses only with me and mom.

Tears burn my eyes, and I squeeze them shut, refusing to let them fall. "I have to go," I whisper. "Everyone will be disappointed in me if I don't."

Kai scoffs and lays on his back next to me, staring up at my ceiling and the fairy lights crisscrossing the space. "That's not true, and you know it."

"How can it not be true? I've always been the disappointment of this family. I can't compete with Rho and Adrian. They're smart and powerful. They aren't scared of talking to people or doing things outside of their comfort zone. They don't have weird quirks. I'm just timid and powerless, and ... and ..." I don't realize the tears are falling until Kai sits up and wipes them away with his thumb.

"Aspen, none of that is true. There is no competition between you and your brothers. We love all of you equally, and we're proud of all of you the same. We don't care if you have powers or not. You're smart and kind and strong. And you as a person are more than enough."

"None of that will matter at LMU," I laugh wetly. "People won't care about how kind I am. All they will see is some weirdo who has no power who can be walked all over."

"Then don't go," he says simply. "We won't be disappointed if you decide to not go to LMU. All we want is for you to be happy in whatever you do."

I shake my head, brushing tears from my cheeks and burying my face in my knees. I don't know how to explain it. I don't know what words to use to describe the utter terror the thought of moving from home into a room on LMU's campus gives me. I've never been able to explain to people who don't have the same kind of anxiety I do, what it feels like to do something your body and mind don't want to do.

"Aspen," Kai says, waiting for me to turn my head to look at him. "Why don't you talk to mom. You know she went through this, too. She understands what you're feeling, and she can help you."

A single tear leaks through my lashes, and I swallow, stopping the urge to shake my head. "She is so powerful now," I whisper. "All of you are so powerful. How can you say I'm not a disappointment? You guys saved the world, and then had me? What a cosmic joke I must be to everyone."

Kai grabs my shoulders. I can tell he wants to shake me, that my words made him mad, but he just shakes his head. "Aspen, you have never once been a disappointment or a joke. You were the light of our family from the first second you were born. There is nothing, *nothing,* you could do that would disappoint us. I need you to believe that, kiddo."

I look into his eyes, the same as mine, and see the emotion in them. I swallow, because I want to believe him. But my brain tells me that it's not possible. There is no way they could be proud of me when I'm nothing.

"Aspen," he breathes, no doubt sensing where my thoughts have gone. He pulls me in for a hug, and I go willingly this time. I need the comfort only my daddy can give me. "The first time I held you and you opened your eyes, that first moment when I realized you were *mine,* I knew there would be nothing I wouldn't do for you." His hands brush my hair and down my back. "I'd burn the fucking world to the ground if that's what you wanted. You are my little girl, and you will always be my little girl. I don't care if you don't have any powers. It didn't stop me from falling in love with your mom, and it won't stop me from loving you."

These are words he's never spoken to me before. We've never talked about *real* dads before. That was a line no one wanted to cross. But hearing him say that, knowing that it doesn't bother him that a child of his blood has no power, it eases something inside of me. I know none of my parents care about power. I know my brothers don't care about that. But it's hard to silence the voices in my head that tell me I'm not, and never will be, enough. So any extra bit of encouragement helps to quiet them, even if just for a little while.

Kai pulls away and wipes my tears again. "Do you believe me now?" he asks, quietly, tucking my hair behind my ear.

I nod, because right now I do believe him. That doesn't mean tomorrow the voices won't convince me to change my mind.

"Will you talk to your mom? I really think she'll help you make the right decision." He searches my eyes, his expression uncharacteristically solemn. I nod again, even though I don't think it will make a difference. He purses his lips like he doesn't believe me, but then stands from the bed. "You can talk to any of us if you need to, okay?" He bends down to kiss the top of my head. "I love you, Aspen."

"I love you, too, daddy," I whisper.

When he leaves, I flop back onto my bed and pull the covers over my head. I really should talk to my mom. She of all people would understand what I'm going through. When she was younger, she also didn't have any magic. It wasn't until she met her mates—my dads—that she came into her power. That's why everyone hopes I'm following in her footsteps. That one day, I'll find my magic like she did.

A sigh climbs up my throat, and my chest deflates, feeling heavier than it has in awhile. It's going to be one of those days, and now I have to go shopping for dorm supplies. I don't want to do anything today. I'm already exhausted even though I just woke up, but I drag myself out of bed and get dressed. Somehow, I'll survive this shopping trip. Then I can crash when I get back.

RHO EYED me the entire trip, waiting for me to talk about what's on my mind. It's one of the reasons we're so close. He gets me. He understands there are times I don't want anyone to touch me. He knows how hard it is for me to break out of my shell and try new things. He may not understand it completely, but he knows it's something I deal with. If I don't want to talk, he won't force me. But he always makes sure I know that he's there.

I'm just not ready to talk about it yet. Even though I'm running out of time. Classes start in less than two weeks. Move in day is right around the corner. But the less I think about it, the less I panic. I'm a pro at burying things in the very back of my mind so I don't have to think about them.

In my room, I drop all of my bags on the floor and sit at my desk staring at the list I made earlier. A pro-con list of all the reasons to go to LMU. The cons far outweigh the pros. Except for that one pro. The one reason I applied to LMU in the first place. The one pro that is also on the con list.

Maybe someone there could help me wake up magic that might be buried deep inside of me.

The mixing of races could very well be the reason I don't have powers. Typically, when races mix, their offspring is usually a human with no magic flowing in their veins. But, my mom is different. She's a harpy. Someone brought into this world to balance the scales of good and evil. She's the only one of her kind, and no one knows how procreation works with a harpy.

Since both of my brothers got magical abilities from their bio dad, we know it's possible for harpies to have kids with power. I, however, did not get any abilities from Kai, except for slightly heightened senses. Like I can smell blood from farther away, and I'm strangely entranced by it. Not enough to drink it, but it definitely doesn't freak me out. I'm also able to read people's emotions better. Not quite an empath, like Kai, but I just kind of get it. I'm also just a tiny bit stronger and quicker than a typical human. But that's it. Nothing extraordinary.

Tuning out the raging thoughts in my mind about what will happen to me if I don't uncover any magical abilities, I turn on my favorite Wandering Fey album and start unpacking my bags. I make a pile in the corner of my room for things that will need to go to LMU—if I go. The rest of it, I put where it belongs. My fingers graze over a smooth, hard surface, and I smile as I pull a statue out of the bag.

I'm not big on tchotchkes usually, but this little gray dove caught my eye, and for some reason I couldn't walk past it. Its wings are painted a shimmery gray that stands out from the rest of the body, and I like the way it catches the sunlight and sparkles. I set it on my desk before unpacking the rest of my haul, but a knock on my door stops me.

"Hey, Pen." Rho slips into my room, closing the door behind him. "How's it going?" He flops onto my bed, head hanging off the edge so he's looking at me upside down.

I narrow my eyes at him and sit in my desk chair. "Fine. How are you?"

"Oh, just peachy." He flicks his hand, waving off my question. "But it's you I'm worried about. I know you don't want to talk, but I'm sick of waiting."

I snort and shake my head. "It's nothing."

"Riiight. Nothing." He clicks his tongue in disappointment. "You know I don't believe that. Talk to me, Pen."

Glaring, I turn my gaze from him to the window. In the distance, a lake nestled between two mountains glitters in the setting sun.

Rho sighs and gets to his feet. "Okay. I won't push... for now.... But you know where to find me."

I nod and wait until he leaves to slouch in the chair. He'd understand if I told him. At least, he'd try to understand, and he wouldn't give me a hard time. But I just can't bring myself to tell him. It wouldn't be anything new. In my 23 years of life, Rho has been there for it all, and he's heard every dark thought, seen through to the very soul of who I am. But, it's still hard to open up and risk judgement. Telling my anxiety that Rho won't judge me, isn't working this time.

Instead of doing what I should do—making a decision about attending LMU—I grab a book and lose myself in a fictional world, because it's better than the real one, and it's easier to ignore my problems than solve them.

IT'S LATE when I finally pull myself from my books. I skipped dinner, and no one bothered to try and get me to join them— Rho's doing, no doubt. So when my stomach growls, I make my way toward the stairs. But voices coming from my mom's library stop me.

Soft light spills onto the floor from the slightly open door. It's not unusual for her to be in here late at night, but she rarely lets anyone else in the room with her. This is her space. A safe place she made for herself after the hell she went through. So when I hear Cade's voice, I stop. Pressing myself against the wall, I ignore the worm of shame that wriggles inside me as I listen to their conversation.

"We have to let her find herself on her own," Cade says, quietly.

"I just wish there was something I could do," my mom says, tears thickening her voice. "I know exactly what she's going through. And if I'm being completely honest, I'm scared for her."

"Scared about what?" Sterling asks. The creak of leather

sounds loud in the silence as someone adjusts their position on a chair.

"If she goes to LMU she'll be defenseless. What if ... what if ..." my mom trails off, a sob caught in her throat.

"She's not defenseless, baby girl," Kai says. His nickname for her always brings a smile to my face. "And just because she doesn't have any magic, doesn't mean she'll get hurt. Especially not how you were hurt."

"Rhory and Adrian will be there, too," Cade reminds her. "You know they'll protect her."

"But they can't be with her at all times." My mom sniffs and clears her throat. "I know how cruel magicals can be. And I know she's strong, but she's also sensitive. I'm scared she's going to get torn down to the point where she loses all sense of who she is."

"And if that happens, she'll build herself back up," Sterling says gently. "Just like you did, kitten. None of us want her to get hurt, but we can't protect her forever."

I'm about to step away, my heart in my throat and tears burning my eyes, when Kai says, "I just wish I knew *why* she doesn't have any powers. Rho and Adrian do, so why not her?"

"Stop blaming yourself, Kai," Cade says, his voice stern but understanding, like this is something they've talked about a lot. "I don't think it has anything to do with race."

My mom sucks in a breath. "What do you mean?"

I can almost picture Cade shrugging his shoulders. "Just that you didn't have any powers until you met us. You had a purpose you didn't know about until it was time for you to know it. Fate has made herself at home with our family, and none of us should be surprised if there's something bigger at play here."

My heart stutters at the implication. That fate has something planned for me.

Kai growls. "She better not have three fucking mates waiting for her at LMU."

Sterling chuckles. "Who are you to get pissy about that? Your beloved is mated to three men."

"Yeah," Kai says, low and dark. "And you know how we are with Ellis. Do you really want our little girl fucked by three guys at the same time? No way in hell."

Silence falls in the room, and even from my position outside, the tension and anger are palpable. I quietly slip away, stomach churning. Not just at the thought of my parents having sex, but at what Kai and Cade were saying. Could I have a mate—or more—waiting for me at LMU? Will I come into some secret power while I'm there?

I don't realize where I'm going until I'm standing outside of Rho's room. I hesitate with my hand raised, fingers shaking slightly, before I knock. When he opens the door and sees me standing on the threshold, looking like a lost puppy, he steps aside and lets me in.

Unlike mine and Adrian's rooms, Rho's is an utter pigsty. Dirty clothes lay in piles on the floor wherever he threw them. On his dresser, plates and cups grow an interesting assortment of mold. And the bottles of beer on the floor make an almost beautiful melody when you kick them as you walk through the mess.

The only thing with any sort of organization is his music collection. Old vinyl, cassettes, and CDs are neatly stacked and displayed next to various record players and boomboxes. His variety of punk, rock, and ska music is truly inspiring, from big name bands to indies that no one has ever heard of.

"What's up little sister?" he asks before taking a hit on his joint.

I knock some clothes from his desk chair onto the floor and sit, perched anxiously on the edge. "I just overheard a conversation between mom and our dads."

One of his dark brows lifts, and a slow grin spreads across his face. "Spying?"

"No," I say vehemently. "I just happened to overhear my name as I was walking past mom's library. You would have stopped to listen, too, if it had been you."

He shrugs. "You're right. What did you hear?"

I take a deep breath and keep my gaze fixed to my bare feet. "Cade thinks fate might be playing a part in my life. Like it did for mom."

Rho releases a breath, smoke clouding in front of him, and he slowly sits on his bed. "He thinks you're a harpy? Like mom?"

"I can't be a harpy. There is always only one harpy in existence at a time. But what if he's right? What if there is a reason I don't have any magic yet? Mom didn't find hers until she met all of our dads."

Rho thinks about this for a moment, smoke wreathing his head. "I wouldn't be surprised. But the question is, what are your powers? And how do you get them? Mom had to find her mates. Is that what you need to do?"

I shrug and slump in the chair. Those questions aren't so different from the questions I've been asking since I was a child. Why don't I have powers? And how can I find them? Rho offers me his joint, but I shake my head. I've never done drugs, and I only drink on occasion. Usually a fruity mixed drink with more sugar than alcohol.

"But this isn't what's been bothering you," Rho says before taking a hit. He exhales and closes his eyes, savoring the high for a moment. "You're torn on whether to go to LMU or not. If you don't go, you're worried everyone will be upset. If you do go, you're worried about ... well, everything."

I huff and rub my face. "I hate how well you know me."

"Psh. That's why I'm your favorite brother. But you know whatever decision you make, we'll all support you. You don't have to go to LMU."

"But if I don't, how will I ever know if I have powers or not? What if someone there can help me?" My words are so quiet they're almost swallowed by the background music from Rho's record player.

He shrugs. "That's the choice you have to make. What's more important to you? Finding out if you have powers or continuing to live your life in this safe space, always wondering if there's more out there? Which one can you accept and not regret later in life?"

I sigh and chew on my bottom lip. That's the question, isn't it? Can I live with not knowing for sure whether or not I have powers laying dormant inside of me? Which fear is worse: living as a human in Lustros or stepping outside of my comfort zone and going to LMU?

Misha

"Are you sure you won't need this?"

I glance at my mom and sigh. She's holding up the desk calendar she bought for me the other day. "Positive mom. I put everything in my phone."

She frowns. "But what if you lose your phone?"

"It's synced to the cloud, just like yours is. Why are you so worried about a calendar? You've asked me about it five times now."

She drops the object in question onto my desk and gives me a rueful smile. "Because, I'm your mother, and it's my job to worry about my baby wherever you go."

"You didn't worry like this when Brayden left for LMU."

"Brayden is different. He's always been independent. Besides, you're my youngest, and even though you're 23, it's hard to see you leave home for the first time."

I shake my head and return to packing the suitcase laying across my bed. I'm not taking much with me to LMU. Clothes, toiletries, a couple of picture frames, and my laptop. I don't need a lot. Besides, anything I need I can get there or order online.

"Did you schedule your classes yet?" mom asks, looking over the contents of my suitcase.

"Yes."

"Do you know your dorm assignment?" She lifts one of the

frames from the bag and smiles. A picture of our family—me, mom, dad, and Brayden—at the beach last summer.

"Yes."

She tucks the frame back inside. "Do you have a map of the school so you can get around?"

I sigh and pinch the bridge of my nose. A headache has been lingering behind my eyes for the past few days. I can't get it to go away and this conversation isn't helping. "I don't need one, but yes."

"You're cranky. Are you feeling okay?" She sweeps her long blue locs over her shoulder and approaches me with her hand raised. Light the color of the ocean wreathes her fingers, undulating like waves.

I duck before she can place her hand on my forehand. "I'm fine mom. Just tired. I haven't been sleeping well." And isn't that the truth. As soon as I received my acceptance letter to LMU, the dreams started.

Every one of them features *her*. I don't know who she is, but she's fucking gorgeous. Tan, curvy, long wavy black hair, and stunning gray eyes. She's sexy and mouth-watering, and so real I can taste her. But I don't know her name. And I don't know why I'm dreaming of her.

Some of the dreams are amazing. Some of the dreams are terrifying. And some of them are straight-up heartbreaking. But every one of them takes place at LMU. There's an instinct deep inside of me that screams she's real, and I'll find her when I get to campus. But I don't know why I'm so sure of that.

"Make sure you're home for dinner tonight. I want all of us to eat together before you leave tomorrow. And tell Ezra and Ari they're more than welcome to join."

I nod in response, and she leaves me alone after one last lingering look. I stretch my neck side to side to ease some of the tension making me stiff and achy. There's an anxious sort of energy rolling through me, half nerves and half excitement. And I have many reasons for feeling both of those things.

Moving to LMU is something I've been waiting for. There's a professor who will be able to help me with my magic. And I desperately need help with it. Then there's this girl. In my dreams, I've taken to calling her Dove because of her gray eyes. I'm itching to know if she's real. And if she is, why am I dreaming of her?

The last reason is perhaps the most serious and scary of all. Finding out what happened to Millie, Ezra and Ari's sister. Thinking of it, I grab four journals from the drawer of my desk and carefully place them in my suitcase. The twins and I have been looking for answers, and the deeper we dig the murkier it becomes. I'm not the only one unsettled by the things we've discovered so far.

I grab my phone and send a text to Ezra and Ari. It's no surprise they pass on dinner, but we plan to meet up after for drinks. We're taking the night off from our searching and planning. All three of us have been at it non-stop this summer, and I think we're all hitting a wall. So before we dive into the waters at LMU, we're going to enjoy ourselves without the worries of what's to come.

I do one last scan of my room for anything I think I'll need on campus, and zip the suitcase shut. I have one hour before dinner, so I hop in the shower to try to clear my head. But like always, the sensation of water falling over my skin drags up the reminders of the dreams.

I close my eyes, and I can see her. Long hair dripping rainwater down her back and leaving a wet splotch on the fabric of her purple shirt. Her beautiful smile, full of joy, as she tugs me out from under the gazebo to dance with her in the rain. The heat from her body pressed against mine, chasing away the chill in the air.

My dick stirs just thinking about her. It's not hard for me to fall into the daydream. I've dreamt of her so often, and most of the time it's raining. With the shower brushing over my skin and the heat swirling around me, I let myself pretend. I take myself in hand and slowly stroke from base to tip. My body shudders just imagining it's her. Her hand, her mouth, her ...

I groan and lean forward with one hand bracing the shower wall. My rhythm increases and becomes less steady. The first tingles in my balls spread outward through my body. I run my tongue over my lower lip, wishing I could taste her in real life. My orgasm slams into me, doubling me over, and I keep going until there's nothing left inside of me.

It's strange that jerking off to the memory of her in my dreams never leaves me satisfied. That doesn't stop me from trying though.

THE SKUNKY SCENT of weed permeates Ezra and Ari's apartment. It's probably so embedded in the stained carpet and peeling paint on the walls that the landlord will never be able to get rid of it. That thought makes me chuckle, as smoke seeps from my mouth on an exhale.

"What are you laughing at?" Ari asks, sitting back on the ugly green couch. His blond hair is impeccably styled as always, slicked back away from his face drawing attention to the golden eyes he shares with his twin.

I shake my head. "Nothing really. Just relishing this unusual sense of calm. Things have been ..." I trail off, not able to find the word I'm looking for in my pot-induced haze.

"Things have been shitty," Ezra chimes in. His blond hair is a mess, sticking up in all directions, and the hand he runs through it does nothing to help.

"I was going for something along the lines of stressful, but sure. Shitty works, too." I tap the ash off the end of my joint into the plastic ashtray on the beat up coffee table. One of the legs is missing and another is duct taped to the tabletop. How it's still standing is a mystery to me.

"We need to be careful when we get to LMU," Ari says. Even high he's the voice of reason.

While the twins look almost identical with their blond hair, golden eyes, and sharply angled cheekbones, their behavior couldn't be more different. Ari is even-tempered, patient, and calculating. If I didn't know he was a tiger shifter, I'd assume he was a hawk. The way he studies his environment and the people in it always reminds me of a bird of prey.

Ezra is every bit a tiger shifter. Hot headed, irrational, and quick to anger. Sometimes Ari is the only one able to calm Ezra down when he gets in a rage. He's always been this way, but things have gotten worse since their sister, Millie, was murdered at LMU four years ago.

Of course, authorities didn't say it was murder. The official reports say Millie overdosed on faeroot, the deadliest and most addictive drug imported into Lustros from the fae lands. But anyone who knew Millie, knew she would never touch drugs after watching her dad with his addiction before he left them when she was young.

Ezra snorts. "Careful my ass. I'm going to do whatever I can to uncover what happened to Millie." His golden eyes stare dully at the coffee table, but a muscle ticks in his jaw. "Whoever did this will pay."

"I'm not saying they won't," Ari says calmly. "I'm just saying unless we want to be the next dead body found on campus, we need to be careful."

"And we need to keep my mysterious dream girl safe as well." I don't know what part she plays in all of this, but after our research over the summer, there is no denying the similarities.

While Millie was born to two tiger shifter parents, she had no powers. The other mysterious murders on campus claimed victims who were also magicless, despite coming from magical families. And in my dreams, my dove has stated she has no magic as well.

"What if she's part of the problem?" Ari asks cautiously. He knows my suspicions about this girl, and the way I've been obsessing over her.

His words spark a fire inside of me. The sudden urge to push to my feet and make him take back what he said by force causes my hands to tremble. I squeeze my fists and take a deep breath. "She's not," I say with a certainty I feel in my gut. "But if she is, we'll deal with it." The words taste sour on my tongue, and I take a hit of my joint to chase away the lingering foulness.

Ari nods, no doubt sensing the volatile shift in my mood at his question, and he lets the subject drop. "We're going to think things through before we act. And we're going to make sure we stay safe. If we wind up dead, there's nothing we can do to uncover the truth behind Millie's death."

Ezra says nothing, but he grinds his teeth loud enough for me to hear across the room. It's as much of an agreement as Ari's going to get. We fall into silence, and I look around the small rundown apartment the twin's share. Things are going to be very different at the LMU dorms.

The twins' dad ran out on them when they were babies, leaving their mom to raise three kids alone. Not that he would have been much help if he'd stuck around. The dude was a drug addict, and frequently beat his wife. At least, that's what Millie always said. But after Millie's death, their mom took a bunch of pills and passed out in the tub. She had already been struggling with her mental health, and losing her daughter drove her over the edge.

Ezra and Ari managed to keep the apartment with the crappy pay of odd jobs and the occasional petty theft. I know it's not something they're proud of, but survival is survival. And no matter how often my parents tried to help them, they refused, not wanting to be a burden on anyone else. Luckily, their shifter abilities are powerful enough to get a full ride to LMU.

But, Ezra and Ari are used to living by their own rules. Moving onto campus won't be easy for them. We've all already attended a local college to get our bachelor degrees, but we lived at home and could do whatever we wanted—within reason. Living on campus will be a step back for the twins. There will be rules to follow. One of which is no drugs or alcohol on campus. Not that that stops anyone.

I take another hit on my joint and close my eyes. Unbidden, the image of my mystery woman flashes behind my eyelids. Rather than snapping them open, I let myself sink into the vision of her. It's been getting harder and harder to fight the urges, and I find myself embracing the thoughts of her, rather than pushing them away. I'm sure it's a dangerous road to travel, one that will be hard to come back from, but it's a mistake I'm more than willing to make, if only for a small taste of what she makes me feel—alive in a way I've never felt before.

A smile tugs at my lips, and the sounds of Ezra and Ari's conversation dim to a soft buzz as a pair of gray eyes ensnare my soul and draw me in.

Aspen

"I forgot how much I hate this place," Kai mutters as we walk under the stone arch at the entrance to campus.

"Why do you hate it?" I glance at the buildings appearing in the fog ahead of us, my arms wrapped around my middle in an attempt to warm myself from the chill in the air.

Located high atop Wraithstone Mountain, low hanging clouds permanently shroud Lustros Magical University's gloomy and oppressive campus. A misting rain dampens everything, and frizzes my hair like a halo around my head. Rolling fog obscures everything in front of me, with only dark outlines of buildings visible in the distance.

Kai chuckles and bumps his shoulder into mine. "Nothing that you need to worry about. They don't allow vampires to drink from the source." He shudders dramatically, making a lock of black hair fall across his forehead. "Blood bags are so disgusting."

"It's awfully ... monochrome." My gaze travels over what I can see of campus. It's all gray, black, and brown. Even the grass looks gray under the cloak of mist dampening everything.

Rho snorts in front of me where he's walking with mom and Cade. "You would comment on the lack of color."

"Not just color," I say. "But plants, too. I'll have to buy grow lights so I can put some plants in my room." Plants give me life. I love tending to them and watching them grow. The extra dopamine boost they give me will probably be needed on this dreary campus.

"You should check out the cemetery," Adrian says behind me. "It's actually quite beautiful, in its own way."

I take in the massive stone and arching wrought iron fence surrounding the cemetery to my right. Fog obscures everything inside. I highly doubt there is anything beautiful on the other side of that wall. Still, I nod my head, if only to appease my brother.

Up ahead, the main building, or Old Main as my brother's call it, looms out of the mist like some enormous monster. The gothic structure is all flying buttresses, piercing pinnacles, and arched breezeways. Like the rest of campus, it's made of dreary gray stones. The only color comes from the ancient stained glass windows. But instead of uplifting and vibrant scenes, the windows are downright creepy. Skulls, bones, candles, ancient tomes and scrolls. A death's-head hawkmoth is displayed front and center of the building in a rose window.

My steps slow as I take in the entire structure. "Please tell me those aren't alive," I quietly say to Kai.

He follows my gaze to the grotesque gargoyles perched at even intervals along the roof and grins. "Not alive but watchful."

A chill skitters down my spine. "And what exactly does that mean?"

"They're enchanted to act as security cameras. If you look closely enough, you can sometimes see their eyes moving."

I shiver and avert my gaze. Doubts creep up on me, and I kick a stray pebble on the path. My brothers have described LMU to me, so this isn't entirely a shock. But I don't think anyone can truly prepare you for how utterly creepy and unsettling this place is. Is this too much for me to handle? This is so far out of my comfort zone. Can I really do this?

Kai takes my elbow and turns me to face him. "It's not too late to change your mind, kiddo. And like I've said before, no one will be disappointed if you decide you don't want to attend." His gray eyes are serious, a rare moment for Kai.

I take a breath and hold it before releasing it. "I'm okay." At least I hope I am. This is the biggest thing I've ever done. I've never lived away from home, and for my first time, someplace this creepy is probably a bad idea. "I just need to get used to everything."

Kai studies me for a moment longer, no doubt parsing through my emotions with his empath abilities. He doesn't look entirely convinced, but he finally nods and tucks a frizzy curl behind my ear. "I'm proud of you no matter what you do."

"Hurry up!" Rho calls where everyone has stopped to wait for me and Kai. "Mom's already crying."

Kai laughs softly and leads me toward the family. "Why doesn't that surprise me?"

"I'm not crying," mom protests, wiping her cheeks. "It's the rain."

"Uh huh. No one believes you, kitten." Sterling throws his arm around her shoulder and kisses the top of her head.

"I don't understand why you're crying now," Rho huffs. "You never cried when you dropped off me and Adrian."

"That's because I was relieved to be getting rid of you for a bit. Aspen is my baby, though. I'm not ready to let her go."

Rho sighs, tipping his head toward the sky. "Pen always gets special treatment because she's the baby. It's not fair."

"Quit whining," Adrian chimes in. "You're a grown ass adult. It doesn't look good on you."

"This is exactly why I didn't cry when I dropped you two off," mom says, giving them an exasperated look. "The house was so much quieter without you guys."

A lump forms in my throat as we continue toward the dorms, and I attempt to swallow it down. *Adrian and Rho will be here with me. It's not like I'm leaving my entire family.* No, not my entire family, just the four people who love and accept me unconditionally. I blink rapidly to stop the tears from falling. Thinking about my daddies' hugs and my mom's gentle smile makes my eyes burn, and I don't want to cry when they'll all see me.

"Come on," Rho whines. "Let's get Pen checked in so I can check out my new room. And get away from all this crying."

THE THREE-STORY DORM building isn't quite as imposing as Old Main; however, it still looms over the quad with its rough-hewn gray stone facade. The arched, leaded windows spill a surprising cozy glow over the lawn out front from the lamplight inside. Pointed dormers and chimneys protrude from the roof, reminding me of broken teeth in the maw of a monster.

After stopping by my brothers' dorms to drop off their belongings, we all head toward my room. The hallways are drafty and dark, composed of the same gray stone as the outside. It's ancient and archaic. One would expect to see wavering torches lining the walls, but electricity was added to the building a long time ago. The brackets that once housed the torches still protrude from the stone, and the ceiling near them is stained black with soot from the many years of fire that burned to light the passageways.

Now, rounded globes mounted on the walls give off an amber-hued glow. But despite them, the hallways remain dim. It's as if they ran out of globes while replacing the torches, or maybe they wanted to keep the perpetual dreary atmosphere. Dark shadows fill the space between the pools of light.

"Would it seriously kill them to add some color to the walls?" I ask, rubbing my arms as goosebumps erupt on my skin. "Or maybe heat the place?" Despite it being the end of summer, the hallways are chilly and damp.

"Get used to it," Adrian says next to me. "The hallways are always chilly in the summer and downright freezing in the winter.

It costs too much to heat the dorms, classrooms, and offices so they forgo the hallways."

"It's like living in the dark ages," I mutter, once again rethinking my decision to attend LMU.

"But every dorm room has a fireplace, and the water heats crazy fast," Rho chimes in, throwing me a wink over his shoulder. "And you won't have to worry about running out of hot water. It's endless here."

I throw him a grateful look for attempting to make me feel better. He always knows exactly what to say and when to say it, even if he can't see my expression.

"This is it," mom says with a cheery smile, stopping in front of one of the endless dark wooden two panel doors. "Hurry up and open it, let's see what we're working with."

I squeeze between my family members and pull the brass skeleton key from my pocket. The ornamental brass door plate and knob match the key, all of them tarnished from many years of use. I shove the key in the lock quickly, hoping no one notices how badly my hand shakes.

"This lock seems really easy to pick," mom says quietly. Her amber eyes narrow on the doorknob, and she worries her bottom lip between her teeth.

"It's the same type of door and lock Adrian and I had when we first moved in. You didn't seem concerned then." Rho places his hands on his hips and stares my mom down with mock outrage. "I'm really starting to learn who the favorite is."

She frowns and tucks a curl behind her ear. "Of course I worried about you boys, but I have less to worry about with you two."

I tune out the banter that ensues from mom's comment and twist the lock. It sticks, and I have to really give it some force to turn. "She's not wrong though," I mutter.

"Don't worry," Cade says. "Most students put some kind of spell on their doors to prevent people from picking the locks. I'll set wards before we leave. They will prevent anyone from entering without your permission and let you unlock the door without a key." He turns to Rho and gives him a flat look. "Just like I did for Rho and Adrian."

The door creaks slightly as I push it open and step over the threshold into my dorm. Luckily, I get my own room and only have to share a bathroom with one other person. The space is cold and barren, lacking personal touch. It's also very gloomy, just like the rest of campus. Two leaded glass windows look out over the quad and let in the dim gray light from outside. A bench seat is tucked against them just screaming for some cozy pillows and blankets.

Already, I'm planning what I'll add to the space to make it my own. A light purple rug will add color and warmth, not to mention a soft spot to walk on the creaking chestnut-colored wooden floor. It will match the violet and white comforter I bought on the shopping trip with mom. I also brought the rainbow blanket I crocheted a few years ago. Despite the occasional frayed string and dropped stitch, it will go perfectly in the window seat.

"Plants for sure," I say, setting my bag on the unmade bed that's pressed against the gray stone wall. "This space is definitely in need of plants."

"And lights," mom adds, peering out the window. "There won't be much sunlight streaming through here."

"But the fireplace will be nice in the winter," Rho says. Once again, harping on the positives of the dorm. "With some plants and lights, a few picture frames, the Wandering Fey merch I know you brought, and bookshelves, you'll be right at home." He gives me a bright grin that makes his icy blue eyes sparkle with warmth.

I turn in a slow circle, imaging where to put the bed and a few bookshelves. Rho might just be right. I can make this room home, even if the rest of campus may forever feel like a foreign country.

"Kai, why don't you and Sterling run to the store real quick and pick up a couple extra bookshelves." Mom sets a box on the empty desk and opens it. "We'll start unpacking."

"And some plants too, please." I smile at Sterling.

Sterling kisses my forehead and spins his keys around his finger. "Any plants in particular?"

"A monstera for sure. And lots of pothos. Oh, and maybe some silver tradescantia. I love the way they shimmer slightly." I glance around the room once again. "And don't forget some grow lights."

Kai grins at Sterling. "You get that? It all sounded like a foreign language to me."

"That's nothing new, Kai. You can barely speak our language as it is." Sterling throws his arm over Kai's shoulder and leads him out the door. He gives me a wink before they disappear down the hall.

"Sterling has no fucking clue what those plants are," Cade says chuckling to himself. "I guarantee he's googling them as we speak."

I smile and unzip my bag. The lump in my throat seems to have grown even bigger. These are the kinds of interactions I'll miss while living on campus.

But at least I'll have my brothers close by.

Aspen

Saying goodbye to my parents was the hardest thing. By the time they leave and I walk back to my dorm, it feels like a grapefruit has been lodged in my throat. The hallway blurs as tears fill my eyes, but I quickly blink them away. I don't want anyone to see me cry.

When I open my door, the ward Cade placed on the knob zinging over my skin, a small smile spreads across my face, and the tears dissipate. Sterling and Kai did a fantastic job buying bookshelves and plants. They even got a few sets of my favorite string lights to help illuminate the space. There are still a couple of hours before orientation, so I get to work unpacking and setting up my room.

I turn the bed so it's no longer flush against the wall and spread out the purple and white comforter. Then I move the bookshelves to flank either side of the window seat and begin the process of unpacking my books, Wandering Fey merch, and the few knick-knacks I brought with me. The smaller plants Sterling bought help fill out the shelves, and the bigger ones add some color and life to the corners of the room.

The little gray dove I bought during the shopping trip with my mom and brothers goes on my desk next to a silver tradescantia. At least when I'm sitting there studying, I'll have a friend to keep me company.

I'm standing on my desk in the middle of attempting to string the lights across my ceiling when my door opens.

"You could have asked for help you know," Rho says, eyeing me with a grin.

I grunt. "Then shut up and help me." I push higher onto my tip toes and strain to reach one of the little hooks I somehow managed to attach to the ceiling.

Before he reaches my side, the lights lift from my hands in a purple shimmer and string themselves along the hooks. "I assumed you wanted them like the ones in your room at home." Adrian's eyes glimmer with swirls of violet before settling back to their amber hue.

I quickly plug them in and hit the on switch, smiling as the soft golden glow spreads through my room. "Perfect," I whisper.

Rhory throws his arm over my shoulder and leads me toward the door. "Come on. We'll walk you to orientation."

"Thank you." I won't ever admit to them how much relief that gives me.

The thought of walking by myself to the cathedral inside Old Main, even though it's a pretty straight forward trek, made my stomach roll with unease. No matter how many times I tell myself I'm not the only first year student and everyone going to orientation is in the same boat as me, I can't help but think they're judging me. It's an insecurity I've always dealt with but have never been able to overcome.

Maybe growing up without magic in a world where everyone else has magic left me traumatized. If my parents had sent me to a human school, maybe it would be different. But they always hoped something would click and my magic would suddenly appear. Maybe that constant pressure of knowing they were hoping for something I had no control over did more damage than anyone realizes.

"Dude, Cade put a crazy strong ward on your door," Rho says, eyeing my door.

"They're worried about her." Adrian takes the lead and heads down the hall. "She's the baby and the only girl. Of course he put a strong ward on her door. It will keep everyone but family out, unless she invites them in."

Rho grunts but changes the subject. "Have you met the girl you share a bathroom with?"

"No." I shake my head, causing my waves to fall over my shoulder. "I'll avoid her as long as possible."

Both Rho and Adrian snort and shake their heads. Together, we make our way across the gloomy campus of LMU. Students flow toward Old Main and greet each other enthusiastically after a month away. I take it all in, shifting my bag on my shoulder. I hope one day I'll feel as comfortable on campus as everyone else appears to be.

"Yo! Grey!" A shout pulls me from my yearning, and I spin around, confused at who would be trying to get my attention.

"Mack!" Rho yells back, jogging toward the guy.

Of course. They didn't want me, but Rhory. The guy is broad shouldered with muscle clearly shifting under his tight gray tee. Two other guys flank him, equally as imposing and large as Mack. It doesn't take me long to realize they must be Rho's lacrosse teammates.

"How was your summer, bro?" Mack asks, slapping Rho on the back.

Adrian sidles next to me and lowers his head. "I hate these guys."

I glance at him with surprise. Adrian is usually the nice one of the family and never speaks ill of anyone. "Why?"

"They're absolute cunt nuggets." He glares, not caring if they see him.

I choke on air as I gasp and whip my head in his direction. "Adrian!"

He shrugs, then runs his fingers through his short curls. "Just wait. And keep your guard up around them. I don't trust them at all."

Mack's gaze slides to me, my coughing apparently getting his attention. "Who's this?" he asks with a wicked glint in his eye that makes my lip curl.

Rho's back straightens, and he takes a step to the side, blocking me from Mack's view. "My little sister," he says, leaving no room for further comment. "I'll see you guys tomorrow at practice."

Adrian grabs my arm and tugs me along, not waiting for Rho to fall in step with us. "Told you. Even Rhory doesn't want them looking at you."

"He doesn't want *anyone* looking at me," I mutter, not that I care much. Finding a boyfriend or girlfriend is the last thing on my mind. Even though my parent's hushed conversation about mates hasn't been forgotten.

Quite the opposite, actually.

As we approach Old Main, my brother's slow their steps. "You can find your way back to your dorm, right?" Adrian asks, studying me closely.

"You're n—" I stop myself before I can ask why they're not going to walk me inside. *Be a big girl, Aspen.* "Yeah, I can. Campus isn't that big."

"Just stick to the lighted paths," Rho says, pulling me in for a hug. "I'll stop by tomorrow. We can head to the bookstore and get all the books and supplies you'll need for the year."

"Thanks." I hug him back, then stand on my tip toes to give Adrian a peck on the cheek. Before I can change my mind, I step away and walk through the massive wooden double doors of Old Main. My stomach twists and turns with nervous nausea, and even the deep breaths I take don't calm it.

Inside is just as overwhelming as outside, if not more so. The interior is poorly lit with more of those rounded globes. The stained glass windows would let in beautiful sunlight if the clouds ever went away. White and gray marble flooring add the only bright color to the space. The walls are the same rough-hewn gray stone as the outside, with nothing hanging on them for ornamentation.

As I follow the crowd of first years heading toward the cathedral, I peer into the niches along the walls only to recoil when I realize they're decorated with skulls—human, animal, bird, you name it. Every nook I pass has a skull in some stage of decay. Some are sitting on ancient books, others are surrounded by unlit, half burned candles. But all of them are very obviously real with deep black eye holes that I swear follow my every step.

I shudder and keep my gaze firmly straight ahead. Why would anyone decorate with real skulls? This entire campus is slightly surreal and dark, and not just in the lighting department.

My fingers ache from grasping the strap on my bag by the time I reach the large wooden doors. I slip inside with the rest of the first years filing into the space. From my periphery, I can tell the cathedral is beautiful, but I don't want to look like a loser gawking at everything. So instead of taking in the architecture and design, I keep my eyes glued to the floor, only looking up long enough to find an empty pew to sit on.

I duck into a row and awkwardly shuffle down, dropping my phone in the process. It lands on the wooden pew with a clatter that echoes through the arched ceilings. Heat immediately suffuses my face and my heart stutters almost to a stop in my chest. With shaky fingers, I pick it up, subtly glancing around to see if anyone is looking at me. While logically I know no one cares, my anxiety rears its ugly head and tells me everyone is now watching and judging me.

My gaze lands on a guy three rows behind me. He's staring at me as if he's seen a ghost. His dark eyes are wide, plush lips slightly parted in shock. I swear his hand shakes as he brushes a loc from his forehead. It feels like wading through waist deep mud to pull my gaze away from him.

To his left is another guy, sitting sprawled out in the pew with his head leaning against the back and his eyes closed. His blonde hair is wild and untamed with one side shaved. Tattoos climb his arms and metal glints in his ears, eyebrows, and nose. Next to him, is ... a carbon copy. They have to be brothers at least, if not twins. This one is more put together though. His blond hair is neatly brushed back from his face and his clothing is unwrinkled and styled nicely. I can't see his eyes either, as he's too busy scrolling on his phone.

My skin prickles with goosebumps, and I glance back toward the startled guy. He's still staring at me as if he's trying to peel back my clothing and skin and peer inside of me. His body tilts forward as he leans closer to me, and I see his shoulders rise on a breath. What if he tries to say something to me?

I shake my head and my hair falls forward, a curtain of wavy black to block my view of him. Quickly, I make my way down the pew and sit, hunching forward to make myself smaller. Taking a breath to calm myself, I pull out my notebook and pen, ignoring how much my fingers shake. I doodle along the edges of the paper while I wait for orientation to start, but no matter how small I try to make myself or how much I try to distract myself, I can still feel his gaze on my back like a brand, burning and sizzling.

Misha

She's real. The girl from my dreams, the one I call Dove, is fucking real.

I smack Ezra's chest hard enough to leave a bruise. He sits up and glares at me, rubbing the spot. "What the fuck, man?"

"Look." I nod toward her three rows in front of us. Of course, he can't see her face, only her wavy black hair. I curl my fingers into fists, already knowing how silky those strands are.

"What am I looking at, Misha?" he growls, his tiger waking up inside of him.

"It's her," I say shakily, never taking my eyes off the back of her head. "The girl I've been dreaming of."

From the corner of my eye, I see Ari look up from his phone. "What?"

"You mean it wasn't just a dream?" Ezra follows my gaze, and he tilts his head to the side, narrowing his eyes. "How do you know it's her?"

"We made eye contact," I mutter. Just thinking about that moment steals the air from my lungs. It was like I'd been sucked into some kind of whirlpool. No matter how hard I fought, I couldn't pull my focus from her. She drew me in and claimed every part of me. "She's real," I whisper hoarsely.

"What does this mean?" Ari asks quietly. "Why were you dreaming about her?"

Before I can respond, the headmaster steps up to the podium, and the cathedral falls silent. What *does* it mean that I was having dreams about her? If she's real, does that mean what happened in the dreams is real as well? She said she didn't have any powers and was attending LMU to find out why. Could she really help us find out what happened to Millie?

Orientation passes in a blur, and I pay absolutely no attention to what the headmaster says. My gaze remains glued on the girl's back. Can she feel my attention? Her shoulders curve inward the entire orientation, and she fidgets with her hair a lot, tucking it behind her ear then untucking it, only to repeat that again and again.

I'm desperate for her to turn around. Could I have just imagined it was the girl from my dreams? Maybe I saw the black hair, so like hers, and my mind decided to play tricks on me. Gods, how horrible would that be? First I have these strange dreams about a girl that I've practically become obsessed with. Then I start seeing her in real life, only to find out it's all some grand joke my mind played on me. That would be so fucked up.

When she stands from the pew and shuffles out the opposite side, I blink. Orientation is over already? My thoughts consumed me so entirely, I didn't even notice what was happening. Glancing around, I find the rest of the first years also standing and filtering out into the misty evening. When I look back, she's gone.

"Where did she go?" I ask, panic rising in my chest and making my palms slick with sweat.

Ari looks around with a frown. "I don't see her."

"Did I just imagine her?" I ask, almost to myself. Rubbing my eyes until stars burst behind my eyelids, I sag in my seat. "Oh gods. I'm losing my fucking mind."

"You're not losing your mind," Ari says soothingly. "We'll figure this out."

Ezra stands and glares at me with his golden eyes. "Let's go. I'd like to walk around campus before it's too late."

What he doesn't say is that he wants to go to the spot where

Millie's body was found. So I push thoughts of my mysterious girl to the back of my mind and follow the twins outside.

Night has already fallen, and a thick mist spreads over the ground, dampening my skin almost immediately. I sigh heavily. It's going to take some getting used to, not seeing the sun or feeling its warmth.

"I already hate this place," Ezra mutters. His shoulders rise tensely around his ears, and his head constantly swivels as he scans our surroundings. I have no doubt his tiger is picking up all kinds of noises.

I open my mouth to say something cheery, like I normally would, something to lighten the mood, but nothing comes to mind. Maybe it's the dark, misty atmosphere. Or maybe it's because we're going to the spot where Millie's body was found. But I have a feeling the real reason is the subtle urgency thrumming just under the surface of my skin, a current of electricity that's making me jumpy and twitchy. And I know it's all because of *her*.

We're quiet as we walk across campus in the opposite direction of everyone else. The silence that surrounds us is at once peaceful and threatening. There could be anything lurking in the dark just out of the reach of the lamplights lighting the brick walkways. When Ezra steps off the path, his eyes reflect the light like a predator in the night, and I shiver.

We tromp through the grass to the northern edge of the cemetery. The brick wall stands tall and imposing over us, and in its shadow, the darkness seems even more threatening.

"What was she even doing out here by herself at night?" I mutter to myself, checking out our surroundings.

"She wouldn't have come here without a good reason," Ari says. He kneels on the ground and pulls a stone from his pocket.

Even in the dark, I know it's about palm-sized, the dark blue surface smooth except for Millie's carved initials painted in gold. I step back and let the twins have a private moment together. While I wait, my mind whirls. How can I uncover more information on my mysterious woman? Knowing she's real and not some figment of my imagination leaves me reeling.

I spent the past two weeks dreaming of this girl, never truly thinking she was real. I honestly thought I was starting to lose my mind. That maybe I was so lonely my subconscious created someone to keep me company. But as soon as I saw her in the cathedral, as soon as our eyes met, something calmed inside of me. Something that had been on edge, like I couldn't settle in my own skin until I laid eyes on her.

And when she disappeared—like she had never been there in the first place—all my doubts came creeping back in, along with the uneasiness inside of me. But despite how I doubt myself on her existence, there is no denying how seeing her made me feel.

Ezra and Ari stand, drawing my attention away from my spiraling thoughts. I ignore the wet gleam in Ari's golden eyes, and the inner fury burning in Ezra's. There will be time to get our revenge. But first, we need to find out what happened to Millie.

THE NEXT MORNING, Ezra and I walk together to class. All first years take the same set of required classes: History of Magicals, Magical Aptitude, Science of Magic, and Applied Magic. We then get to enroll in three or four additional courses of our choice. Ari, however, is a total nerd. He already tested out of all of his first year required classes, leaving Ezra and I to suffer through them alone while he enjoys taking classes of his choosing.

"How did Ari get so smart?" I ask Ezra as we traipse to Old Main in the early morning hours. "Did he steal all of the smartness in the womb and leave you with nothing?"

Ezra snorts and kicks a rock out of the path. "He didn't steal it, I gave it to him. That way I could make him do all the hard work, and I could slide through life in his shadow."

"Wow, that's quite the goal to have." I crack a grin and shove him with my shoulder. "Seems to be backfiring a bit now, though."

He grunts and rolls his eyes. "Having a nerd for a brother is really fucking weird sometimes. Especially since we're so similar. It's like looking at the version of myself that I could be if I actually put effort into ... well anything."

I want to argue with him, but now isn't the time or place. Ezra has always lived in his twin's shadow. Ari is incredibly smart and athletic. He has a drive to *do* that most people don't have. Ezra is quite literally the opposite of Ari in that regard. It doesn't matter how hard he tries, he can never catch up to his brother. I think that's why he gave up a while ago. He accepted it, and now leans into the persona of someone who doesn't care about anything.

But I know deep down he cares a lot. And I also know how much it scares him to care so much. Everyone he's ever loved has disappeared. The only person he really trusts is Ari. He doesn't even completely let his guard down around me, and we've been friends since second grade.

"What class are we going to again?" Ezra asks, scanning the facade of Old Main.

I pull out the slip of paper I scribbled my class list on and glance at it. "History of Magicals. Room 16."

Ezra groans. "Why the most boring class first thing in the morning?"

"Look on the bright side. We're getting it out of the way for the rest of the week."

"How are you always so cheery? Especially in the morning?" he grumbles, side-eyeing me.

Laughing, I throw my arm over his shoulders and pull him inside the building. It's like a kicked ant hill inside, with students scrambling to find their classes and professors quietly weaving through the throng to their offices with sure steps.

"Let's just get through this morning and meet up with Ari for lunch. We all have time this afternoon to discuss our first steps." I know I don't need to mention what those first steps involve. I also know mentioning our purpose for being here will help focus him.

We find room 16, which turns out to be a giant lecture hall with auditorium style seating, and take seats near the middle. Ezra immediately slouches in his chair and lays his head back, closing his eyes. I sigh. I should have known any classes with him would mean I'd be the one taking the notes and helping him pass.

The class is as boring as we expected it to be. By the middle of the lecture, Ezra is snoring softly next to me, and it takes all of my self control to not elbow him awake. I have to remind myself he's only attending LMU to find out what happened to his sister. He has no desire to further his education, even if it means making himself a more powerful shifter. Ezra will always be content doing the least required to survive.

As pointless as it seems, I take meticulous notes. I may have agreed to help them find out what happened to Millie, but I have another purpose for attending LMU, and the twins know this. Ever since the "incident," I've been terrified of my magic. Of course I'd never admit that to anyone other than Ezra and Ari. But it's the truth. And I'm hoping I can learn better control while I'm here.

When the lecture ends, I kick Ezra awake and we head to our second class of the day. The only two classes we have together are History of Magicals and Science of Magic, and both are Monday mornings, go figure. As I take notes in this class, I can tell I'm going to be asking Ari for help. Science is not my strong subject, I'm already confused. And it's only the first day. Wonderful.

With my head spinning, I kick Ezra awake for the second time, and we head to the library to meet Ari. It rivals Old Main for gothic beauty. The five-story building with soaring spires and arched doorways boasts magnificent carvings on the cream-colored facade. The only building on campus that isn't gray. Vines climb the side, but the gardeners prune them back from the front so the carvings can be seen. Carvings of books, scrolls, parchments, feather quills, inkwells, and ancient scholars. And intermixed with the 'normal' carvings, are depictions of skulls, violence, and death.

It wouldn't be Lustros Magical University without the skulls and death.

"Ari said he's on the second floor," Ezra says, pocketing his cell. "He bought us lunch." A rare smile blooms on his face as he takes the lead. Anytime his brother does something nice for him, Ezra's soft spot emerges.

The second floor of the library is for any student to use. It contains shelves of general books, study areas, and a couple conference rooms. The third floor holds the knowledge of more in-depth topics, while the fourth floor is for third-year students only working on their big projects. The fifth floor is strictly off limits to students.

Rumors abound on what the fifth-floor is like. Anything from professor lounges to books on summoning demons. If you're caught on the fifth-floor, the punishment is rumored to be severe, but no one knows exactly what that punishment is. Anyone who's been caught up there has never been seen again. Everyone says those students are murdered. I think they've just been expelled. But again, it wouldn't be LMU without the creepy rumors.

Ari claimed a study space in a back corner. It's surprisingly nice, with a couple of brown leather couches, a wooden table, and even a window with a small seat that lets in whatever light is shining in the murky sky. Two floor lamps provide the rest of the needed light from magical lighted globes.

"I brought sandwiches," Ari says, sliding two across the table for Ezra and me. "I also already pulled any books that might be helpful for us. One of the librarians showed me where LMU records are kept, and she gave me free access to it."

"How the hell did you pull that off?" Ezra asks, unwrapping his sandwich.

"You'd be surprised what a smile and a wink can do. You should try it sometime."

I huff a laugh and shake my head. "You got access to LMU records by flirting? You never cease to amaze me, Ari."

Ari's cheeks turn a light shade of pink, and he glances down at his sandwich, picking a stray onion off of it. "Just because I'm a nerd doesn't mean I can't flirt," he mumbles defensively.

I hold up my hands in surrender. "Sorry. Didn't mean anything by it. I've just never seen you flirt before."

Of all of us, Ari is the shyest, and I don't think he's ever had a girlfriend, but it wouldn't surprise me to find out he kept one a secret to avoid the ribbing Ezra and I would have given him. Ezra also has never had a girlfriend, but that's because he prefers to fuck them and leave them.

Ari shrugs off his embarrassment and points to the different piles of books and ledgers on the desk. "I thought I'd take the LMU records. Misha, you can take the research on magical creatures since you've been dreaming about them. And Ezra, you can take the police reports filed on campus and in surrounding areas." He then slides a smaller book toward me and ducks his head. "I thought you might be interested in this as well."

I pick up the volume and suck in a breath. *Soul-bonds: A Comprehensive Look at Mages and Their Bonds.* "Comprehensive, huh?" I flip the book over and crack a grin that feels forced. "It's awfully small for a comprehensive look."

"I think soul-bonds are pretty straightforward. At least as far as most mages are aware." Ari shrugs and picks up a ledger. "Of course, just because it's not mentioned in the book, doesn't mean it can't be true."

I stare at the book for a moment before tucking it into my bag. The possibility this girl could be my soul-bonded is outrageous. Soul-bonds are essentially soulmates for mages. Shifters have mates. Vamps have beloveds. I'm sure other magical creatures have specific bonds as well, but those are the only ones I know.

There's still a small part of me that wonders. And obviously Ari does too if he sought out this book. I keep coming back to the same questions over and over. Why would I dream of someone I've never met before? Why would I feel such anxiety when she's not in my sight? And why do I feel the desperate need to find her anytime I think about her?

Shoving those questions to the back of my mind—again—I pull a stack of books toward me and dig in. My focus right now needs to be on helping the twins. I don't have a single doubt in the world that my dream girl is connected to all of this. It's a gut feeling I can't explain. So the more information I can gather before she gets dragged into this, the better.

Aspen

"How are you finding LMU so far?"

"It's good," I say, forcing a smile. How can I possibly have an answer to that question when I haven't even had a full day on campus yet?

My counselor smiles and pulls her glasses from her nose, setting them on her desk. "Good. I looked over your schedule, and I think the courses you picked are appropriate, but I wanted to add an extra course. Would that be okay?"

An extra course? I swallow and nod, not quite sure about it. Every new student is assigned a counselor to help them navigate their first year at LMU and make sure they're on the right path. Ninety-eight percent of students never meet with their counselor. I'm one of the special few who has to because of my 'situation.' The main reason—well, honestly the *only* reason—I'm attending LMU, is to find out why I don't have powers.

"Don't worry," Mrs. Hancock says with a gentle smile. "It's not an actual class. I've talked with Professor Malvanado, and he's agreed to be a sort of mentor, or tutor, for you. He's a brilliant mage, and if anyone can help you figure out your magic situation, it's him."

A wave of uneasy nausea rolls through me. One-on-one sessions with a professor? A male professor? I've never felt comfortable around men. Anyone I've had to have close contact with, like my doctors, have always been women. If I've ever had to see a male doctor, I always made my mom go with me. And it's not because I'm worried about them taking advantage of me. I mean, that might be a small part of it, but just in general, I'm uncomfortable near them. It's something I've never been able to put into words. Just another of my weird quirks.

But instead of standing up for myself and requesting a female professor, I agree. Because agreeing is easier than stepping out on a limb and being judged or risking her brushing me off and making me feel ridiculous.

She gives me another smile, and jots down the day, time, and location for my one-on-one tutoring sessions before shooing me out the door for her next meeting. As I step into the hall, I run into someone—someone who is obviously male by the broad chest I bounce off of.

"Oh shit, I'm sor—" the guy cuts off with a sharp inhale.

I look up and take a quick step backward. It's him. The guy I made eye contact with at orientation. The guy whose gaze sucked me into a vortex of ... of ... I don't even know what. And as I meet his eyes now, it happens again.

A sensation of falling overcomes me. Like the floor has suddenly disappeared, and I'm free-falling through time and space. My blood rushes in my ears, and it's all I can hear, like the wind howling through an abandoned forest. He looks just as stunned as I do. His dark eyes are wide, filled with shock and something else that looks a lot like awe.

I swear it's like everything is moving in slow motion. His hand floats up and he reaches out a finger, as if to brush it down my cheek. His mouth parts as he reaches closer, and I somehow find the presence of mind to jerk backward. The spell snaps, and we both stagger.

The guy blinks and closes his mouth with an audible click of his teeth. He looks at his outstretched hand and quickly shoves it in his pocket. Before he can say anything, I duck around him and rush down the hall with my heart pounding in my chest. I fight the urge to turn around and look back at him. Is he still standing there, watching me? Or has he already moved on?

I dart around a corner and plaster my back to the rough stone wall. My heart is beating so hard I can feel it under my palms. I let my head thunk back against the wall and close my eyes, sucking in lungfuls of oxygen. It feels like I've just run a marathon. What the hell was that? Why do I lose myself every time I look at that guy?

My phone buzzes in my back pocket, and it jerks me out of my spiraling thoughts.

Rho: you free?

Me: I have class in 20. Why?

Rho: nvm call me when ur out

I put my phone away and take a breath. As always, that little bit of conversation with my brother helped to center me. My second class of the day is an elective; Physiology and Magic. When I chose my elective courses, I picked ones that I thought could possibly help me figure out my issue with not having magic. Also, because Kai is my bio dad, I've always been more intrigued with blood and the body. So I'm actually kind of looking forward to this class.

Before I head for the stairs, I peek around the corner. The guy is gone, probably in Mrs. Hancock's office. I let out a breath, a strange mix of relief and disappointment warring inside of me. I've seen this guy twice, but I didn't really get a good look at him either time. Dark eyes. Dark skin. But that's all I've gathered. Every time I see him, I get sucked into that spell-like sensation that takes over everything.

I almost trip on the first step. *Spell-like.* Is he a mage? Is he doing something to me to make me fall into a trance or something? I swallow and wipe my palms on my leggings before gripping my bag strap tightly. I'll have to keep an eye out for him and be more careful next time I run into him.

My class is on the second floor in a smaller lecture hall than the ones on the first floor. Instead of holding hundreds of students, this one looks to hold only about fifty. There are two parts to this course, one is a lecture and the other is a lab which is on a different day in a lab setting, I'm assuming.

I take a seat near the middle of the room in a spot where I won't have to move if someone has to go to the bathroom in the middle of class, but also far enough back where the professor won't be able to single me out for answers. Picking seats is almost a science to me. I think about every possible scenario before I choose, and try to pick a spot where I'll be the least noticed.

I'm pulling my notebook out when the sensation of eyes on me crawls over my skin. I look up only to find *him* striding up the steps while searching for a seat. I quickly look away, breath hitching in my chest. If I don't look at him, maybe he can't use his magic on me. I peek from the corner of my eye, watching as he stumbles when his gaze lands on me. I tear my eyes away and focus on the paper in front of me, heart racing.

Please don't sit by me. Please don't sit by me. Please don't sit by me.

He climbs further up the steps, and I sag in my seat. But it doesn't take long for the sensation of being watched to hit me again. He's not next to me, but he's behind me somewhere. And he's looking at me, if the crawling between my shoulder blades is any indication. I squeeze my eyes shut and try to ignore the sensation. But it's hard when I can literally feel his gaze burning into the back of my head.

I don't know what possesses me, but I turn around to look at him. I was right. He's four rows up, staring at me, an expression like he's seen a ghost painted on his features. As the weird spell-like fog begins to settle around me, I pull my gaze from his. Instead, I look at the rest of him. His black hair is styled in short locs that fall over his forehead. The red and black Altair LAX shirt stretches tight across his chest and biceps. And holy shit. His lips. My cheeks immediately heat when I imagine what they would feel like against my own.

I whip my head around and scoot down in my seat. *What the fuck, Aspen. Why would you even think that?* But no matter how hard I try to focus on the professor, I can't stop picturing him now that I've seen more than just his eyes. He's cute. He's really fucking cute. But that doesn't matter. He's most likely using his magic on me. And why the hell is he doing that? I obviously can't trust him.

The rest of the lecture passes in a painful blur. I have no idea what the professor talked about. My notes are just random doodles and words, anything to try and keep myself distracted from the guy sitting behind me. The entire lecture, I forced myself to sit still and not fidget like I wanted to. By the time the lecture ends, sweat pools between my breasts and the back of my shirt sticks to my skin.

I've never packed up and left a class so fast in my life. In record time, I have my notebook and pen put away, my bag slung across my shoulder, and I'm weaving between students to dart down the stairs while grabbing my phone out of my pocket. My fingers shake as I pull up Rho's contact and press the call button.

"What's up, Pen? How was class?"

"Where are you?" I ask right away, trying to sound like nothing's wrong.

I obviously fail, because Rho turns serious. "I'm in the library. Why? What's wrong?"

"It's nothing," I say quickly. In reality, it probably is nothing. I'm sure I've just worked myself up into thinking the worst possible scenario. It wouldn't be the first time I've done that.

"Where are you?" he repeats, voice low and serious.

I hear him packing his bag, and immediately regret calling him. "Stop, Rho. Don't leave the library just because of me. I'll meet you there. We can study together." After all, I need to figure out what this lecture was about before lab on Thursday.

"I'll meet you outside," he says almost hesitantly. "Are you sure you're okay?"

I glance around as I step out of Old Main, but there is no way he beat me outside. I practically ran to leave that lecture. "I'm fine. I'll see you a few."

Halfway to the library, I glance behind me. My eyes snag on someone in the crowd wearing a red and black shirt, but there are too many people between us so I can't tell if it's him or not. I hurry my steps so I'm practically running, and by the time I reach the library, I'm out of breath and sweating even more.

Rho waits for me on the front steps to the library with his hands on his hips. As soon as he sees me, his shoulders relax. I throw my arms around him and sag in relief. As long as he's here, I'll be fine.

"What the fuck, Pen?" He pushes me away to get a closer look at my face. "Why do you look so terrified?" The thought of explaining to my brother why I ran the entire way here, makes my cheeks heat in sudden embarrassment. Rho catches my shame and shakes his head. "Come on. I got the best study spot in the library."

He leads me across the first floor, and I take in the beautiful gothic design of the space. The high ceilings are lined with massive wooden beams that sit atop carved marble pillars. Separate rooms branch off from the main space, each housing a specific section of books. A winding staircase is the main feature of the library. It spirals all the way to the fifth floor with intricately designed handrails.

Rho leads me past the winding staircase, though, to the back of the library where an old set of steps have been carved into an alcove. It's dark in the stairwell, and I grab the back of Rho's shirt as fear spikes inside me. It doesn't take long to emerge at the second floor, and I relax as the gloomy light of day filters through the arched windows spaced evenly along the walls. Floor lamps provide additional light, and the soft glow they emit helps to fight back the ever present gloom.

The study space Rho has claimed is by a big bay window with two wingback armchairs on either side, and a table sitting in between. I sink onto a chair and close my eyes, taking deep breaths to center myself.

"Okay, Pen. Talk to me." Rho sits across from me and leans his elbows on his knees, studying me with his icy blue eyes.

"It's stupid. Just forget it." I pull my textbook and useless notes out of my bag, hoping Rho will drop it. I should know better though.

"I'm not going to forget it. You called me and sounded completely freaked out. Then practically ran to the library to find me. You're pale and sweaty, and your hands are shaking." He raises one brow and tilts his head to the side, looking very much like the wolf he can shift into. "If you don't tell me, I'll call our dads."

"You wouldn't!" I lift my head and glare at him. "You can't threaten to call our parents when you don't get your way. We're not children anymore, Rho."

"No, we're not. But something clearly scared you. And as your older brother, I'm going to protect you. And if that means getting our parents involved, then I sure as hell will. Now tell me what happened."

I sigh and lean forward to rest my elbows on my knees. He's not going to drop this. I bury my face in my hands and rub my eyes hard enough to see stars. Through my hands, I mumble, "I think someone is following me. Or at least, every time I run into him, I swear he's using magic on me."

Rho pushes from his seat so fast his cell phone hits the ground. "What?" The wild look in his eyes makes me shrink back. His wolf is rising to the surface, and I can tell he's fighting for control as he makes a fist, claws poking from his skin. "It's illegal to use magic against people on campus. It's the one rule they never take lightly. If someone is using magic on you, you have to let a professor know."

"I don't know for sure that he is." This was a mistake. Of

course Rho would take this to the extreme. I never should have said anything.

He sits on the edge of his chair and gives me a look that I remember seeing from him when we were kids and he was about to lecture me. "Tell me what happened? Why do you think you're being followed, and why do you think he might be using his magic on you?"

I set my books on the table and tell Rho of the three times I've seen this guy, and the weird sensation of losing all control over my thoughts when I look into his eyes. Rho frowns and pulls his bottom lip between his teeth.

"Three times in two days. That's not too uncommon on this campus, especially if you're in the same cohort and similar classes. But the magic thing ..." he trails off and gives me a sly grin. "Could you maybe just have a crush on him?"

"Seriously?" I grab my books and start to shove them back in my bag. If he's going to act like that, I'm leaving. "Just because I'm a girl you think I lose all my faculties over a cute guy?"

"Guy or girl, yes." He shrugs, then sighs. "Stop packing your bag. You're not leaving. I'm not downplaying your feelings. It could be suspicious. Definitely keep your guard up. And let me know if anything else happens. I'm not going to risk your safety, Pen."

I relent and set my books back on the table. "I just don't want you to make a huge deal out of it or freak out and start following me around to make sure I'm safe."

"Well, I'll always take your safety seriously, so get used to it. But I won't do anything crazy unless it's called for." He gives me a wolfish grin. "Deal?"

Rolling my eyes, I grab my textbook and flip it open. "Deal."

Aspen

I groan when my alarm goes off Thursday morning and hit snooze. The past two days have been blissfully clear of my mysterious stalker. While they weren't exactly easy days since I still had to experience 'first days' with my new classes, they were less stressful without his presence. I'm slowly getting into a routine, which unfortunately involves waking up earlier than I would like so I can get a shower before my bathroom buddy.

We've run into each other twice now, but I still don't know her name. Mainly because I'm so awkward I just run when I see her. She's a cute blonde, tall and skinny. Her toiletries basket is full of makeup and hair products. She is the exact opposite of me.

I'm in no way a girly girl. My favorite color is black. I have no idea how to do makeup, and when I do, it looks like a child put it on. My wardrobe consists mostly of leggings, baggy tees, hoodies, and black boots. I wear my hair in a rotation of four different styles—down, half up, in a claw clip, or a messy bun on top of my head. I'm simple and low maintenance. At least when it comes to fashion.

When my alarm goes off again, I drag myself out of bed and into the shower. Today is my first tutoring lesson with Professor Malvanado. I slept horrible last night because all I could think about was this morning. Having to meet one-on-one with him is literally my worst nightmare.

I take a little longer in the shower trying to calm my nerves, but it doesn't work. So I hop out and quickly get dressed. I forgo breakfast because I'll probably just puke it all up anyway, and head straight to Old Main.

It's chilly this morning, but luckily it's not raining. The clouds still hang heavy in the sky though, giving everything a dreary gray appearance. I love weather like this, but not every single day. A warm, sunny day sounds pretty nice right about now. There aren't many people up and moving this early in the morning, so campus is quiet and still. I find I kind of like it like this. It's almost peaceful in a strange, eerie way.

When Old Main comes into view, slowly creeping out of the fog, my steps slow. Nerves writhe in my gut like snakes twisting and tangling together. I swallow back the nausea that climbs up my throat and take deep calming breaths that do nothing to actually calm me. *I can do this.*

I'm too preoccupied with my anxiety to notice the beautiful interior of Old Main like I usually do. But it's quiet inside, and I make my way to Professor Malvanado's office. Outside his door, I pause and take more deep breaths. My heart pounds so hard it's almost painful, and I'm seconds away from throwing up. Maybe I could just skip it. Say I'm sick or something. But, I know eventually I'll have to do this. Especially if I want to figure out why I don't have any powers. Before I can talk myself out of it, I knock on the heavy wooden door.

"Come in," a deep voice booms from inside.

I step inside the office, but keep my gaze to the ground. The floor is tile, like the rest of the building, with a burgundy plush rug covering the surface.

"Ms. Grey, sit down please."

I take one of the chairs in front of his desk. "Thank you," I mumble, setting my book bag in the other chair. Hesitantly, I glance up. Professor Malvanado is probably in his late forties. His dark hair is sprinkled with salt and pepper, and his goatee is completely gray. He's wearing a pair of tortoiseshell glasses, and a sweater vest over a white button-up shirt. In short, he's the epitome of a college professor.

"So, Ms. Grey. It sounds like you're having a problem with your magic. Mrs. Hancock suggested we meet to figure out what's going on. Is that correct?"

"Yes, sir," I nod, keeping my gaze just over his shoulder.

"Okay, so tell me about yourself. What's going on with your magic?"

I shift in my chair, butterflies erupting in my stomach. Didn't Mrs. Hancock tell him already? Did he not look into my file before this meeting? Or is he just putting me on the spot?

"Um, well, I don't … I don't have any magic."

I swear Professor Malvanado pauses, but it's such a short pause I'm probably just imagining it. "No magic? I saw in your file that your dad is a vampire. What about your mom? That information wasn't provided."

"My mom also has magic," I hedge, hoping he lets it drop even though I know he won't.

"What kind?"

Ah. I hate explaining this. We've always kept my mom's abilities secret and only told the people who absolutely need to know. But we agreed it would be important for me to share all the information when I came to LMU in the hopes of figuring out what's going on. "Well, she's a harpy."

Professor Malvanado rears back in his seat. "A harpy? You're sure? That is extremely rare." His eyes narrow on me, taking on a glint that makes me want to squirm.

Am I sure? Seriously? "Yeah, I'm sure."

He makes a note on a piece of paper in front of him. "Well. It's common knowledge that when two races procreate any offspring will be essentially human."

I take a breath and prepare for the part I always have to explain to people. "Yes, I know. But my brothers both have powers. My oldest brother is a mage, like our dad Cade. My other brother is a wolf shifter, like our dad Sterling."

Professor Malvanado hums as the dots in his head connect. "That's right. Your brothers have different fathers. Your biological dad is Malakai Thorne."

Dude seriously didn't look at my file at all. What a joke this entire thing is. "Yes." And now I wait. Because I know what will come next. My dads aren't exactly unknown in the magical community, although we keep a pretty low profile.

Malakai, my bio dad, is the prince of the vampires, which means my granddad is the king. Cade has a super rare magic and is insanely powerful, which means my brother also has this super rare magic. And Sterling is the alpha of the Iron Shadows pack, the biggest pack in Lustros. And yes, that means Rho is next in line to be alpha. And on top of all of that, my mom is a harpy, not that most people know that fact. Harpies are so rare most people don't even know they exist.

I watch Professor Malvanado's face closely, and there it is. The calculation in his pale blue eyes as he realizes just how powerful my family is and ways he can use it against me. Okay, maybe that's a bit of an exaggeration, but I know he's thinking one of two things: either I'm a lazy spoiled brat who thinks I deserve everything handed to me, or my family will raise hell if he doesn't solve the problem of me not having any magic.

Neither of which is true, of course. Well, I may be a bit spoiled.

Professor Malvanado nods slowly and jots down a few more notes. "Okay. Let's start with the basics."

I'M LATE FOR LAB. Professor Malvanado took extensive notes on my family history, digging as deep as I could go, which isn't very deep. But it took a lot longer than I anticipated. So as soon as I leave his office, I have to run. Luckily, it's also in Old Main, but it's on the third floor.

By the time I run up the flight of stairs, my thighs are burning and so are my lungs. I work out with Rho a lot, but mainly just lifting weights. I absolutely despise cardio, and this is why. I'm sweating and panting when I reach the room.

I check my phone real quick before I push inside. I'm only five minutes late, but still. Walking into the class when everyone else is already in there and knowing they will all turn to look at me makes me want to turn around and leave. My skin suddenly feels too tight on my bones, and the nausea is so bad I have to swallow to keep from vomiting. I take a breath and open the door.

The room is filled with large wooden lab tables and metal stools. Cabinets and shelves line the walls with various instruments and supplies. Professor Anderson is standing behind another lab table in the front of the room, but it doesn't look like she's started class yet. I release a breath and look around for a seat.

And my heart stops.

Oh no. No. No. No. No! There is only one open seat, and it's next to *him*. I whimper quietly and try to think of a way out of this situation, but nothing comes to mind. He's watching me with the same shocked expression he always has when he sees me. Today he's wearing a gray LMU hoodie and a pair of jeans that hug his thighs and make me swallow.

"Okay, class. Let's get started," the professor calls.

My feet drag, and each breath I take catches in my lungs as I head toward the only open stool. Dropping my bag on the ground, I pull the stool as far from him as possible before perching on top. The entire side of my body closest to him burns with awareness. I reach up to fan my hair to hide the side of my face, but of course I wore it in a bun today so I can't.

"Welcome to the lab portion of Physiology and Magic. The person sitting next to you today will be your lab partner for the year, so hopefully you chose your seats wisely." Professor Anderson grins at us, then clicks on the projector. "Before we dive into the meat and potatoes of this lab, we'll start with some basics. I'm assuming most of you have had some sort of lab experience in the past, but just in case we'll start easy." She dims the lights, then hands a stack of papers to someone in the front. "Take one and pass it on. I want you to work with your partner and use the projected case study to come up with a hypothesis for the cause of the subject's illness."

Before I begin working with *him*, I send a quick text to Rho letting him know what's going on. Just in case. At least if something happens, he'll know who the last person I had contact with was. Grim thoughts, but I can't help but think them.

"You might have to scoot over a bit," *he* says. "We only get one paper." He shakes said paper to get my attention, but his voice is what grabs me. It's deep and smooth, and it slides over my body like silken sheets.

I swallow thickly and drop my phone into my bag before scooting my stool just a tiny bit closer. He chuckles, and I swear I almost drool all over myself. Nothing has ever sounded so sexy.

"Hi," he says, leaning forward far enough I can see him in my peripheral vision. "I'm Misha."

Okay. I can't be rude. As much as I want to get up and run as far from here as possible, I can't. And since I'm stuck with him for the rest of the year, I better play nice. I turn to face him, keeping my gaze firmly over his shoulder and away from his eyes. "I'm Aspen."

Misha sucks in a breath and actually shudders. But when I blink, he's looking at me like nothing weird just happened. "Aspen," he breathes. "That's a really beautiful name."

I shrink back, heat climbing up my neck and into my cheeks. "Uh, thanks?"

He grins at me, and I find myself drawn to look at him. But I stop myself. I can't let him use his magic on me. He taps the paper on the table with his pen. "So, what do you think?"

"About what?" I blurt, then realize he's talking about the case study. "Oh! Um. I don't know." I cringe and look away, turning to face forward again. Why am I so awkward around people? Instead of worrying about what an idiot I'm being, I read the case study and try to focus on what it's saying. When I'm done, I turn back to Misha.

He's watching me with an expression I can't put a name to. It's like a mix of awe, disbelief, and something else. Something like ... desire? I quickly look down at the paper between us, ignoring the fluttering in my stomach.

"So, uh, it seems like some kind of magical attack against his bloodstream," I say quietly.

Misha jerks and shakes his head, muttering something to himself. Then he straightens and returns his focus to the paper. "Yeah. I agree. But based on the symptoms, I don't think it's just a random magical attack. It sounds like red magic."

"That's what I was thinking, too." I watch him jot the answer down, his penmanship narrow and precise, if only slightly sloppy.

"The next question asks how we would treat it." He frowns as he thinks through possibilities.

"A violet mage." The answer comes quickly to me. "They have unique particles in their magic that can counter attack magic in the body."

Misha stares at me for a moment, mouth parted. Then says, "But they are very rare. Where would you even find one?"

"There's a clinic in Altair with a violet mage." My dad, I don't say. I also don't add that my brother is studying at LMU to follow in Cade's footsteps.

"Seriously? That's awesome." Misha quickly scribbles the answer on the paper. "Are you from Altair?"

"Yes."

He nods. "I'm from Crescent Falls. But I've been an Albatross fan since I was a kid."

That explains the lacrosse shirt he was wearing the other day. The Altair Albatross is my brother's favorite team as well. His dream is to play for them after LMU. "Do you play lacrosse?" If he does, that would mean Rho probably knows him.

Misha snorts. "No. I tried out in high school, but it turns out I have horrible hand-eye coordination."

"My brother plays for LMU," I offer. Then I bite my cheek. Why did I just open myself up for further conversation about my personal life? *Idiot, Aspen!*

"Really? Who's your brother?" The excitement in Misha's voice almost makes me smile. He sounds like a little kid learning his superhero is real.

"Um, Rhory Grey." Great. Now he knows my last name, not that he wouldn't have figured it out eventually.

"No way! He was a first year student last year, right? He made huge waves in the lacrosse world, surprising everyone with how good he is."

I nod. "Yep. That's my brother." I roll my eyes because if Rho could hear Misha talking, he'd never stop bragging about it.

"So, do you like lacrosse then?" he asks, scooting his stool a little closer to mine.

Tingles spread through my side closest to him, like my body can sense how close he is to touching me. And it's confusing, because half of me wants to pull away, and the other half kind of wants to lean closer, just to see what it would be like to touch him. I shake my head vigorously in an attempt to clear the absurd thoughts from my mind, which Misha takes as confirmation that I don't like lacrosse.

"So you never go to your brother's games?" he asks, sounding suspiciously put out by that thought.

"Huh? Oh, no. I don't mind lacrosse. I went to his games in high school, but I haven't been to any at LMU." Just don't ask me to play it. I don't mind working out with Rho, lifting weights. But there's too much cardio in lacrosse. And like Misha said, too much need for hand-eye coordination.

"Really? LMU games are wild. Maybe w—"

"Okay," Professor Anderson calls, interrupting what Misha was going to say. "You should have your paper filled out. Let's go around the room and share our hypotheses."

Misha

Aspen Grey.

I finally have her name. Her voice is just as low and hypnotic as it is in my dreams. Her beautiful gray eyes are captivating, and I want to stare into them until I'm lost.

My thoughts are all over the place as Professor Anderson makes her way around the room to hear everyone's hypotheses. When Aspen first walked into class a few minutes late, her cheeks were flushed, and her eyes were wide as she scanned the space for a seat. My heart almost stopped at the sight of her. I'd been praying she'd be in my lab, but when she didn't show up, my hope evaporated. That hope flared back to life when she stepped into the room. But something ugly coiled in my gut when she realized the only seat left was next to me.

Her eyes had darted wildly around the room, and her throat worked on a swallow. It didn't take much for me to realize she was scared. I thought back to our past encounters, but I can't think of why she'd be afraid. Besides, we really haven't had many encounters. When she scooted her stool farther from mine, I knew I'd be working to break down the wall she had already built to protect herself from me. I don't mind working hard to do that.

I barely hear Professor Anderson ask me and Aspen for our hypothesis. From the corner of my eye, I see Aspen's shoulders curve inward, and she looks down, tucking a strand of black hair behind her ear. Glancing at her, I find her cheeks and ears tinted pink, and she's chewing on her bottom lip. Shaking myself out of my thoughts, I take the paper and share our answers without actually thinking about what I'm saying. When I'm done, Professor Anderson moves on to the next group, and Aspen visibly relaxes. Interesting. I don't think she likes to be the center of attention.

As the rest of the class shares their findings, I notice Aspen subtly packing her bag, slipping her notebook, textbook, and pens away. I glance at the clock and see we have a couple minutes left, and I'm guessing Aspen is going to make a run for it to get away from me. I smile to myself. *Good luck, dove. I'm not letting you go so easily.*

I was right. As soon as Professor Anderson dismisses us, Aspen dashes out of the room. "Shit," I mutter to myself. I should have been prepared. Quickly, I shove my things into my bag and hurry after her.

She's already heading into the stairwell when I exit the lab. I jog down the hall, and catch her on the stairs. "Hey, Aspen," I say, stepping up to her side.

She jumps, her hand flying to her throat as she gasps in a breath. "Oh my gods, you scared me."

"Sorry," I grin. "I didn't mean to. You left so fast, I didn't have time to ask you if you wanted to meet up to study. I can already tell this course is going to be a struggle for me. I'm not the best with sciencey things." Not entirely a lie. But I thought learning about the human body and how magic works within it might help me to understand my magic a bit more.

"Um ... I ..." Aspen's eyes dart back and forth as we step out of the stairwell and into the main hall of Old Main. The flood of students and professors forces me to walk behind her, giving her the time she needs to come up with an excuse.

Son of a bitch. How am I going to convince her to study with me? Now that I know she's real, and I've talked to her, I want to know everything there is to know about her. I need to know if her lips are as soft as they were in my dreams. Does she really fit into my arms like a puzzle piece? And, even though I know what it feels like in my dreams to be buried deep inside of her, I'm positive it won't compare to reality.

When we finally make our way through the crowd and step outside into the misty, cloud-covered campus, I step up to her side again. "So, studying." I hold my breath, praying she didn't think of a good excuse. "We could meet in the library." Where there are lots of people and she'd be safe.

"I ... um ..."

"Pen!"

Her head shoots up, and everything about her body language screams relief. Her shoulders sag, and her head lolls to the side. A small smile pulls her lips up, and she darts forward, wrapping her arms around a tall, broad shouldered guy.

Insane jealousy burns through me, molten lava spreading through my veins as his arms go around her. My fingers curl into fists and squeeze until they shake. This possessiveness doesn't even take me by surprise, because somewhere along the way, my subconscious decided this girl is mine. Seeing her in another man's arms almost makes me lose my shit. And seeing her relaxed with him, is like a hot knife spearing right into my heart.

The guy looks over her shoulder, and his eyes narrow. He possessively tugs Aspen behind him, and it takes all of my self-control to not yank her away. My fingertips tingle, and I squeeze my hands harder, willing the sudden spike of my magic to go away. *She's not yours, asshole. She doesn't even want to study with you.*

"Is there a problem here?" the guy asks. His blue eyes are sharp as knives as he stares at me like he wants to cut me into ribbons.

I shrug as nonchalantly as possible with the possessive rage tearing through me. "Not that I'm aware of."

"Then why is my sister so terrified of you?"

Sister? Sister! A laugh bubbles in my chest, but I swallow it down and focus on keeping my knees from buckling in relief.

Now that I take a closer look at them, I can see the similarities. Sure they have different hair and eye color, but the facial structure is the same. I release a breath and fight to keep the smile from my face. Smiling at his question won't do me any good.

"Rho," Aspen mutters, looking down at the ground. She peeks up at me through her lashes, pink tinting her cheeks.

She's so fucking adorable when she's embarrassed. "I'm not sure how I've scared her, but I never meant to. And I'm sorry that I have." I keep my gaze on her, trying to make sure she hears my words and believes them.

Her brother snorts. He's wearing an LMU lacrosse shirt, so I take a wild guess and assume it's Rhory. Does she have any other siblings? Yet another thing I want to find out. I need to know everything about this girl.

"Look, I was just asking her if she wanted to study together in the library." I lift my hands in surrender, but I have no intention of giving up. "If she doesn't want to, I'm not going to force her." But I will do everything in my power to change her mind. I turn my gaze to Aspen. "I'm sorry I scared you. I really thought you might be able to help me with our class, but if you don't want to, that's fine." How the hell did I scare her? What did I do? I need to figure that out so I can make sure to never do it again.

She looks at me, half hiding behind her brother. She reminds me of a timid mouse, and something about that doesn't sit right with me.

"Just stay away from her," Rhory says, a low growl lacing his words. He turns to Aspen and tucks her under his arm. "Let's go."

I watch them walk away, silently fuming. A boyfriend might have been easier to deal with. As they walk away, Aspen looks over her shoulder at me. I quickly school my face into something pleasant, not wanting to scare her again. Fuck. What the hell did I do? Just having her gaze on me is like standing in the rays of the sun, warm and inviting. But then she turns back around, and I shiver in the sudden loss of that heat.

I sigh and head toward my dorm. Fuck me. This is not going how I wanted it to go.

THIS FIRST WEEK of school has been a little hectic. Ezra is moodier than usual because we haven't done anything to work on finding out what happened to Millie. Ari has been immersing himself in his classes because unlike Ezra, he actually wants to get something out of school besides avenging their sister. And I'm stuck obsessing over someone who is apparently terrified of me.

I pinch the bridge of my nose and let my head fall against the back of the chair. A headache has been steadily brewing for the past two days and nothing seems to make it better. Normally when my head hurts, I just want peace and quiet, but the library right now is too quiet. I find my mind wandering in the silence with nothing to focus on. And of course it wanders right to Aspen.

Groaning internally, I pull my headphones from my bag and turn on some music to help drown out the quiet. I really meant what I said to Aspen. I'm going to have a hard time with Physiology and Magic, and talking with her about the hypothesis and the way she talked about violet mages, I can tell she's smart. Not only would it be nice having someone to help me through the class, but being able to spend time with her and getting to know her would be the cherry on top.

I pull my textbook closer and pop the lid off my highlighter. Chapter one is basic human anatomy: bones and muscles. I make it through the first two pages, highlighting things that seem important, before the hairs on the back of my neck prickle. Someone's watching me.

I turn in my seat and freeze. Aspen is standing at the door to the second floor, her gray eyes trained on me. That warmth spreads over me, the physical manifestation of being the center of her attention. She bites her bottom lip, and I clench my hand trying to erase the urge to walk over to her and tug it from between her teeth. The uncertainty in her gaze, her posture tense and prepared to turn and run, causes my stomach to sink like a stone in the river.

Now is not the time to try and convince her to study with me. If I push too much, I'll push her away for good. I need to be patient. Slow and steady wins the race, right? Fuck. Try telling that to my heart. It pounds against my ribcage as I turn around and get back to studying. Not that I'll be able to focus knowing she's right there.

I read the same sentence four times, never once actually processing what I'm reading. This is fucking pointless. Her presence behind me is like a lodestone drawing a magnet. I want nothing more than to stay in her orbit for every second of my day and night.

"Do you still want a study partner?"

I jump and turn around again, pulling my headphones from my ears. She's standing right behind me, white-knuckling the strap of her bag across her chest. Her discomfort and uncertainty are written plain as day across her face and posture. She's fighting every instinct she has.

I choose my words carefully, and shrug one shoulder. "I'm sure I can get by just fine on my own." I give her a self-deprecating smile. "Don't feel like you have to study with me if you don't want to. I don't want to pressure you into anything."

I turn back to my book, holding my breath. She's going to walk away. I gave her the out she so desperately wants, and she's going to take it. I'll have to figure out a different way to get close to her.

I'm shocked when she sits down on the couch across from me. Every muscle in my body freezes, scared to move even an inch for fear of spooking her. She doesn't look at me, but she sets her bag down and digs through it, pulling out her textbook and a notebook. Each of her movements are small and controlled, like she's doing everything she can to keep attention off of herself. Too bad it doesn't work. My gaze is glued to her, no matter how hard I try to look away.

She's so much more beautiful in person. So real and ... alive. Her tan cheeks flushed with nerves and her chest lifting faster than it would normally as she breathes unsteadily. Those curves make my mouth water, and I remember how it feels to hold her in my arms. To touch her skin with my own. My dick twitches and I grimace. *Get it the fuck together, Misha.* I pull my book onto my lap and force my gaze down to the letters that refuse to come together in my mind to make any sort of coherent thought.

"You're brother isn't going to hunt me down for this, is he?" I ask with a wry lilt to my voice.

Her cheeks flush further, and she keeps her attention strictly on the book in front of her. "I'm sorry about that," she says quietly. "My brother's tend to be a bit protective of me."

"Brothers? There's more than one?" That could be problematic. "Do I need to be worried?" Protective siblings are not something I want to deal with.

She smiles at her book, and I desperately wish she'd direct that smile toward me. "I have two older brothers. Both of them attend LMU." A strand of hair falls forward from her messy bun and she tucks it behind her ear. "Rho is a second year, as you know. Adrian is a third year." She shrugs and looks up, but still doesn't meet my gaze. Instead, her eyes shift up and to the left. "The only one you really need to worry about is Rhory. Not that he'd actually do anything. He's all talk. Mostly."

I stare at her open-mouthed before I click my teeth together. That's the most I've ever heard her talk. Her voice is so seductive, sliding over my skin and sinking into my bones. I clear my throat and ask the one question that's been plaguing me all day. "How did I scare you? I really didn't mean to, and I want to make sure I don't do it again."

She looks back at her book, fingers fidgeting with the pages.

"Um ... I thought ... well ..." She shakes her head and looks back up, this time her eyes shifting to the right. "What are you?"

And to think I've never even thought about what she could be. A mage. She has to be, right? "I'm a mage," I say, praying she doesn't dig further into it. But instead of asking the next most common question—what type of mage—she tenses. "You don't like that," I say slowly, reading the discomfort in her body language.

Aspen chews on the inside of her cheek for a moment, eyes going distant as she looks in front of her. "I thought ... um ... have you used your magic on me?" The question leaves her in a rush of breath, as if she has to get it out before she changes her mind.

I sit back in my chair and study her. Why would she ask that? First of all, it's against LMU policies to use magic on another student. Second of all, what the hell would I have done? "No, I have not used my magic on you." I will never let my magic near her. "Why would you think that?"

She takes a breath like she's preparing herself to do something. Then she lifts her gaze to meet mine. The shock of electricity that zaps through my body actually makes me jerk. I lean forward, drawn into her gray eyes and needing to be closer. Her lips part, a soft inhale of her breath makes me think of all sorts of things I shouldn't think about. In my dreams, she'd make that exact noise when I kissed her throat. And fuck, I want to hear her do that again.

My brain is screaming at me to look away. I'm probably freaking her out by staring at her so intently, but I can't physically make myself do it. I'm trapped in her gaze, washed in the heat of her attention and wanting even more. I want all of her. The need is so visceral my stomach clenches. Tendrils of my magic snake through my bloodstream, gray mist that searches for an exit. I'm so caught up in her, I can't even clamp down on it.

Someone smacks the back of my head, and I'm ripped out of the magnetic pull of her gaze. I hear her suck in a shaky breath, but I turn around to find Ari standing next to me.

"I've been calling you for an hour now."

Aspen

THE TENSION BETWEEN ME AND MISHA SNAPS AS SOON as he looks away. I sag on the couch, breath rushing from my lungs as my muscles turn watery, and I close my eyes. Being this close to him and having the foresight to pay attention, I was able to watch his eyes. They didn't change. If he was using his magic, his eyes would have changed to the color of his magic. Just like Adrian's do. Misha's eyes stayed a beautiful dark brown.

"Sorry," Misha says, "I was studying."

"Riiight," the new guy says.

I snap my eyes open and find him watching me. His blond hair is longer on the top than the sides, and it's swept back away from his face. Golden eyes take me in, and I can't stop the chill that works over my body. Those eyes are animalistic. There's nothing human about them. His face is sculpted in all sharp plains and angles. In short, he's just as beautiful as Misha. He's also one of the guys I saw at orientation.

The guy takes the chair next to Misha's and gives me a smile. "I'm Ari."

I lick my lips and swallow, trying to work moisture back into my mouth. "Aspen."

"Dude, her brother plays lacrosse for LMU." Misha slaps Ari on the chest with a grin. "Rhory Grey."

"Oh yeah? That's pretty cool." He sits back in the chair, but keeps his gaze on me. There is something about the way his brows are slightly furrowed that makes my hackles rise. But, I also could be imagining things. I am paranoid after all.

Misha turns to me with an easy grin. "Ari is one of my best friends from back home, along with his twin brother, Ezra, who also attends LMU."

Twins? That makes sense. But it's definitely not good. It's bad enough sitting and talking with Misha, but add in two more gorgeous guys, and I know I'll make an absolute embarrassment out of myself. My brain tends to just shut down around new people, especially if they're guys, and double especially if they're hot guys. Put me in a situation with three of them, and I'm goner.

"So why were you calling me?" Misha asks Ari.

"Ezra is on a rampage. He stormed out of my dorm after I told him I was going to finish studying before I helped him. By the time I was done and went to his room, he wasn't there. I imagine he's stomping around campus by himself, probably getting into trouble."

The look Ari gives Misha is filled with hidden messages and layers of secrets. I quickly look back at my textbook, but I don't actually see any words, just a blur of black and white and highlighter pink. Thanks to the meager supernatural abilities Kai passed on to me, I use my heightened sense of hearing in an attempt to overhear what Ari's whispering to Misha, but he's pitched his voice too low, and I can't quite make it out.

"Well, he's going to have to learn we're both here for another reason as well. If that means he throws a few extra temper tantrums, we'll just have to deal with that." Misha shakes his head and sighs. "It's not like we didn't warn him before we came."

Here for another reason? What could be another reason for attending LMU besides continuing your education? Not that it's any of my business. I don't want to get involved in anything or anyone. I've done just fine in life keeping my head down and staying in my own lane, and I have no plans to change any of that now.

Ari grunts. "Easy for you to say. You're not the one who has to try and calm him down when he gets like this."

"It's not that I don't want to help you," Misha says, then throws his hands up in surrender at the raised brow Ari gives him. "Hey, I've tried, and I only made it worse."

"I know, I know." Ari sighs, running a hand through his hair and slightly mussing up the blond strands. "It just gets tiring after a while. And then I feel guilty for thinking that."

"Nah, it's nor—" Misha cuts off as the door to the stairwell bangs open.

The sudden loud noise in the hush of the library makes me jump, and my heart almost beats right out of my chest.

"Oh, shit," Ari mutters. "Here we go."

The guy who stomps over to our study area is most definitely Ari's twin. They look identical, except Ezra has an edgier look with the messy hair, tattoos, and piercings.

Their animalistic eyes are the same golden color, but his gaze is sharp enough to cut diamonds.

"Are you fucking serious?" Ezra growls, not bothering to keep his voice down. "I spent the past half hour searching for you both, only to find you here with *her*?" He barks a laugh that sounds anything but humorous, flinging his arm in my direction. "I shouldn't be fucking surprised that I'm the only one who cares about what we're supposed to be doing here."

My mouth falls open in shock for a moment before I get myself under control and look back at the book in my lap.

"Ezra, take a breath," Ari says calmly. "Give us a chance to at least defend ourselves before you berate us. And lower your voice. We're in a library."

I peer at Misha from under my lashes and find him wincing. He glances at me and I quickly avert my gaze. That wince could have meant a myriad of things.

"Ezra—" Misha begins, but he doesn't get any further.

"Fuck that," Ezra spits. "I'm the only one taking this seriously. I'm not surprised to find you going back on this, Misha. I knew she'd become a problem in the end. But, Ari, I can't believe you're acting this way."

She'd be a problem? Is he talking about me? He can't be. There is no way he knows who I am. And what would I have done to cause a problem?

Ari stands up and grabs his twin's shoulders, shaking him slightly. "Ezra, you need to calm down. You're drawing attention to us." He looks around pointedly, noting the students watching this interaction. "Misha and I both told you from the beginning we were coming to LMU for two purposes. One of those is to learn and graduate. We have three years to figure out ..." he glances at me and swallows. "To figure out the other thing."

I shouldn't be intrigued. I shouldn't be wondering what it is they're not mentioning. But I've always been nosey, and I love drama as long as I'm not in the middle of it. These three are mysterious, and they are definitely hiding something.

Ezra shakes his head. "This is unbelievable. I always thought you'd be on my side, but apparently I was wrong." He gives me one more disgusted look before storming off.

Ari sighs heavily and pinches the bridge of his nose. "Well, that went just about as I expected it to go." He plops into the chair and lets his head fall against the back. "I should go after him."

"I'd give him some time to cool off," Misha says, settling more in his seat. "Trying to talk to him when he's like this never ends well."

Ari grunts and closes his eyes. I take the opportunity to study him more without him looking at me. He really is quite handsome even with his jaw clenched tight and strain bracketing his mouth. He's clearly worried about his brother. I get the impression from their conversation that Ari is the one to keep things running smoothly. And it looks to me like it's worn him down.

"So," Misha says, drawing my attention away. "That was

Ezra." He grins at me and tosses his book onto the table. "And it was a pretty good first impression, all things considered."

Ari snorts but keeps his eyes shut. First impression? That implies there will be opportunities for further impressions. I never agreed to that. But of course I don't say anything, because that would require me to not only talk to them, but to also disagree, which is even harder for me to do. Always the people pleaser, despite my fear of attention.

"I've completely lost my focus for studying now." Misha leans forward and snags my gaze.

It takes all of my self-control to not stare into his eyes, and that absolutely floors me. Never in my life have I had an easy time with eye contact. With my family, I do okay depending on how I'm feeling. But with strangers? No way. I always look up and to the left. But now, I find myself wanting to look into Misha's deep brown eyes. The realization makes me squirm, suddenly uncomfortable in my own skin.

"How was your first week on campus?" Misha asks me.

I shrug. "It was fine."

He smiles. "Just fine? What electives are you taking?"

"Um, besides Physiology and Magic, I'm also taking Psychology of Magic and Magical Theories."

Misha makes a face. "Ew. That sounds incredibly boring. But, I'm also taking Psychology of Magic. We must be in different classes, though."

"Magical Theories?" Ari asks, lifting his head to look at me with his unsettling eyes. "With Professor Strand?"

"Yes." I swallow and fight the urge to fidget with my textbook.

"I thought you looked familiar. We're in the same class." Ari gives me a warm smile that only makes his eerie gaze even more chilling.

"Oh. That's nice." I cringe inside. Why am I so awkward with socializing? I should talk about the class with him. Ask him a question. But no, I just bring the conversation to a screeching halt. Sometimes I seriously hate myself.

The guys exchange amused glances that make my cheeks heat. I quickly look back to my book and pretend to study, but it's impossible to focus when I know they're looking at me.

Ari sighs again. "Okay. We really should go look for Ezra before he gets into trouble."

"Fine," Misha says reluctantly. "If you insist."

"I do. Let's go."

They push to their feet, but before they leave, Misha turns to me.

"You're okay here by yourself?" he asks, looking around the quiet space.

"Yeah. I'll just be studying." His concern for me makes my belly flutter, and I shift on the couch to get more comfortable.

"Okay. I'll see you later?"

I nod and turn back to my book. Part of me hopes I never see them again. Another part is strangely looking forward to it.

I COMPLETELY LOSE track of time while studying. When I finally look up it's dark outside the windows. Glowing orange globes have been lit, casting the library in a cozy light. There are still a few students buried in books, but they all look half asleep. I grab my phone and check the time. Holy shit. It's almost midnight.

I quickly pack my things and shoulder my bag. Rhory and Adrian would be pissed if they knew I walked back to my room by myself in the dark, but seriously, what could happen on campus? I'll stick to the main paths.

Outside, the chill soaks straight through my sweater, and goosebumps prickle my skin. It's like campus is part of its own little atmospheric bubble. It's September, and in Altair, it would be sweltering hot. But at LMU, it feels like November. Luckily it's not raining right now, but the occasional gusts of wind are almost as bad. And to top it off, those gusts sound like the moans of something undead as they blow around the buildings.

I hurry my steps, doing my best to keep to the puddled light cast by the magical lamp posts. But, there are large gaps between them, and the shadows in those gaps are dark and eerie. My senses are on high alert, my head on a constant swivel. I'm halfway to the main walkway that connects to the quad when I hear a rock skitter behind me.

I whirl around, but I'm standing under a lamp post, and everything outside of the light appears even darker than normal. Turning back around, I quicken my pace. The hair on the back of my neck stands on end and my shoulder blades prickle. I roll my shoulders in an attempt to ease the sensation, but the soft tap of shoes on concrete behind me makes its way to my straining ears.

I whirl around again, this time standing in the shadows. A dark human-like shape quickly ducks out of the light and out of sight. I can still sense their gaze on me, and the unsettling feeling of being watched doesn't ease, so I know they're still there. Waiting. If it was another student walking back to the dorms, why would they hide when I turned around?

Someone is following me.

My heart kicks in my chest and fear spreads through my veins like poison. I turn around and practically jog to the main lane on campus. Behind me, the footsteps match my pace. My fingers dig in the bag at my side for my cell, but they're shaking so badly I can barely shuffle through all the shit I shoved in there. Why didn't I have the phone in my hand?

Are the steps closer? They seem louder. I don't dare look behind me. But the urge to run gets stronger, so I don't second guess myself. I dart forward, almost to the main walkway. The cafe sits on the corner, and I rush around it, desperate for more light, more people, anything.

And I run straight into a hard body.

Misha

It's too cold outside for this shit. I curse Ezra under my breath, but I keep moving. He instructed me and Ari to walk campus at night to look for anything suspicious. What he thinks we'll find is beyond me, but if it keeps him appeased, I'll do it. My only request was to take the northern portion of campus. I hadn't thought about the strain the cemetery would put on my magic until I got here and experienced it first hand.

And it fucking sucks.

Groaning for the hundredth time, I shake off the chill as the night air tries to creep inside my hoodie. I just want to go back to my dorm, put on my sweatpants and climb under the covers. Fuck this middle of the night shit.

Deciding I'll check the library and then call it quits, I round the corner of the cafe only for someone to run right into me. They scream as they bounce off my chest. A scream so terror-filled it sinks inside me and raises my hackles. I know before I get a good look at their face who it is. Even without the black hair in a messy bun on top of her head, my body reacts to her on a cellular level.

"Whoa, Aspen. Are you okay?" I grab her shoulders and steady her, squeezing harder than I need to, but that scream still echoes through my body.

She gasps and looks up at me with wide, fear-filled gray eyes. "Misha?"

I don't have time to revel in the sound of my name on her lips.

She sobs in relief and grabs the front of my hoodie before burying her face against my chest. Her body trembles like a leaf, and she gasps for air against my shirt.

My arms wrap around her instinctively, and I have to fight the shudder that tries to work down my body. It's just like in my dreams. She fits perfectly in my arms. "Aspen, what's wrong?"

"Someone is following me." Her voice is muffled in the fabric of my hoodie, but I hear her words clearly.

I stiffen and try to pry her away so I can see her face. She fights me though, clinging even harder. "You're sure?" I look around but we're the only ones outside on this part of campus. Now would be a wonderful time to be a shifter, to have some kind of animal sense to send out into the world.

She nods. "I saw them," she says, pulling away to look up at me, silver lining her lashes from unshed tears. "When I turned around to look, they ducked out of the light before I could see any details."

"Where are you coming from? And why are you out so late by yourself?" My grip on her tightens, and my mind whirls faster and faster. Was she really being followed or was it her mind playing tricks on her? This campus is certainly creepy, and it wouldn't surprise me if her fear got the better of her. But …

"I was at the library. I got distracted studying, and didn't realize how late it was."

I nod and study her. In the lamplight, her face looks sickly pale, and I can't tell if it's the unnatural light or the fear that's drained the blood from her face. "You're okay though?" The need to scour campus and find whoever was following her makes my muscles tense.

Seeing her so scared hit a primal part of me that I've never experienced before. My magic flared to life the second I heard her scream, and it's taken all of my control to shove it back down into the deepest pits of myself. I don't like seeing her scared. And I need to know she isn't hurt.

Aspen shakes her head before burying her face in my chest

again, body sagging as she finally quits trembling. "I'm okay. It just ... it scared me."

Her voice is so small, and she's so delicate in my arms. I hold her tighter, resisting the urge to run my hands over all of her curves. She's safe now. And she took comfort from me. I can't stop the smile that spreads across my face, despite the situation.

"Come on," I say gently. "I'll walk you back to the dorm."

She nods and steps away, and I instantly miss the feeling of her in my arms. "Thank you."

Her shoulder presses against my arm as we start the walk back to the dorms, and I act before I think. I lift my arm and wrap it around her shoulders, tugging her close to my side. Once I realize what I've done, I tense and expect her to pull away. But she doesn't. Instead, she snuggles closer, and my heart almost leaps out of my chest. While I hate that someone may have been following her, I'm glad I was there and have been able to experience *this*.

We're quiet on the walk back, and her eyes constantly scan our surroundings while I strain my ears to listen for any little noise. But campus is eerily peaceful aside from the occasional gust of wind that howls between buildings. An owl hoots in the distance and nighttime bugs sing their lullaby. I could get used to this, walking with my arm around Aspen and her body pressed against mine.

"What were you doing out so late?" Aspen asks cautiously, like her mind is now catching up to what's happening and she's suddenly suspicious of running into me.

"I couldn't sleep. Back home when I would have nights like this I'd take a walk." It's not a complete lie. I did take walks at night when I couldn't sleep. When the darkness felt too cold and alive, and my blankets felt like dirt covering me, suffocating me. It's been a long time since I've had to walk off the paranoia. "The sound of crickets and cicadas has always been soothing to me." Because it's proof that something is alive in the darkness.

I'm not sure if she's convinced but she doesn't pull away, so I take that as a win. The breeze blows her scent to me, earthy tinted with something sweet, a flower I can't name. My magic claws up my spine, spreading down my arms and into my fingers, gripping me so tightly I gasp. Aspen looks up at me with concern, and I force a smile to my face while also shoving my magic down, down, down.

By the time I get it under control, sweat slicks down my back and the dorm looms before us. I haven't had to wrestle my magic this much since that fateful night years ago. I hold the door open for Aspen and follow her to the second floor. She stops in front of a door, and I memorize the number.

"Thank you for walking me back," she says quietly, looking at her feet.

Again, I act without thinking. I tilt her head up with my fingers under her chin. "You don't have to thank me for that," I say, or at least that's what I think I say. Honestly, I have no idea if I even speak.

As soon as her gray eyes meet mine, I'm swept away. The world disappears, and it's just me and Aspen. Her mouth parts on a small inhale as her pupils expand. I watch her cheeks flush rosy pink, and I find my thumb tracing the soft skin of her jaw. What is it about her that does this to me? She's like a drug I've developed an addiction to before I've ever had a taste. Well, at least a taste in real life. I'm not going to count the dreams, because as great as those have been, they really don't compare to her being right in front of me.

A strand of black hair has fallen from her bun and rests against her cheek. With my free hand, I take it between my fingers, feeling the silken strands in real life. Aspen sways closer, and my hand on her cheek slides to the nape of her neck. Desire, hot and needy, floods my system. With her looking up at me with large doe-like eyes, I find myself wanting to drop to my knees to beg this girl for *everything*. Gods I want to taste her. Does she taste as good as she did in my dreams? Better?

Before I can lean forward, Aspen closes her eyes. "Is this ... are you ... is this your magic?" Her words are husky, and my cock twitches in my pants at the sound.

But then her words register, and I blink. "Magic?" I breathe, almost as husky as her.

She swallows, her throat clicking in the silence. "Magic." She nods, still not opening her eyes, but also not pulling away.

"This isn't my magic."

She sucks in a breath, her chest brushing against mine. "Then what ..."

"I don't know," I answer honestly. And before I can do something too stupid, I lean forward and press a gentle kiss to her forehead. "Goodnight, Aspen."

I'm halfway down the hall before I hear her door open and close. The smile on my face doesn't last long. Under normal circumstances, I'd probably not worry about her thinking someone was following her. But considering everything else ...

If my dreams are true—which so far they have been—then Aspen doesn't have any magic. Just like Millie. Cold fear grips my spine in an iron fist making it difficult to draw in breath. Somehow, I need to figure out more about Aspen while also keeping her safe and not drawing attention to what the twin's and I are doing.

The next morning, I drag myself out of bed despite it being the weekend and having stayed up way too late the night before. I send a quick text to the twins, not really expecting either of them to be up yet, and head to the cafe for breakfast. Coffee is a must if I'm going to get any work done. I haven't been pulling my weight on this whole Millie thing, and with Aspen possibly being in danger, I need to get my act together. So I pull out Millie's notebooks and a textbook on mythical creatures and dive in.

I haven't found anything useful when Ari slides into the chair across from mine an hour later. "Find anything good?" he asks, setting his tea on the table.

"No. Nothing we don't already know." I sigh and flip the book closed. "But I ran into Aspen last night during my walk around campus."

Ari raises one brow and takes a sip of his tea. "And?"

"She was terrified. She said someone had been following her. It was almost midnight and there was no one else around that I could see, but her fear was off the charts."

Ari frowns and pulls out a notebook and pen. "So we know Millie had no magic, despite being from a magical family. She wrote about being followed while on campus, and mentioned seeing ghost-like beings." He jots a few things down in the notebook. "We suspect Aspen has no magic, and we know her family is magical if Rhory Grey is her brother. She claims she was being followed last night. Do we know if it was human or ghost?" He sets the pen down and looks up at me. "Because if things progress the same way they did for Millie, she will be seeing ghosts next."

I shake my head, unsure what exactly was following Aspen. The coffee in my stomach churns threateningly, and I regret drinking it. "We have to keep her safe." The desperation in my voice is obvious even to Ari.

He sits back and rubs his chin. "There is so much going on here I don't understand, and I don't like it. The similarities between Aspen and Millie. Your dreams of Aspen and the way you're so ..."

"Obsessed?" I ask with a wry grin. He's not wrong. The way I feel about Aspen borderlines obsession, and that mildly freaks me out. I don't even know her, but I'm already in so deep there's no turning back now.

"It's like we're missing just a few key pieces and everything will fall into place. At least I hope so." He sighs. "Have you heard from Ezra?"

"No. I assume he's still sleeping. You didn't find anything suspicious on your walk last night?"

"Nothing."

We fall silent as we both get lost in our thoughts. Ari's most likely trying to solve this puzzle. Mine obviously about Aspen. She's all I think about these days. And last night didn't help. I couldn't sleep after I returned to my room on the first floor. I could still feel her in my arms. My lips still tingled where I'd pressed them against her forehead. I'd thought maybe finally touching her would ease the ache of wanting her, but it only seems to have made it worse. And what about her asking me if I was using my magic on her? Could it really be possible ...

Shaking my head vigorously, I shove that thought away. Whatever the reason, now I've had the tiniest taste, and I want more.

I want all of her.

Misha

Fuck.

I need to wake up. I don't want to see what's coming. This isn't going to be one of the good dreams, I can already tell.

My heart races in my chest as I take slow steps through the cemetery. The fog is thick, like it always is, swirling and eddying around my feet. A misting rain quickly chills me and makes my shirt stick to my skin uncomfortably. I strain to hear any sounds that don't belong. A voice. A hushed breath. A scream. But there's nothing. Just an eerie silence that sits heavy on my shoulders.

I keep walking in no direction in particular, letting my instincts lead me, even though I want to ignore them and run away. The deeper into the cemetery I head, the thicker the fog and the louder the silence. With each step, my heart pounds faster and my anxiety rises.

In the distance a large dark shape takes form in the gray mist. It slowly emerges from the fog the closer I get. The more it shows its facade, the more I'm drawn to it. The more I'm drawn to it, the more I want to scream and run.

It's a mausoleum that looks like a decaying miniature version of Old Main. Crumbling marble pillars support an arched roof and flying buttresses. Broken stained glass windows open to pitch black insides where anything could be watching. Waiting. But my gaze doesn't stay on the building for long. A figure laying in front of the mausoleum draws my attention, and my breath freezes in my lungs.

Aspen is sprawled on the marble steps, pale and motionless. Her black hair is splayed around her head, wet from the misting rain. I trip over my own feet as I rush forward, falling to my knees next to her. The world crashes to a halt when I see the open, gaping wound on her chest. An empty, bloody pit where her heart should be. The ground underneath me shifts until I have to brace my hands on the marble steps to keep from toppling over.

"Aspen," I breathe, my hands shaking, hovering over her body. "No. Please, Aspen. No."

Inside, my magic goes deathly still. A frozen cloud that spreads ice through my veins. A second later it explodes.

MY THIRD CUP of coffee of the day doesn't help to improve my mood, but I know nothing really will. Even knowing I'm going to see Aspen later doesn't help shake the unease I've felt since I woke from my dream, sweaty and shaking. I don't know why I had another dream after so long of not having one. I thought it was all over after meeting Aspen.

However, this one was different. It's not the first time I dreamt of Aspen dying. But it is the first time my magic has reacted that way in a dream. It was like … like I couldn't control it. Like seeing Aspen's lifeless body had made my magic take on a life of its own. It exploded from me in a wave of gray light, destroying everything around me. Mausoleums and gravestones crumbled to dust in the wake of that blast, leaving Aspen untouched.

I release a huge breath, attempting to clear my mind and relax the tension in my shoulders. It doesn't work. So instead, I try to ignore the thoughts plaguing me and focus on my upcoming meeting with Professor Schaffor. It's hard, though, especially since my magic continues to sit inside of me, unsettled and queasy. I've been sick to my stomach since I woke up this morning, and it's because my magic is on edge.

When I step into Professor Schaffor's office, I haven't done much to ease the tension inside of me. I swallow back the nausea that burns in my throat, regretting that third cup of coffee.

"Good morning, Misha," Professor Schaffor says, smiling as he sets down his pen. "How have things been?" His brown eyes are kind but shrewd, they take everything in as I step inside, from my rumpled clothing to the dark circles under my eyes.

I shrug and take my usual seat in front of his desk. His office is sparsely decorated. A picture frame of a young girl is the only thing on his desk besides a notebook, pen, and laptop. His shelves are filled with scholarly books, all neatly organized by title. There are no wall hangings, artwork, or plants to liven up the space. It looks like he could up and leave at any moment.

"Things have been fine, I guess," I say, setting my bag at my feet.

Professor Schaffor cocks his head to the side. "Is everything okay? You seem ... off."

"Just tired," I sigh. "Didn't sleep well last night."

He hums thoughtfully before opening the notebook and scanning the words written on the last page. "So last time we met, we worked on meditating to clear your mind in an attempt to dampen your magic. Have you practiced at all? Any success in blocking out the pull from the cemetery?"

"Yeah, actually. I was able to a couple times, but only for a few minutes."

Professor Schaffor jots that down in his notebook. "And why could you only manage for a few minutes?"

I frown as I think back to those few attempts. "It was exhausting. Like my brain had exercised all day, and I just couldn't do it any longer."

"That makes sense," he replies, studying me. "Your brain is as much a muscle as say your biceps or quads. When you first start to train it, it will exhaust quickly and require time to recover. Keep practicing. The more you do it, the easier it will become and the longer you'll be able to manage."

Professor Schaffor isn't a gray mage, like me. He's a blue mage, like my family. However, he's dedicated his life studies to all things mage. He is the only person who has been able to help me even a little bit. I'm truly grateful for his knowledge.

"I'm guessing based on the lack of sleep last night, you don't want to try meditation today?" he asks.

I snort. "Probably won't get very far with it."

"Okay," he replies. "Let's try something different. I'm not sure you're ready for this yet, but it's worth a shot." He sits back in his chair and directs me to close my eyes. "Feel deep inside of you, where your magic lies. What does it feel like?"

Right now? Like a ball of snakes squirming, making nausea churn in my gut. Instead of telling him that though, I tell him what I usually feel. "A slight chill in my gut, like I swallowed an ice cube."

"Hmm, and does that chill have any form? Substance?"

"It's ..." I scrunch my nose trying to find the right word to describe what my magic usually feels like. "Puffy."

"Good. Everyone's magic feels different to them. For example, mine feels like waves as it does with many blue mages. Knowing the base form of your magic will help you to manipulate it. Now, I want you to focus on that puffiness. What can you do to take hold of it? I scoop mine in my hands, like cupping water. What about yours?"

If I were to try and grasp mine now, I imagine it would be like wrestling an oiled alligator. It wants to do what it wants, and it's not listening to me. Still, I try. I imagine hands reaching out and grabbing a chunk, only for it to pull away in agitation. When I try again, the same thing happens. I grit my teeth and shake my head, releasing a frustrated sigh.

"It's okay," Professor Schaffor says. "Keep trying. Don't give up. It's never easy the first time."

I nod, and try again. This time, I clamp down tight, squeezing my fingers around a strand of gray. As soon as it's in my grasp, I yank. I don't know why I pull it. I just do. And the next thing I know, a flash of gray light erupts from me. Wind blows the papers in Professor Schaffor's notebook and his gray streaked brown hair ruffles on his head.

His thin lips pull into a delighted smile, and his eyes glow with excitement. "Excellent, Misha. Excellent."

Misha

TWO DAYS LATER, I CHECK MY PHONE FOR THE millionth time and curse under my breath. My plan to catch Aspen as she walked past the cafe was spectacularly foiled by the long line for coffee. As I step outside into the misty gray morning, I manage to tug my hood over my head while holding both coffees in one hand with the bag of donuts under my arm.

Luckily, I know where her first class of the day is, and I cut between buildings, ignoring the soggy grass that dampens the bottom of my jeans. By the time I reach the steps of the small lecture hall, I see Aspen heading my way, and I grin. The shortcut worked. I watch her make her way toward the steps, a weird tumbling sensation clenching my stomach. I can't wait to see her reaction when she sees me with the coffee.

Aspen doesn't notice me at first. Her gaze remains on the ground before her, so she almost bumps into me when I step in front of her. She lifts her head, eyes wide with shock and embarrassment, and I give her a cocky smirk as she takes me in.

"Coffee and donuts," I say with a small bow.

Aspen's mouth parts in surprise, and my gaze drops to her lips, desire tightening my gut. "Why?" she blurts.

"Because I know how much you love your coffee." The girl has at least one cup a day, usually two. It doesn't take a genius to connect the dots. "And, I've never seen you turn down a donut." My observational skills are not always the best, but when it comes to Aspen, I could be a detective with how much I'm learning just from watching her.

"You didn't have to do that," she breathes, taking the coffee and white paper bag from me. Her cheeks take on a pinkish tint, and she ducks her head to hide herself from my view.

I grind my teeth together and refrain from gripping her chin to lift her face to mine. One day she won't hide from me. One day she'll feel confident enough to be herself around me.

I smooth my features before she looks up and give her a smile. "I mean, it was kind of for myself too. I also love coffee and donuts." My heart flutters in my chest when she giggles breathlessly, and her cheeks darken further. She looks good flushed. I can't help but imagine what she'd look like with that blush and her hair mussed from my hands. "Come on. Don't wanna be late for class."

She stumbles a step before catching up to me. "What? You don't take this class."

I shrug and take a sip of coffee. "I need somewhere out of the rain to enjoy my donut."

Aspen's shocked expression makes me chuckle, and I walk straight to her lecture hall as she incredulously follows behind me. When I take a seat and cross my leg over my knee, I toss her a dazzling smile and pat the chair next to mine.

She sits slowly, donut bag crinkling in her grasp. "Are you crazy?" she whispers, looking around. "Someone will notice."

"Doubtful. No student pays attention to who is in class with them. And the professor is too busy and has too many students to remember every face." I hold my hand out and wiggle my fingers.

Aspen looks at it with a raised brow. "What?"

"There are two donuts in that bag," I reply. "Now, I know you could eat both of them, but I did buy one for myself."

She hesitates like she's debating giving me one, but she finally reaches in and blindly pulls out a pastry. I take it, our fingers brushing in the process, and Aspen jerks her gaze to mine.

"Thanks, Dove."

When we leave the lecture hall after class, the drizzling rain has stopped, and the sun has made a surprise appearance in the sky. Aspen grins as she tips her face up and lets the rays bathe her skin in warmth.

"How about we find a spot to study outside. Maybe the quad?" I ask.

Aspen nods her head in response, and we make our way across campus. "I can't believe you sat through a class you don't even need," she mutters. "Shouldn't you be studying or something?"

I shrug. "Probably, but donuts are more important."

She laughs softly and shakes her head. "I don't get you, Misha."

My breath catches hearing my name on her lips. I swallow the obstruction in my throat and ask, "What's there to get?"

"Why—" She stops to clear her throat then starts again. "Why did you buy me coffee and a donut then sit through my lecture with me?"

I let my smile fade and lock eyes with her, hoping she can see the sincerity in my gaze. "Because I wanted to. I like spending time with you, even if that means sitting in a boring lecture. And I wanted to do something nice for you. Coffee and donuts seemed like a good choice."

"That's always a good choice," she mutters, hiding her blush by focusing on the ground and letting her hair fall forward.

"Misha!"

I spin around at the sound of Ari's voice and wait for him to catch up. He gives Aspen a smile and a nod, then falls into step on the other side of her.

"Where were you this morning? I thought we were meeting at the library." He looks past Aspen toward me, a knowing glint in his golden eyes.

"Oh shit." I smack my forehead and grimace. "I completely forgot." And I did. Buying Aspen coffee was way more exciting, and the library slipped my mind. "Please don't tell me Ezra is pissed."

"Oh, he's pissed alright. But I managed to get him off your back. You slept in because you were up too late last night looking through the journ—" he cuts his gaze to Aspen and quickly changes what he was going to say. "Books. For your class. The books for your class."

Ari winces, and I bite back my laugh. Smooth, brother. Real smooth. "So you're saying I better have something to prove for my late night cram session the next time I see him."

Ari grins at me. "If you don't want Ezra to kill you, then yeah."

"Lovely," I groan. From the corner of my eye I notice Aspen looking at me with a raised brow. "What?" I ask.

"So you had somewhere to be but you sat through my lecture with me instead?"

Ari whips his head toward me, eyes wide with incredulity. "Seriously?"

I give them both a sheepish grin and rub the back of my neck. "It was more fun than the library?"

Ari shakes his head, and Aspen hides a smile as she faces forward again.

"So, where are you two heading?" Ari asks, glancing at me with a knowing smirk.

"The quad," I answer. "Since the rain has stopped and the sun is actually shining, we thought we'd take advantage of it and study outside. Wanna join?"

Ari agrees, and when we get to the quad, I run inside and grab a blanket from my dorm to spread in the grass. We all settle down on the soft fabric to study. Although Aspen's form of studying is quite different from mine. She promptly laid on her back and closed her eyes. The sun's rays bathe her tan skin in a golden glow, and her black hair glimmers tantalizingly.

"You know you're not getting any studying done looking at the inside of your eyelids," I say, watching her.

A slow smile spreads across her face. "I don't typically enjoy the sun. Cloudy and rainy days speak to my soul. But every now and then I need to recharge. This is the best way to do it."

Looking at her reminds me of a cat lounging in the sun, stretched out on its back, belly warming in the sunlight. I have to refrain from patting her stomach. When I turn my attention to Ari, I find him watching her, too, a strange expression on his face. I can't quite put a name to what it is. Not desire necessarily, but longing. It's like he's seeing something that he *needs*. I ignore the slimy jealousy that slithers through me and refocus on the book in front of me.

Aspen sighs, drawing my attention back to her. "I'm not going to lie," she says with a small smile. "I never thought I'd be hanging out with you two and actually enjoying myself."

I gasp dramatically and place a hand over my heart. "I don't know whether to take offense to that or not."

Aspen giggles. "No. It's just that I'm usually not big on interacting with other people. I prefer to be alone most of the time. It's not normal for me to enjoy being around people who aren't my family."

My chest warms at her words. It didn't take me long to realize how shy Aspen is. And for her to admit that she enjoys being around us, well I'm going to take that tidbit and run with it.

Today is one of those days.

Every little thing is pissing me off. I slept through my alarm, so I was late for class. Since I was already late, I stopped for coffee. They got my order wrong. It's raining, which is nothing new, except instead of the usual drizzle, it's a full on deluge. And when someone bumped into me on my way to class, I stepped in a puddle. My sock has been soaked since then.

The cherry on the cake, though, was knocking on Aspen's door and her not being there. After the shitty morning I've had, seeing her face would have done wonders to cheer me up. But instead, I'm sent further into my grumpiness. Groaning, I head toward my room, my steps heavy and shuffling.

When I get to my dorm, the sound of a video game just barely reaches me from behind the wooden door. Great. Now I'll have to deal with either Ezra or Ari, or maybe both. When I had the ward placed on my door, I thought it was a good idea to give them access to my room. At the time it seemed like a smart idea. Now? I'm regretting that decision.

But it's not Ari sitting on my couch, feet propped on the coffee table with a controller in his hands and a goofy smile on his face that makes me stop in my tracks when I step into my room. It's Aspen sitting next to him with the second controller in her hands. Her legs are crossed under her, and her messy bun lays crooked on her head. She lets out a half laugh, half scream, and tilts her controller to the side like that will help her character run.

My mouth drops open, and I stand in the doorway for a minute taking in the picture. Aspen's eyes glitter with happiness even as she bares her teeth in a snarl and smashes the buttons on the controller. Ari laughs freely as he easily maneuvers his character through the game, dodging bullets and hiding behind walls expertly.

"Follow me, Aspen," Ari says a second before her character dies.

Aspen growls in frustration and then sticks her bottom lip out in an adorable pout. "I told you," she says, setting her controller in her lap. "I'm much better at racing games."

Ari laughs. "Yeah, but this was funnier." He turns his head and finally notices me standing in the doorway. "Hey, you're back."

I step into the room and let the door close behind me. "You know, when I gave you and Ezra access to my room, it wasn't so you could come in here and play video games whenever you wanted." I toss my bag onto the floor and cross my arms over my chest in mock annoyance.

Aspen turns her pout onto me, and if I had really been upset, there is no way I would have been able to hold onto my anger with that look. "Don't be mad," she says. "I ran into Ari on my way back to the dorms. My umbrella broke, and I guess I looked miserable enough that he felt he had to do something to cheer me up."

I huff a laugh. "I had a pretty shitty morning, too. I actually went to your room looking for you, but I guess you were here."

Her smile brightens the entire room when she beams at me. "Want to help me figure out this game? I'm determined to not lose again."

Ari snorts. "Good luck. You're pretty bad."

She elbows him in the side without looking at him.

Smiling, I cross the room and sit on the floor in front of her. "How about I just watch for now. I could use a good laugh."

And laugh I do. All three of us laugh so hard tears leak from our eyes. Aspen is truly horrendous, and her exclamations of frustration and occasional excitement have me sinking further into ... whatever this is that I'm feeling. Her laugh settles inside of me and gives me such joy I can't stop smiling.

Spending this time with her and Ari is something I didn't know I needed until now. As we sit together, playing video games and laughing, I can feel my soul healing from things I wasn't aware were even bothering me. I only hope this is the first of many times we do things like this.

Aspen

The past two weeks have been uneventful. I've attended my classes, studied in the library, and nothing nefarious has followed me. Although, I've made sure to be in my dorm before it gets dark. Ari is indeed in my Psychology of Magic class, and I won't lie when I say it's been nice having someone to sit next to. Even though we don't talk too much. Nothing else has happened between me and Misha, and the weird sensation of falling whenever I look into his eyes has gotten better.

The best part, though, is how much time I've been spending with Misha and Ari. We've found excuses to see each other pretty much every day—whether studying, playing video games, or watching movies. Slowly, the walls I built to protect myself have been crumbling. Misha and Ari are becoming people I want to be around. People who, instead of draining my social battery, help to recharge it by letting me be myself.

I'm currently walking to my one-on-one meeting with Professor Malvanado, and I want nothing more than to turn around and go back to my dorm. My meetings with him are awkward and anxiety provoking. He's been nothing but nice to me, yet I can't help but feel uncomfortable around him. We've been digging into my past and trying to figure out if I have a mental block that's preventing me from accessing my magic. So far, we've gotten nowhere.

As I step onto the quad, a shadow falls over me, and Ari falls into step beside me. "Where are you headed?" he asks quietly.

"Um," I hesitate. This is something I haven't told them and only my brother's know about. "I have one-on-one meetings with Professor Malvanado." *And please don't ask why.*

Ari's brow furrows, and his golden eyes squint. "And what do you have after that?" His voice has gone distant, like his thoughts are somewhere else instead of on the question he asked.

"Lab with Misha. And after that we typically go to the library to study." I glance at him from the corner of my eye.

As he walks, his arm brushes mine, and warmth spreads from the point of contact, like the sudden flare of a bonfire. He looks down at me, eyes wide, and he rubs his chest. "Do you—" he cuts himself off with a shake of his head. "Never mind."

"Would you like to join me and Misha at the library?" The question pops out before I can even think about not asking it. Another sign this guy has become someone I want to be around. Not only do I find comfort in his and Misha's presence, but I just enjoy their company.

I'm not one to typically like spending time with people, except for my family. I had a few friends in high school I would hang out with, and a girlfriend, but it was always draining to be around them. My capacity to handle social situations is almost non-existent. Trying to be social, trying to act quote-unquote normal and not worry about what people think of me, is exhausting. But I haven't experienced that drain with Misha or Ari, and I think I like that.

He swallows and looks unsure for a moment, then nods. "Sure. I can join you."

"Great." I smile up at him, and he blinks, looking like a startled owl.

Ari walks me all the way to Professor Malvanado's office and stops me before I knock on the door. "Aspen, if you ever need anything, you can always ask me, okay?"

Looking into his eyes sends a streak of warmth through my

body. They're kind and sincere as he glances down at me, and I have no doubt he means what he says. So I smile at him and nod. "Thank you."

When he walks away, my nerves double down on me. While walking with him, I was at ease. The anxiety about this meeting, the constant worry of what people think about me, it was all gone. I realize now as I stand in front of Professor Malvando's office, just how comfortable I am around Ari and Misha, and that thought makes me nervous. Why am I so okay with their company? Why do I feel like I can just be me around them, when I barely know them?

Shaking my head and taking a steadying breath, I knock on the door.

"Come in, Aspen."

The door creaks when I push it open, and I hide my shaking hands by shoving them into the pocket of my Wandering Fey hoodie. I take the seat I always sit in and stare at the top of Professor Malvanado's desk.

"How has your week been?" he asks, shuffling through some papers.

"Fine."

He looks up at me, his light brown eyes seeing way more than I want him to. He nods, but his mouth pulls down into a frown. "Any luck with finding your magic?"

"No." How could I? We haven't done anything but delve into my childhood and my family history. So far, there's been nothing weird, except my mom being a harpy.

"Are you adjusting well to being on campus?" Professor Malvanado removes his glasses and sets them gently on his desk. "I know the first couple of weeks can be disorienting. But by now you should be adjusting."

"I think I am." My words don't sound quite as convincing as I'd like them to. It's not that I'm not adjusting, I just never feel like I fit in anywhere except at home with my family. Maybe, just maybe, I'm creating a space where I belong, but I don't know for sure yet.

He hums, not sounding reassured. "What are some things you enjoy, Aspen?"

I swallow and refrain from shuddering. It feels too personal when he calls me by my first name. "Reading, mostly. And plants. Crochet isn't terrible, even though I'm not good at it." For some reason, I don't think he'll accept being alone as an answer.

"Plants? Have you visited the cemetery?"

I must make some kind of face because Professor Malvanado chuckles.

"That does sound weird, doesn't it? But the cemetery is filled with tons of old plants and flowers. A lot of them have been growing there for hundreds of years. I don't know much about flora, but I've heard there are some in our cemetery that can't be found anywhere else."

Okay, that does pique my interest. And Adrian mentioned the cemetery to me when we moved in, so maybe it's not a horrible idea. "I'm allowed to visit? I thought it was off limits."

"Oh no. Students are more than welcome to visit the cemetery. In the past, some students have left flowers at various gravesites. It's quite peaceful, to be honest."

I nod my head. "Thank you. I'll do that."

He smiles and I resist the urge to shudder once again. My gut tells me to be careful around him, and my visceral reactions to him only solidify that instinct.

We go through another painful session of me dredging up memories of my childhood, much to no avail. Although Professor Malvanado still fills two pages with notes. When he catches me checking the clock, he smiles.

"It's time for lab, correct?" he asks, setting down his pen.

"Yes. I don't want to be late."

He nods. "You're free to go. Keep thinking about things that may have happened in your past that might make you suppress your magic. We can discuss anything you think of next week."

"Okay. Thanks."

I rush out the door and heave a breath when it closes behind me.

"WHAT ARE YOU DOING?" Misha looks up from his book as I start to pack my bag.

"I need a break," I say, rubbing my eyes. "We've been studying for two hours, and my brain hurts."

I blink when Misha begins packing up his things as well. "Where are we going?"

"We?" I watch him and try to force down the mixture of nerves and excitement.

"If you get to take a break, then I do, too. It's only fair." He grins at me and stands, shouldering his backpack.

It's that damn smile that does me in and the way his eyes crinkle at the edges. I sigh and push to my feet. "Professor Malvanado mentioned the cemetery has a lot of plants."

Misha's smile falters, but a second later it's back, if looking slightly forced. "And you like plants, I'm guessing."

"I do. He said there are a few that can't be found anywhere but campus, and I want to see if I can find them."

He frowns before nodding. "Then let's go plant hunting." Misha holds out his hand, and I only hesitate a second before I take it.

Walking across campus holding Misha's hand is ... oddly nice? But strange at the same time. I keep looking around, expecting to see one of my brothers, but they don't appear, luckily. I don't want to know how much they'd freak out about this. In fact, I should probably be freaking out as well. What does this mean?

"So, I'm assuming based off of the Wandering Fey hoodie you wear all the time, you like F-pop?" Misha asks.

I close my eyes and bite my bottom lip, feeling my cheeks warm. "Yes?"

He chuckles. "Are you blushing?"

I shrug. "I always feel like I'm too old to listen to fairy pop, and be as obsessed about The Wandering Fey as I am. I don't usually admit that to people."

"Eh, just like what you like. Who cares what people think. I listen to SubFae, which is basically F-pop, just grungier."

"Oh, I do really like The Sidhe." I frown then glance at Misha. "You're right. SubFae is basically grungier F-pop."

He laughs. "Told you so. I saw The Sidhe in concert a few months ago with Ari. They were great live."

"I've never been to a concert before," I admit, shyly. "I don't really like crowded places or loud noises. Although, I'd endure the discomfort to go to a Wandering Fey concert. Actually, Rhory makes fun of me because I'm such a homebody, but I will stand in line at the store for hours to get their album when it releases."

Misha smiles and bumps my shoulder. "Nothing wrong with that. We all have our own things we're secretly obsessed with. And if the Wandering Fey is what brings you happiness, then lean into it, and don't be ashamed."

Warmth pools inside me at his words, at the way he so easily accepts that strange quirk of mine. "What is your secret obsession?" I ask him.

He looks down at me with an adorable pout. "Promise you won't laugh?"

"Promise." I give him a reassuring smile, and he sucks in a breath.

"Well, I love musicals."

I gawk at him in surprise. "Really? I do, too! I sing to them in the shower at home. Badly, I might add."

"Oh, I've been known to put on a shower concert or two," Misha laughs. "Going to musicals is something my mom and I do together. We've done it since I was kid. She would plan an entire date night with dinner and a show, and educate me how to treat my future girlfriend."

"Smart woman," I say with a grin. I wonder what kind of person his mom is. She sounds lovely for taking Misha to plays like that and trying to raise her son the right way.

The cemetery gates loom before us, and we slow to stop. "You're sure you want to go inside?" He scans the massive metal structure with a frown, rolling his shoulders. "It's so creepy."

He's not wrong. The arched black iron gate with intricate swirls and whirls is topped with sharp pointed spikes. On either side of it, gray stone standing at least seven feet tall spans as far as I can see in the gray mist. Crawling ivy digs into the cracks and attempts to pry the stones apart. Add in the billowing fog and you have the set-up for a scene in a horror movie.

I purse my lips and shrug. "It's just a cemetery, right? What can go wrong?"

The look Misha gives me is layered with hidden message upon hidden message, and I have no clue what any of them mean. But he sighs and plasters a grin on his face as he reaches out to grasp the iron gate. He pulls it open, making us both wince as the ear splitting screech of metal on metal grinds against our eardrums.

"Ouch," I laugh, sticking my finger in my ear. "I can add that to the list of the sounds that make me cringe."

Misha takes my hand again and pulls me into the cemetery. "What other sounds are on that list?"

"Styrofoam rubbing together, velcro, crayons when they rub against the paper just right and squeak, and any repetitive sound."

"Good to know. I won't color around you, just in case." His words are light, but I don't miss the way his eyes scan our surroundings, as if he's searching for something.

I bump my shoulder against his with a soft laugh, but my attention has already turned to the cemetery. Gravel crunches under our feet as we head further inside. Everything around us is mostly new-ish. And by new, I mean a couple hundred years old.

Small gravestones mark the resting places of the dead. The trees are just like the trees on campus.

"I think we have to go further to see the good stuff," Misha suggests when he sees the disappointment on my face.

But looking deeper into the cemetery doesn't yield any hints. The fog lays thicker here than it does on campus. It obscures everything that isn't a couple feet ahead of us. So we continue down the gravel path with the gray mist swirling under foot. Sounds are dampened in the fog, lending everything an even eerier vibe.

"It's not too late to change your mind and turn around. I promise I won't tell anyone we chickened out." Misha's shoulders are tense, and strain brackets the corners of his eyes.

"Are you scared?" I joke. "I'm not going to chicken out, but you certainly can. I don't promise I won't make fun of you though."

He huffs and sets his shoulders. "I'm not chickening out," he mutters under his breath.

The deeper we go, the older the gravestones become. Instead of the more polished marble markers with legible carvings, the monuments appear more distressed and weatherworn. Inscriptions are difficult or even impossible to read, and cracks and broken pieces mar each surface.

I'm still not seeing any plants that are particularly fascinating. Trees sprout from the ground, but they are common oak and ash trees. Wildflowers and tall grasses have taken over the green space. But that's it. I'm about to suggest we turn around when I notice something looming in the fog ahead.

I squeeze Misha's hand and pause. "What is that?" I whisper.

"It looks like ..." He tilts his head to the side and squints, like that will help him see through the thick mist. He tugs me forward a few more feet. "It's a gazebo." His voice is quiet, muted in the fog, but I can hear a faint tremor in the words.

The fog parts the closer we get to it, and the structure

becomes clear. White marble pillars support a bronze roof turned green with exposure to the elements. Vines climb the pillars and cling to the roof with fat blooms of dangling white wisteria.

"Oh," I breathe, reaching up to brush my finger down the white petals. "I love wisteria."

Misha steps under the gazebo and pauses. "Aspen, come here."

The gazebo is small, probably only five feet in diameter, and standing next to Misha in the space makes me all too aware of how isolated we are. Just the two of us. Alone. But my thoughts stop in their tracks when I realize what he's looking at.

On the other side of the gazebo, is a completely different world. Ancient towering trees with wide sweeping branches stand sentinel over beautifully decrepit monuments and statues. Cattail moss and hanging lichen drip off branches like delicately folded fabric. The world is green and earthy and dark. And it speaks to my soul.

I step out from under the gazebo as if in a trance. I feel so small in this world of weathered marble and ancient flora. The air is rich with wet earthy scents that I draw deep into my lungs. I turn back to Misha under the gazebo and find him watching me with an expression I can't describe. He looks as if he's been hit in the gut.

"This is ... this is beautiful." The smile on my face must stretch for miles. I spin in a slow circle, taking it all in.

"Stunning." His words are hushed, and hold a quality of reverence that has me turning back to him, only to find him staring at me.

The breath leaves my lungs in a rush, and awareness spreads through my body. Awareness of the way Misha is looking at me, the way his dark eyes drink me in. The way his lips part and his chest rises more rapidly than usual. I'm reminded again of the remoteness of our location and how alone we are out here. Surprisingly, the thought doesn't scare me.

"Misha?" I whisper.

"Aspen." He whispers back, before taking a step out from under the gazebo. Then another and another, until he's standing in front of me.

Misha

I can't breathe when I look at her. The memory of Aspen standing just outside of this gazebo in my dreams overlaps with reality. In my dream, it was raining and she was spinning in circles, laughing. Right now, though, she's very, very real, and she's absolutely breathtaking.

The pull of the cemetery on my magic is forgotten as soon as she spins around and whispers my name. Instead, she becomes the lodestone to which I'm drawn. The sun that pulls me into her orbit. I don't even realize when I take that first step toward her.

"Aspen," I whisper back, afraid to break this spell that's fallen over us in this hauntingly beautiful cemetery. Before I know it, I'm standing in front of her, looking down into those mesmerizing gray eyes. "Dove," I breathe.

She stares at me with wide-eyed wonder, her cheeks blushing a pretty pink. Overhead, a raindrop falls, then another until it becomes a light drizzle. Still, neither of us move. We're locked in the moment, in the silence of nature and the peace of the resting dead.

Droplets of water gather on her lashes, falling to her cheeks like tears when she blinks. I wipe them away with my finger, her skin warm and smooth. When she leans into my touch, my breath catches. She doesn't pull away, so I cup her cheek before sliding my hand to the back of her neck, tangling my fingers in her black hair.

I move as if I'm floating in water, my limbs feeling as if they belong to someone else. But Aspen's body pressed against mine is very real. With my other hand on her lower back, I pull her tighter against me, and she gasps before bracing her palms against my chest. The heat of her burns everywhere she touches, even through my clothing. It's not enough. It will never be enough. But it will do for now.

Her eyes stay wide open when I lean down and gently press my lips to hers. And fuck! It's so much better than my dreams. She's warm and soft. Her breath fans over my mouth as she stands frozen for a second. It's a short kiss. Just a gentle brush of lips. But when I pull away, she chases my mouth, standing on her toes in an attempt to not let me go.

It does me in.

I take her face in both of my hands, tipping her head back and diving in for more. This time, she meets me halfway. This kiss sears me to my very core. She tastes like strawberries and sugar, and I know I've found my new favorite fruit. All it takes is a small brush of my tongue against hers and she whimpers, almost dropping me to my knees. I'm not a religious person, but I would gladly worship this woman just to hear her make that sound again.

I have no clue how much time passes, I'm so lost in Aspen, but when I pull away, we're both breathing heavily and the rain has soaked us through. It takes a moment for her eyes to flutter open, the gray darker than usual. Her lips are puffy from my kiss, and I can't resist running my thumb along her lower lip.

She swallows and opens her mouth to say something, but she doesn't. She just stares at me with wonder in her eyes. I tuck a wet strand of hair behind her ear and smile.

"We should head back. You're soaking wet." So maybe my smile was more of a wicked grin, and her blush tells me she caught that innuendo. Fuuuck. How badly do I want to know just how wet she is?

Aspen nods and steps away, and I instantly want to pull her

back to me and never let her go. I grab her hand in mine and tug her under the gazebo, then onto the path that will take us to campus. We don't bother to hurry our steps, we're already drenched, but as the sun sinks lower to the horizon, I realize there are no lights in the cemetery.

A chill spider-walks down my spine and the spot between my shoulder blades itches. I glance behind us, but between the clouds, the fog, and the setting sun, it's too dark to see anything. I pull Aspen a little closer to me and quicken our pace. She looks up at me with a frown.

"It's getting dark, and there are no lights here. I don't want to get caught in the cemetery at night. Plus, your teeth are starting to chatter."

"They are not!"

I grin and bump her shoulder with mine. "Okay. Maybe not. But I don't want you to get sick."

Even though I couldn't see anything behind us, my hair still stands on end when I turn my back to the darkness. The telltale chill in my gut only solidifies my fears. If my magic is reacting, then something is behind us. I try to remind myself we're in a cemetery and it wouldn't be uncommon for a spirit to wander toward me. But I've never been good at telling myself that.

When we make it back to the cemetery gate, I quickly push it open and gently shove Aspen through before tripping over my own feet to get out. The metal clangs loudly, echoing through the night, making us both jump. She looks almost longingly into the darkness past the gate, like she can see the beauty of the untamed trees and moss from where she stands.

"You can go back again," I say, taking her hand once more. "Just promise me you'll only go during the day."

Her throat works on a swallow. "Is there something I should be worried about at night?" She glances over her shoulder as I lead her away.

"Nothing in particular. But it *is* a cemetery, and spirits can sometimes get restless. It's better to be safe than sorry." A motto I've lived by for 23 years now.

"You're saying spirits are real?" The doubt in her voice is obvious.

Somehow, I have to make her believe me without giving too much away. "They are very real. Spirits, ghosts, and even otherworldly creatures. They rarely make themselves known. But that doesn't mean they won't try to cause problems if they get too restless." I squeeze her hand reassuringly. "During the day you'll be fine visiting. Just make sure you're out of there when it gets dark. And don't go by yourself."

"How do you know so much about this?" she asks, glancing up at me.

I open my mouth then close it. This is a conversation I really don't want to have. Not with anyone. "I just do." And I'm learning more every week in my meetings with Professor Schaffor. If it hadn't been for his lessons, I never would have been able to set foot into the cemetery tonight. His guidance alone taught me what I needed to block some of the pull of the cemetery on my magic.

My answer doesn't appease her, and why would it? She narrows her eyes, and I wrack my brain for a way to distract her. But when she pulls her bottom lip between her teeth, my brain short circuits. I do the only thing that comes to mind. Tugging her to a stop, I turn her to face me, lean down, and kiss her. She squeaks in surprise, but doesn't resist. Her arms wind around my neck, and her mouth eagerly parts for my tongue to slip inside.

I need to get her back to the dorms and out of the rain, but with her warmth pressed against me, her lips molded to mine, and her taste in my mouth, I can't think of anything but *her*. The soft patter of rain on my skin disappears as I lose myself in her again. The world coalesces into one point, one single moment, and it's Aspen kissing me like she's trying to steal my breath to survive.

"Well, isn't this romantic?"

Aspen gasps and pulls away at the sound of Ari's voice. Her cheeks flush a deeper red, and she ducks her head.

"It was romantic," I say, pulling up the hood of Aspen's sweatshirt to help her hide inside of it, even though it's soaking wet. "Until someone interrupted us."

Ari laughs and slaps my back. He's just as wet as we are, his blond hair stringy and hanging in his eyes. "I'm just doing my civic duty and trying to prevent you two from getting pneumonia."

I groan but tug Aspen down the walkway. Distraction mission successful. We hurry to the dorms and inside the relative warmth of the hallways. At least it's dry inside. Ari follows us to Aspen's room, and when I throw him a look over my shoulder he gives me an evil grin. Cock blocking bastard.

Aspen turns to me with a shy smile. "Thank you for taking me to the cemetery."

From the corner of my eye, I see Ari jerk in surprise. I have some explaining to do for sure. Giving Aspen a little bow, I say, "It was my pleasure. Call me if you need anything."

She nods and swallows, gaze traveling to Ari before returning to me. "Goodnight, Misha. Ari."

"Sweet dreams, Dove." I wait until her door closes before rounding on Ari. "Thanks, fucker."

He chuckles and turns back down the hall. "You're welcome. I'm just helping you take things slow, keeping it interesting. Half of the fun is the chase."

I grumble under my breath, but really, I'm glad he was there. Things could have very quickly gotten out of control between us, and he's partially right. I don't want to rush things with Aspen. Not to mention, she deserves someone who will take their time and get to know her first.

"I'm actually glad I ran into you," Ari says.

"Yeah, what were you doing out in the rain?"

"I snuck into the admissions office."

I turn to him, stopping in the middle of the hallway. "What the hell for?"

"I walked Aspen to one of her classes earlier. A one-on-one lesson with Professor Malvanado."

I frown, something about his words sound familiar. "I'm assuming she's meeting with him because she doesn't have any magic? I haven't confirmed this with her, but I'm willing to bet my dream was true."

Ari nods. "Yeah, that's my guess, too. But I wanted to pull her schedule and compare it to Millie's." He hands me two pieces of folded paper, one crisp and fresh, the other worn, creased, and weathered.

I scan both of them. The newer paper is Aspen's first year schedule. The other is Millie's. Besides the normal first year classes, Millie took different electives than Aspen. Except ... "Millie took the same one-on-one with Malvanado," I whisper.

"Why did you take Aspen to the cemetery tonight?" Ari asks, taking the schedules back and putting them in his pocket.

"She wanted to see the plants ..." I frown again. "Actually, Malvanado told her about the plants in the cemetery."

Ari whips his head in my direction. "And Millie's body was found next to the cemetery."

My blood turns to ice in my veins. "Is Aspen ... Is she ..." I can't finish the question. My throat closes up, threatening to choke me.

"There are too many coincidences here," Ari says. "I think she's somehow connected to all of this."

ARI DROPS another book on the table, a little cloud of dust puffing into the air from the worn leather cover. I sigh and pull the tome toward me, adding to the pile I still need to go through.

Ezra grunts and crosses his arms. "We should be prioritizing our time. And by we, I mean you two."

Ari sighs as he takes the seat across from me, but he doesn't engage with his brother. We've talked to Ezra many times now, but he doesn't agree with us actually trying to learn and graduate while we're at LMU.

I bury my nose back in the book in front of me, furiously scribbling notes in the notebook I've designated to Millie's case. "I'll have to cross reference this info with Millie's journal entries, but I'm positive these are the creatures she mentioned. And with what I've seen in my dreams ..." I shudder and push that thought away.

Before coming to LMU, the dreams I had of Aspen being stolen from my arms by malevolent spirits, of blood running down the walls, Aspen's screams and her body broken and lifeless in the arms of an angel statue plagued me. Those dreams—no, nightmares—I won't be able to forget anytime soon.

"So you're positive spirits could have been following Millie? All of this is really possible?" Ezra asks, leaning forward with his elbows on his knees.

He's asked this question before. Many times. I know he knows how possible it all is, and I don't fault him for doubting it. I know he just wants me to verify that Millie was not going insane and that she wasn't hopped up on drugs. "I am. The majority of myths and legends are based on real spirits, usually malevolent." I shake my head and set the pen down. "But even peaceful spirits can easily become restless, and when they do, they can be just as dangerous." I yank my hand away from my chest when I realize I'm rubbing the scars under my hoodie.

The twins both look away and wisely don't talk further on the subject. I sigh and sit back in my chair, rubbing my eyes. The print in this book is tiny and the language is old and the spelling wonky. Poring over the pages for the past hour has done me in.

"I felt a presence when Aspen and I were leaving the cemetery." Goosebumps prickle on my arms under my hoodie, and I shove my hands into the front pocket. "I don't know what it was, but it didn't feel like a normal spirit."

"Was it malevolent?" Ari asks.

"I wouldn't say that exactly. It didn't really feel good or evil. Just ... off." I shrug, remembering the way my shoulder blades prickled and the magic in my veins woke with a sleepy stretch. "I didn't like it though. And neither did my magic."

"This weekend we should head to the cemetery at night. See what we can find." Ezra leans back and crosses his arms over his chest.

My stomach clenches at the thought, and a cold sweat beads down my back. "I'm not sure I should join you for that," I say quietly.

"We need you there," Ezra says, his tone harsh with no-nonsense. "Your magic is exactly what—" Ezra cuts off sharply and glares over my shoulder. "What do you want?"

I turn around and find Aspen standing behind me, a pile of books clutched tightly in her arms. Her cheeks flush with red, and she drops her gaze down to the ground, letting her black waves hide her face.

"Seriously, Ezra? There's no need to be an ass," Ari mutters.

I push to my feet and walk around the chair to grab Aspen's arm. "Hey. What are you doing here on the weekend? Shouldn't you be enjoying your free time?"

She peers up at me with a shy smile and shrugs. "I had nothing better to do, so I thought I'd get ahead on some reading." She looks behind me at the twins. "Besides, I could ask you the same thing."

Danger. Danger. Danger. I gape at Aspen like a fish out of water, desperately trying to come up with an excuse why the twins and I are studying in the library on the weekend, something none of us are known for.

"It's none of your business," Ezra blurts. "We're busy." He flaps his hand like he's shooing her away, and I grind my teeth.

As much as I want to tell Ezra to fuck off and let Aspen sit with us, I can't. If Aspen is in danger, I need to be prepared. I need to find out as much as possible so I can protect her. Tucking her black hair behind her ear, I let my fingers brush against her cheek.

"I'll call you later, okay?" I say, quietly.

Her expression falls and she tries to hide the hurt, quickly pasting on a bland smile. But her eyes give it away. "Okay."

I watch her walk away, her ass in those black leggings drawing my attention. Hot damn, I want to grab that thing in my hands and squeeze. Ezra clears his throat, pulling me from my thoughts, and I whirl around to face him.

"Don't be an asshole," I growl. "I won't hesitate to rip off you're fucking dick if you so much as look at her wrong."

Ezra snorts and rolls his eyes. "Whatever, dude. Get your head in the game, and not your cock. Now, tell me what you've found so far."

Aspen

MY CHEEKS STILL BURN HOTLY THIRTY MINUTES AFTER Misha so coldly blew me off. Okay, maybe he wasn't cold about it, but it stung all the same. This is why I hate getting close to people. I have a hard time reading social situations and frequently make a fool of myself. I also tend to get attached to people too quickly, especially if I feel comfortable with them, and when I fall, I fall hard. Misha has every right to not want to hang out with me. Just because he's kissed me a few times, doesn't mean we're dating. We aren't dating, right? Shit. Maybe I should ask him?

Sighing, I let my head fall forward, thumping on the bookshelf in front of me. I ran to the third floor as fast as I could when Misha shot me down, and hurried to the darkest alcoves. If I could crawl into a hole in the earth and bury myself I would.

Just thinking about that night in the cemetery and the way he kissed me makes my body flush hot. There wasn't a single ounce of hesitation on my part. Nothing screaming inside of me to pull away, to avoid his touch. In fact, it was the exact opposite. I was drawn to him, to get closer, to bathe in his attention. Thinking about it kind of freaks me out.

With more effort than it should take, I push my head up and scan my surroundings. I've never been this deep into the stacks and the lighting here is sporadic at best. Orange globes leave pools of light between the darkness, but the darkness is ... well it's very dark.

The silence is eerie, so when the sound of fluttering paper greets me, my heart lodges in my throat. I whip my head to the left but there's nothing there. Turning around, I make my way toward the main area, but immediately walk through a patch of cold air. The hair on my arms stands on end, and my skin prickles. I need to get out of here, but when I try to take a step, my feet won't move.

Gasping, I stare wide-eyed at my feet and yank my legs harder, but it's as if I'm frozen to the floor. Behind me, I hear a soft rustling, and my hair blows in a phantom breeze. Fear spreads through me, and rises like a wave of acid crawling up my throat. With my heart thundering painfully in my chest, I slowly turn around. There's nothing behind me, but the chill in the air increases until I can see my breath puffing in white clouds in front of me. I whimper and try to yank my feet free again with no success.

Something trails down my spine, something that feels like a finger. I jerk forward with a muffled cry and lose my balance with my feet stuck to the floor. Flinging out my arms, I drop my books and brace myself as I hit the ground. Pain shoots through my knees and wrists, and my ankles twist sharply as my feet rip free. But all of that is secondary when a sudden pressure pushes on my back. What the hell is happening?

I'm slowly forced down, and soon I'm flat on the floor. The pressure doesn't let up, though. Squirming does me no good, now my entire body is frozen to the ground. Actually frozen. Frost spreads from underneath me, and my body shivers as much as it is able to within the binds of whatever this is. I try to reach for my phone, but I can't move. It's getting harder to breathe, harder to expand my lungs with the force on top of me. Before the pressure gets any worse, I suck in a breath of air and scream.

I scream so loud it echoes in the quiet of the library, but I don't stop. I keep screaming until my throat is raw, and the pressure increases until it squeezes the air out of my lungs. Soon, I can't suck in any breath at all. Fear explodes inside of me, hoarfrost spreading over my body. This is it. This is how I die. Frozen to the floor and squished to death by ... by what? What is doing this to me? A sob crawls up my throat, but without air, I can't get it out. Within seconds, my vision darkens, and my lungs burn with fire.

I hear the sound of running footsteps. Or maybe that's just my heartbeat in my ears. At this point I can't tell. Spots dance in my vision and my eyelids droop heavily. It would be so easy to just close my eyes and fall asleep. But I know I won't wake back up. I give it one more try, one more fight to free myself. It's too hard. Everything hurts. Everything is going dark.

"Aspen!"

My name sounds so distant, like I'm hearing it underwater, and it's not enough to pull me from the fog. Suddenly, the pressure is gone, and I'm able to drag air into my starved lungs. Then there are hands on me. I'm rolled over, but I can't get my eyes to open. It's still too hard.

"Aspen, talk to me. Open your eyes."

I like that voice. It's nice and deep. It soothes me, and I want to fall into it. Hands caress my face, and I hear more voices in the background.

"Keep breathing, Dove. Keep breathing and look at me. Please, open your eyes."

The voice sounds panicked, and I don't like that. I don't want the person with this voice to be scared. So I take a deep breath that burns the entire way down and pry my eyelids open. Above me, Misha hovers with concern painting every inch of his face. He holds my cheeks in his hands, his thumb caressing gently. It makes me want to close my eyes again, but he asked me to open them.

"Aspen," he breathes, shoulders sagging in relief.

"What's going on here?" A stern female voice says from down the aisle.

Suddenly, it all comes back to me. Why I'm lying on the floor. Why Misha is hovering over me, worried and afraid. Why my lungs hurt. I gasp for breath and tears pool in my eyes, blurring my vision. What was that? What happened? My breaths come faster and faster, and soon my body starts to tremble.

"Hey," Misha says soothingly. "You're okay, Dove. Take a deep breath."

"Wh-wh-what—" My teeth are chattering too hard to form words. And even if I could speak, I have no clue what to say.

Misha reaches behind his neck and yanks off his hoodie. He quickly pulls it over my head and helps me thread my arms through. "It's okay, Aspen. You're okay."

I let his words fall over me like soothing caresses. Heat from his body lingers in the hoodie, and I snuggle into it, letting it warm my frozen limbs. When the voices behind him get louder, I can't tune them out anymore.

"What's going on here?" that stern female voice asks again.

"It's not what it looks like," Ari says hurriedly. "We heard her scream and came running. There was no one here when we arrived."

"Can you stand?" Misha asks me quietly.

I'm not sure what he sees in my expression, but instead of letting me try to get to my feet, he scoops me into his arms. And, oh. Oh. The instant sense of safety that drapes over me causes all of my muscles to go lax. Exhaustion sweeps over me, and I close my eyes, nestling against Misha's chest.

"Excuse me, sir." That damn woman won't stop talking. I want her to go away so I can snuggle against Misha and forget what just happened.

Misha ignores her and carries me down the aisle into the well lit portion of the third floor. I expect him to set me on one of the couches, but instead, he sits and keeps me in his arms. Curling into a tight ball, I squeeze my eyes shut and let Misha's warmth soak into me, driving away the chill that's settled into my bones.

"It's okay," he keeps saying. "You're safe."

"Excuse me. I need someone to tell me what's going on."

I grind my teeth together. Why won't she go away? When I slowly open my eyes, squinting at the brighter lights, I find it's the head librarian with her black heels, black slacks, white button down shirt, and hair in a severe bun on top of her head.

"Nothing's going on here," another deep voice says. "You can go back to your job."

I turn my head and find Ezra standing behind Ari, hands on his hips and looking pissed at the world. I cringe. Of course I had to go and inconvenience the angry one.

The head librarian's eyes almost pop out of her head. She slowly turns to Ezra, cheeks flushing in anger. "Young man. This is my job. You'd do well to remember that and the rules of the library. I will not be leaving until I know what happened."

"I tripped," I say quickly, wincing at the hoarse sound of my voice.

She turns to me with a raised brow, clearly not believing me. "That was quite a ruckus for someone to make just because they tripped." Her gaze travels to Misha, and she narrows her eyes. "If you need protection from these men, you just have to say it."

I almost laugh. First of all, if I truly needed to be protected from them, would I say so out loud in front of them where they could hurt me? It's not like this woman could do much to protect me if I really needed it.

"Um ... I uh ... I have epilepsy?" Stupid Aspen. It's not a question. "I have epilepsy."

Misha's arms tighten around me, and I lay my head against his shoulder, praying this woman just leaves. She purses her lips and studies me before switching her burning gaze to the guys. Each one gets a solid three seconds of glaring before she turns back to me.

"If that's the case, you should go to the infirmary."

I nod. "I will. I just need a moment."

The librarian hesitates before nodding. "Remember, if you need *anything* just let me know." With that, she turns and stomps away.

No one else is around, and if I had to guess, I'd say Ari and

Ezra made sure we have privacy. The energy radiating off of them is enough to make me want to run away.

Misha's palm cups my cheek. "Aspen, tell us what happened?"

I shrink in his arms. I can't tell them I was attacked by something that wasn't there. They'll think I'm crazy. *I* think I'm crazy. But what can I tell them that they'll believe? I don't realize I'm shaking again until Misha gently forces me to look at him. Instead of shrinking away from his gaze, I fall into it. I take comfort in his presence and the way he makes me feel safe and protected.

"You can trust us, Aspen," he says with a small smile. His thumb strokes back and forth across my cheek. "I promise, there is nothing you can't tell me."

My shaky breath gets stuck in my too tight chest, and I close my eyes before I speak. There is no way I can watch his reaction as I try to explain what happened. If I see any look of amusement or disbelief, I might just crack. But I think I need to tell him. I need someone to tell me I'm not crazy. To give me an explanation of what just happened.

"I was looking for a book." *Also known as hiding from myself and the world,* I don't say. "I heard rustling in the aisle, but there was no one there. It got really cold. Like *really* cold. I could see my breath. When I tried to walk away, my feet were frozen to the floor. I fell over, and then something pressed down on my back, hard enough that I couldn't breathe, and I started to black out. That's when you showed up." By the time I finish, my words are no more than a whisper, but I can tell by the way Misha's gone still that he heard everything I said.

It's silent in our little area of the library. So quiet I can hear my ragged breathing. Shame beats down on me, and I bury my face in Misha's chest so I don't have to face the world. I shouldn't have said anything. The guys are probably looking at each other thinking I'm insane. Misha will probably never talk to me again. I should have just made up something or stuck with the epilepsy story.

Misha's chest expands as he takes a breath and positions me so he can look at my face. I duck my head, still not able to meet his eyes, but he lifts my head with a finger under my chin.

"Look at me, Aspen." It's like his command worms inside of me, and I have no choice but to open my eyes. His face is serious, but I catch no hint of derision in his gaze. "I believe you."

Those three words crack me open and everything inside of me spills out. Tears burn my eyes and fall over to track down my cheeks. Misha believes me. He doesn't think I'm crazy. Hearing him say that lifts the weight of fear and uncertainty off my shoulders. He wipes the tears from my cheeks, but more follow.

"We have something to tell you, but it's not going to be easy to hear. Do you want to know now? You've been through a lot tonight." Misha keeps wiping my falling tears as he speaks.

Ari sits on the couch next to Misha. His golden gaze compassionate and understanding. I know Ezra is still here, I can feel his presence like something watchful and ready to pounce in the background, but I can't imagine his gaze being as calming as his twin's.

I swallow down the rest of my tears and force myself to take deep calming breaths. "I need to know what happened tonight."

Misha nods. "Okay. We'll start with that, and then if you want to know more, we'll tell you."

Misha

My heart won't stop thundering in my chest. When I heard the screams echo through the library, I knew instinctively who it was. I have never run so fast in my life. And when I rounded the aisle and saw Aspen pinned to the ground by the drogue, cold fear spread through me. Ice spiderwebbed out from her prone body, and I could see how hard it was pressing against her back, restricting her lungs from expanding.

I have no doubt she is somehow connected to all of this now. And that thought utterly terrifies me.

Holding her in my arms now, I still feel the little tremors that wrack her body. I shift on the couch, positioning her so she can see me and Ari better, while still keeping her against my chest. What we're about to tell her will undoubtedly freak her out, and I need to keep her as calm as possible.

"It wasn't your imagination tonight," I begin. "When I rounded the corner, I clearly saw what was pinning you to the ground, even though you saw nothing. Ezra and Ari also saw nothing." Shit. I didn't even think about how I would need to explain my powers to her after this. And subsequently, my failings when it comes to my magic. "It was a drogue, a zombie-like ghost that possesses incredible strength. The more powerful of them can also manipulate weather, hence the cold and ice."

Aspen goes very still in my arms, a soft gasp the only noise she makes. But her gray eyes widen until I see white all the way around them. "A ghost?" she whispers hoarsely.

I nod, keeping my expression calm despite the way I want to bundle her in my arms and run far, far away from here. "An evil spirit, essentially. Their only purpose is to satiate their thirst for blood and death. People who were wronged in their past life and wish to seek revenge are more likely to become drogues when they die."

"I- I-" Aspen swallows thickly and closes her eyes.

"It's a lot to take in. Here," Ari says, handing her a bottle of water.

We wait in silence, Ari and I patiently letting Aspen process what I just said. Ezra sits across from us with a frown on his face and his arms crossed over his chest. I'm sure he'll yell at us for telling her. But, we don't have any other choice. She needs to know what's going on since she is apparently in the middle of it.

Aspen looks at me, eyes glassy with unshed tears. "How come you could see it but no one else could?"

I shift uncomfortably and take a breath, not meeting her gaze. "I'm a gray mage. I can see and interact with ghosts." My words are quiet, and I pray she just takes my answer and lets the rest of her questions about it go. I'm not ready to share everything with her yet.

Luckily, Aspen only nods, although I see a hint of awe in her features that's quickly swallowed by her fear. "So why did I get attacked by an evil spirit?"

I open my mouth to answer, but nothing comes out. We don't know why, but that doesn't seem like a good enough answer.

Ari notices my loss for words and says, "There is a lot to that question, and we don't have all of the answers, yet. Do you want to hear all of it tonight?"

Aspen hesitates, glancing between me and Ari. "If I say no, you'll tell me later? You won't change your mind?"

"I promise, we won't change our minds," I say, rubbing my

hands up and down her arms. When Aspen looks like she's going to hesitate, I press a kiss to her forehead. "You've been through a lot tonight, Dove. Why don't we take you back to your room so you can get some sleep? We'll meet up tomorrow and tell you everything."

Aspen bites her bottom lip, but eventually nods. I give her a reassuring smile and help her stand. When she wraps her arms around her middle, I tug up the hood of my sweatshirt over her head, letting my fingers trail over her cheeks that are paler than usual.

The walk to the dorms is tense. I have Aspen tucked against my side, while Ari walks next to us. Ezra follows behind, a threatening presence that would make most people hesitate to approach. I know the tiger shifters have their senses tuned into the environment, parsing through every noise, scent, and minuscule movement. It gives me some reassurance having them with us. Although I'm not sure they'd be much use against a ghost. I'm hesitant to pull my magic up from the depths of my core. Not only because I don't want to draw anything to us, but there isn't guarantee I can control it.

My meetings with Professor Schaffor have been beneficial. He's been helping me feel more confident in my magic, but not enough to risk Aspen's safety. I'm more comfortable on campus now, the pull of the cemetery not as draining thanks to his lessons on shielding. But I haven't yet mastered how to use my magic and shield at the same time to prevent drawing spirits toward me.

Aspen shivers under my arm, and I hurry our steps to get her inside and out of the cold drizzle. All four of us heave a sigh of relief as we step inside the dorm. Ezra immediately heads down the hall toward his room without a backward glance. Ari and I share a look. We'll be hearing about all of this later, that's for sure.

"Want me to come with you?" Ari asks.

I shake my head. "We'll be okay. I'll drop her off and head to your room."

Ari nods and gives Aspen a small smile before following Ezra.

I lead her up the steps to the second floor, and down the hall to her room.

"Do you have wards on your door?" I ask, looking at it like I'd be able to see anything there.

"Yeah. My dad put some on it. Adrian and Rho said they're pretty strong." Her voice is distant, as if she's lost in her thoughts, and she stares at the door, but doesn't move an inch toward it.

I file away the information that her dad is mage. Something tickles the back of my mind, but I ignore it. "You'll be okay then. Nothing should be able to get into your room uninvited."

Still, she doesn't move.

"Aspen?"

She looks up at me, tears clumping her lashes together. "I don't want to be alone," she whispers.

My heart cracks at the raw vulnerability of her tone. I hesitate, because I don't trust myself to be alone in her room all night. "Can you go to one of your brother's rooms?"

She shakes her head, causing a tear to slip free. "I can't tell them what happened. They'll freak out."

She's right. I should have thought of that. If she tells them about tonight, they'll have too many questions that will lead to the bigger picture. So I wipe her tear away and smile. "I'll stay with you."

Aspen's shoulders slump and she finally pulls away to open her door. Her steps are stilted and sluggish, and she stops in the middle of the space like she doesn't know what to do. I go straight to the fireplace and light a fire, hoping to chase away the chill. Then I tug Aspen to the chair in front of the hearth and gently push her down into it.

She's wearing leggings and my hoodie, which falls almost to her knees, and she looks comfy enough to sleep in what she's wearing. I unlace her boots and pull them off, then sit back on my heels and study her. Her eyes are dull, and she's staring off into space. I'm not a doctor, but I'm willing to bet she's going into shock.

Without thinking, I run my hands up the sides of her calves to her thighs. Her lashes flutter as she blinks, then drags her eyes to mine. Some color returns to her face as a blush darkens her cheeks. I want to make that vacant look disappear. I want to see her smiling again with sparkling eyes. Knowing what I'm about to do is a horrible idea, I do it anyway.

Pushing to my knees, I slide my hands behind Aspen, memorizing the curves of her ass and hips. She leans forward and brings her hands up, hesitating briefly. I wait patiently, my heart in my throat, while I let her take her time and come to a decision. I see the moment she does. She tugs her lower lip between her teeth and gently runs her fingers down my cheeks.

I want to close my eyes and lean into the touch, but I force myself to keep them open, to watch every movement of her eyes as she traces my features with her fingers. She slowly follows the angle of my cheekbones, the curve of my jaw, and finally, my bottom lip. The reverence of her actions makes me shiver, and I realize just how hard I'm breathing.

"Aspen," I whisper. I plead. I beg.

She slides her fingers to the back of my head, tangling them in my locs. My heart freezes in anticipation, and it takes all of my self control to remain still. I want to lean up and claim her, to devour her, but I'm letting her make the moves here. She does so slowly, watching me closely as she leans in. I'm not even ashamed of the noise I make when she finally presses her lips against mine.

It's a soft brush, feather light and teasing. When she pulls away, I tighten my grasp on her hips, growling softly. That wasn't near enough. Aspen uses my hair to tilt up my head. I'm on my knees before her, begging her to give me whatever she's willing to give. I'll take it all, gladly.

This time when she kisses me, she parts my lips with her own, and I greedily slide my tongue against hers, desperate for that strawberry and sugar taste. My stomach tingles, a sign that my magic is coming to life, but I ignore it. I'm too consumed with

Aspen, with her taste, her scent, the feeling of her tongue tangling with mine.

When a quiet moan slides up her throat, I almost snap. What would she look like completely undone? No. I don't have to ask that. I already know. But would it be the same as in my dreams? I doubt it. Nothing with Aspen even remotely compares to my dreams. In real life, she blows those dreams out of the water.

I push to my feet and pick her up. She starts to pull away, no doubt to protest, but I silence her by tugging her bottom lip between my teeth. On instinct, her arms and legs wrap around me as she tries to get closer. I carry her to the bed, the soft curves of her body rubbing against me driving me fucking wild.

When I lay her down, she pulls me on top of her, and I willingly tumble after her. Aspen's hands slide under my shirt, and her fingers tracing my back muscles are cool on my overheated skin. I want to return the favor, to slide my hands under her clothing, but I somehow find the strength to resist.

I don't know how long we lay on her bed, a tangle of limbs and tongues. But when I finally pull away, Aspen is flushed. Her hair is a mess from my fingers, and her lips are kiss swollen. She looks at me with gray eyes so dark they're almost black, and I'm tempted to dive back in for more. But instead, I close my eyes and take a deep breath.

"We need to stop," I say, breathing heavily. "If we keep going, I won't be able to."

I swear, she looks like she's about to argue, but a log pops in the fireplace and it breaks the spell. She jumps, and I see the moment the reality of what happened tonight crashes back down on her.

I run my knuckle down her cheek before gently kissing her lips. "Get some sleep, Dove. I'll be right here."

As much as I want to climb into bed with her, I force myself to get up. I don't trust myself—or my magic—to lay next to her all night. Instead, I turn one of the chairs by the fireplace to face the bed and I settle down. I wait for her to snuggle under the covers before pulling out my phone and sending a quick text to Ari. I'll never hear the end of it, but there is no way I could have said no when she stared at me with such fear in her eyes.

Tomorrow we'll have to tell her everything. Tomorrow I'll bring more fear and uncertainty into her life. The thought curdles my stomach. But instead of dwelling on that right now, I watch Aspen sleep. I listen to her soft breath as it evens out. And I think about her kiss and how I've never felt more alive than I do with her.

Aspen

Misha was true to his word. When I wake the next morning, he's asleep in the chair. The fire has died down to flickering embers, and a chill permeates my room. I take a moment to study Misha's sleeping form. His features are relaxed in sleep, not as severe as usual. But his strong jaw and plush lips are still just as enticing as always. I find myself smiling, fingers covering my mouth when I think about the kisses we've shared and the way he makes butterflies come to life in my belly. It's a sensation I'm not used to.

"It's rude to stare," he mumbles, not even cracking his eyes open.

I gasp and quickly pull the blankets over my face so just my eyes peek over the edge. My cheeks heat at being caught looking at him.

Misha chuckles and stretches, arms raised over his head. The movement lifts his shirt, exposing the taut muscles of his abdomen. He smirks, lingering in his stretch longer than necessary.

"I have to shower," I say quickly, throwing the blankets and jumping from my bed to rush to the bathroom. His laugh follows me.

Luckily my bathroom buddy isn't in here, so I strip and hop in the shower without a second thought. The hot water and steamy air help to loosen tense muscles. Memories of yesterday float to the surface, and I shiver despite the heat. I need answers. I need to know what's going on and why I was attacked by a vengeful ghost. Seriously, a ghost? It sounds like something I made up. How am I supposed to wrap my head around something that sounds like a children's story?

Sighing, I shut off the water and reach for my towel. It's not until I step out that I realize I don't have clean clothes.

"Shit," I mutter, picking up the leggings I wore yesterday and the hoodie Misha gave me. The black fabric of the leggings is dusty, and there's a hole in the knee from where I fell. I bring Misha's hoodie to my nose and inhale. A smile spreads across my face involuntarily. It smells like him, like sandalwood and citrus.

Sighing I let my arms drop. I can't put dirty clothes back on. The thought makes my skin crawl. But I also can't walk back into my room wearing nothing but a towel. Maybe Misha left already. I creep to the door and push it open just enough to peer through the crack. My heart sinks. He definitely didn't leave.

I have two options here. Run out as fast as I can, grab some clothes and run back to the bathroom. Or own every bit of this situation. Normally, I'd do the first option. I'd run as fast as I could, keep my gaze averted from Misha, and let my skin heat to the point you could roast marshmallows on it. Then, I'd be awkward and weird the rest of the day. But ...

But Misha seems to actually like me. At least, he likes kissing me. There's power in that, if I can only dig deep enough to find it. Maybe I can work up the courage to saunter out of here like I own the place. *Come on, Aspen. You can do this. For once in your life, do something daring. Be brave.* I square my shoulders and double check to make sure the towel is firmly tucked around me. It's not a very big towel, so I tug it down as best as I can without exposing the girls.

One. Two. Three. Go, Aspen. I lift my chin and push the bathroom door open. The cold air hits my skin and I instantly shiver. Instinct makes me want to rush across the room, and not entirely just because Misha is here. It's fucking freezing. But, I slow my steps and walk to the wardrobe. If my steps are slightly jilted and unsteady, I can't help it. This is so far from my comfort zone.

I hear a sharp intake of breath, and I know Misha has spotted me, wet and clothed in only a towel. This time, I shiver for an entirely different reason. I can practically feel his gaze traveling over my body. Every part of me wants to turn around to see his expression, but I force myself to remain facing forward.

I quickly rifle through my wardrobe and pull out clothes. When I turn around to head back to the bathroom, I gasp. Misha's standing right there. I didn't hear him move because I was so focused on my embarrassment. But. He's. Right. There. I take a step backward until my shoulder blades hit the wardrobe door, and Misha follows with a smirk.

His eyes are so dark as he stares down at me. "What are you doing, Dove?"

I gasp as his deep voice travels over my skin. It's raspier than usual, and when I swallow, my throat clicks. "Getting dressed," I say, cheeks heating at the breathless sound of my own voice.

Misha makes a noise in the back of his throat, and his gaze drops to my bare shoulders. When he raises his hand and runs his finger down my throat and over my collarbone, I have to lock my knees to keep from collapsing into a puddle on the ground. Heat pools in my belly, and I try to squeeze my legs together without letting Misha notice. But by the way he grins, he knows.

He lowers his mouth to my ear and whispers, "Get dressed and meet me at the cafe for breakfast." His lips brush against the shell of my ear, and his breath warms the side of my face. When he pulls away, his eyes are almost black. He stares at me for a moment before turning around and walking out of my room like nothing happened.

I release a shaky breath and let my head thunk back against the wardrobe. Clutching my clothes to my chest, I wait until my body temperature has cooled and my heart slows, then I do as he ordered.

THE CAFE ISN'T AS busy as I thought it would be on a Saturday morning, and I quickly spot Misha sitting at a table in the corner. His gaze meets mine across the room and he winks, causing my cheeks to flush for what feels like the hundredth time already this morning. Ari sits across from him, looking as polished as ever with a book in front of him and a pair of glasses perched on his nose. That leaves Ezra as the one with his hood up and head on the table.

Before I beeline to them, I head to the counter and order myself the largest cup of coffee I can get. I have a feeling I'm going to need it today. And the way Ezra grunts and glares at me when he sits up as I slide into the booth next to Misha, just confirms my suspicions.

"Morning," I say quietly, inhaling the steam from my cup. That scent alone has magical powers that help bolster my spirit and gives me the courage I need to face what's coming.

Misha throws his arm over my shoulders and tugs me against his side. "Good morning, Dove. How'd you sleep?"

Ezra snorts. "Let's cut the crap. We have things we need to do today."

"Seriously, Ezra. Would it kill you to show a little kindness?" Ari asks, elbowing his twin.

I level a stare at Ezra, somehow managing to meet his golden eyes. "Okay. I'm waiting."

He gives a little huff of a laugh and turns to Ari. "After you, my oh-so-chivalrous twin."

Ari rolls his eyes, but settles into his seat. He looks around once before leaning forward and lowering his voice. "What we say today has to remain between the four of us. You cannot tell your brothers or your parents. I mean it. This is ... well, it's dangerous."

I swallow the fear that climbs up my throat, bitter and burning, but I nod. "I understand."

"This will probably be a lot for you, so if at any point you need me to stop, just tell me." Ari's eyes are serious but kind. He looks like he doesn't want to divulge this information, but he's doing so as a courtesy. When I nod, he continues. "Four years ago, mine and Ezra's sister, Millie, was murdered on campus."

I jerk, my gaze bouncing between the twins. My heart instantly breaks for them. If I ever lost one of my brothers, it would be like losing a limb. That loss would rock me to my core. The thought of it makes my heart stutter in my chest.

"Authorities ruled it a drug overdose," Ari continues. "But Millie wouldn't do drugs. She experienced too much shit in her life because of drugs, so we have no doubt that was a cover up." He pulls out a stack of worn notebooks from his bag, the covers creased and torn from being flipped through so many times. "When we got her belongings, I looked through her journals. I just had this strange feeling that something wasn't right. Something wasn't adding up."

He slides a journal across the table to me, but I don't touch it. It feels too personal. I watch him closely, my nerves making my stomach clench uncomfortably.

Ezra looks at me, and for the first time, there's no hostility in his gaze. Just anger at the death of his sister. "There are entries in these journals that confirm our suspicions. Something was going on with Millie before she died. And her death was definitely not a drug overdose."

I glance at the journal before me and my fingers shake as I slowly flip through the pages. With just a quick scan, I pick out words like 'ghost,' 'scared,' 'creatures,' and 'darkness.' A stone settles in my stomach, the few sips of coffee I've managed turn to lead.

"The thing about Millie is, she was born from a magical family," Ari continues with a pointed look in my direction. "Both of our parents were shifters. Ezra and I are shifters. But Millie had no power to her name."

I jerk my head up, staring at Ari with wide eyes. Millie had no powers? And she went through all of this, ultimately to end up murdered? Looking at Ezra and Ari, I can tell they already know about me and my lack of powers. I turn to Misha, wiping my palms on my leggings. "How did you know?" I breathe. "How did you know I don't have magical abilities?"

He doesn't flinch or look away. "Ari got access to your records. We were curious why you were attacked by a drogue. That's how we found out."

Do they think ... do they think the same thing is happening to me? Before I have a chance to ask, Misha squeezes my shoulder.

"Millie wrote about things in this journal that most people have never heard of," he says calmly. "Things that are more myth than reality. Unfortunately, they are very real. And we believe she was being hunted by them. One of those things she described were drogues."

Hunted? I suck in a breath that gets lodged in my throat. "Are you—" I stop to clear my throat painfully. "Are you saying what happened to Millie is happening to me?" Am I going to end up dead on campus?

I don't realize how badly I'm shaking until Misha takes my hands in his. The warmth from his skin soaks into my freezing body, and he squeezes me gently, trying to keep me from shaking apart into millions of pieces.

Ari gives me a small smile that does nothing to ease my fears. "We think it's possible. There are too many coincidences, in my opinion. And it's not very common to have someone born from a magical family but have no powers."

"Wh-why was Millie ... hunted?" The word comes out as a hoarse whisper.

"That's why we're here," Ezra says. "Our goal in coming to LMU is to find out what happened to Millie and why."

"And there's more," Misha says quietly, rubbing my arm. "Millie was attending LMU to figure out why she didn't have any powers. Ari just found out Millie had to take a one-on-one class with Professor Malvanado. Just like you do."

Fear snakes through my system, and I can do nothing but close my eyes against the wave that threatens to take me out. "Is he part of all of this?" I ask shakily.

I feel Misha shrug. "I don't know. But he told you to check out the graveyard, right? When we were leaving, I felt something following us. It was too far away to tell if it was evil or not. But, I wouldn't be surprised if he set that up somehow."

Fear and exhaustion sweep through me. If what they say is true, what happened last night was only the beginning. I whimper and slump in my seat, leaning on Misha for support.

Ari takes the journal back and places it in his bag. "I know that's a lot to take in. And I know it's scary. But we're here, Aspen. We're going to keep you safe through this."

I don't really know these boys. Ari is nice enough. Misha ... well Misha is Misha. But Ezra has never been nice to me. Still. As I look back and forth between the twins, something inside of me settles, something that gives off a warmth of trust and comfort. I don't know what it is, but my gut tells me to trust it. So that's exactly what I'm going to do. I don't really have much of a choice anyway.

Misha

THE NEXT NIGHT, I WALK HAND IN HAND WITH ASPEN to the cemetery. It took a lot of convincing to get Ezra to agree with her coming along, but in the end the thought that she may draw something to us is what changed his mind, which is exactly what makes my stomach churn with anxiety. I really don't want her with us when we explore the cemetery for that very reason. But, she deserves the right to choose if she wants to be part of the investigation.

It doesn't surprise me she decided to join us. While I know she's scared—I can feel the tremors working through her body— she's also incredibly brave. I'm proud of her for taking the risk.

By the time we reach the foreboding iron gates, I'm distracted by the pull of the cemetery on my magic. With professor Schaffor's help, it's been easier to ignore when I'm far from the cemetery. I was able to ignore it when Aspen and I visited because it was mostly daylight. But as the sun set that night, the pull became greater. Now, this close and in the middle of the night, it's a sharp tug on my gut, making my magic writhe like a pile of snakes inside me.

As we step through the gate, I clench my free hand and shove hard on my magic, hoping to keep it contained. I meet Ari's glowing golden gaze, and he nods, letting me know he remembers the talk we had before we left the dorm. If something were to happen with me and my magic, he'll get Aspen far away from me. I won't risk being the reason she gets hurt.

"I think we need to go to the older part of the cemetery," I say quietly, trying not to disturb the peace. "My gut tells me that if we're going to find anything, it will be there."

A thin layer of a mist swirls on the ground under our feet as we walk along the path to the gazebo that acts as the dividing line between old and new. There isn't a sound around us, except the pebbles crunching under our feet and Aspen's unsteady breathing. Not a single nighttime insect chirps or sings, and it raises the hairs on the back of my neck. I squeeze her hand in reassurance, and she takes a step closer to me.

As we step under the gazebo, we all come to stop and stare out at the other side. During the day, the older part of the cemetery held a beautifully desolate atmosphere. The trees with hanging lichen and the monuments cracked and crumbling were something stunning to behold. At night, in the dark with the fog swirling thicker, it's unsettling. The large oak trees with sweeping branches look like monsters reaching arms through the mist, gnarly fingers ready to snatch unsuspecting victims.

Before I step out into the wild, untamed section of the cemetery, I unspool a tiny thread of my magic and send it forth into the night. It's a risk, but one we have to take. If a spirit senses it, they'll be drawn to it. But without it, we'll be wandering aimlessly without knowing what direction to go.

I frown as I work through the sensations my magic picks up. Darkness. Stillness. Quiet. And ... "Southeast," I whisper hoarsely. "There's something there. Almost like a void, or something ... heavy."

Ezra nods and steps into the fog. He almost disappears immediately, and we all hurry after him. I keep my magic closer to the surface now, using it to help me sense what's around us. So far, I've felt nothing out of the ordinary besides whatever it is we're heading toward. But, I'm not getting my hopes up that this will continue to be a peaceful exploration.

Gravestones and mausoleums slowly appear in the shroud of white as we move closer to them. Broken statues and monuments jut from the fog like jagged crags of a barren peak. Aspen takes it all in with wide gray eyes that hold a combination of fear and curiosity. I bet she would love to see this during the daylight. The gothic beauty of it isn't lost on me, despite the creepiness.

In front of us, a statue slowly becomes visible, and as soon as I see it, my blood runs cold. My feet freeze to the ground and a lump forms in my throat. I stare at it, horror creeping up my spine. It's an angel, somber face upturned toward the heavens, and the discoloration of the marble makes it appear as if she's crying tears of dark blood. Her arms are outstretched in front of her, and white robes flow around her body. One of her two wings has broken, the feathers ending in jagged slashes.

I've seen this statue before, in my dreams. It was in those very arms Aspen's broken and bloody body was cradled. I can still feel the dampness on the knees of my jeans from the dewy grass as I hit the ground in agony. My magic recoils inside of me like it does whenever this vision pops into my head. But seeing the actual statue, knowing it exists, sends a chill of terror through my body that leaves me trembling.

I pull Aspen close, wrapping her in my arms and holding onto her tightly. She starts in surprise, her brows lowering in confusion. I don't bother to explain. I just hold her in my arms and frown at the statue over her shoulder, wanting nothing more than to bash it into pieces. *She's alive,* I remind myself. She's alive, and she'll remain alive. I won't let anything happen to her.

Ezra and Ari notice that I've stopped. Ari looks between me and the statue, his mouth pulled into a frown. I never told them about this dream, but it doesn't take a genius to realize there's something about the angel statue that I don't like.

"Misha?" Ari asks quietly.

I tear my gaze from the angel of death and shake my head. "It's nothing." I don't let go of Aspen, though. Letting the warmth of her body remind me everything's okay, I tighten my grip on her shoulders.

Ezra shuffles on his feet, glancing around. His golden eyes pierce the darkness, although I don't know how much better his tiger can see in the fog. "How far?" he asks gruffly.

I hesitantly send out a tendril of my magic. "Another five minutes or so," I guess.

We continue on, and even putting the statue behind us doesn't help me feel at ease. Are the dreams I had before coming to LMU prophecies? So far they've come true. I've met Aspen, who doesn't have any magical powers. She's been attacked by a ghost. Will I one day find her lifeless body in the arms of that angel statue or on the steps of a mausoleum?

A violent shudder works through me, and Aspen peers up at me.

"Are you okay, Misha?" she asks quietly.

I tug her closer to me and nod. "Yeah. I'll just be glad when we're back in the dorms." One day I'll have to tell her about the dreams, but not now. Not anytime soon.

We come to the edge of the cemetery and all stop in our tracks. There's nothing here. Just the same stone wall that circles the rest of the cemetery, this portion covered in hanging lichen like the trees surrounding it. My magic wants us to be here, though. It's alive inside of me, swirling and spiraling like the fog around us.

"What now?" Ari asks.

Aspen tips her head to the side and steps forward out of my arms. I reach for her, but she shakes me off. "Aspen?" I ask, following her closely.

"It's ... I ..." She rubs her chest and shakes her head, her messy bun flopping around. "I ..."

As if in a trance, she reaches the wall and lifts her hand, fingers brushing over the lichen and tangling in the mossy strands. When she pulls it to the side, we all freeze. The lichen acted as a curtain, hiding an opening in the cemetery wall. Behind it is a small, darkened alcove. Standing in the middle of the space is a stone altar, with skulls and dancing demons carved on the sides.

I take an involuntary step forward, morbid curiosity drawing me in. Silver candle holders crusted with red and black wax lay haphazardly around the altar. The top of the platform is carved with shallow grooves that combine into one deep channel that drains into a collection bowl sitting on the ground at the head of the stone. Even in the dark, I notice the stained brownish color of the grooves.

It's not just an ordinary altar.

Ezra steps up to my side. "What the fuck? Why is there a sacrificial altar on LMU's campus?"

A light breeze blows through the space, the wind chillier than usual this close to the cliffs on the edge of campus. We're so close I can hear the waves crashing against the rocks in the distance. It would almost be peaceful if it weren't for the altar and creepy factor.

"It doesn't surprise me," Ari says, walking around the perimeter of the little alcove. "LMU is old. Like, really old. People used to believe magic required sacrifices, so places deeply ingrained in magical history tend to have old relics like this." He comes to a stop on the other side of the altar. "The question I have is, why is there fresh wax on the candle holders?"

Ezra brings one to his nose and inhales. "It does smell like it's been lit recently." He drops it, the metal clanging in the silence, and he leans forward. "And there's still a very faint smell of blood."

Aspen steps closer to me. "You're saying someone has been sacrificed here recently?"

"It hasn't been too recent. A few years maybe." Ari gives her a reassuring smile. "And not necessarily a person. Could have been an animal."

But judging by the grimace on Ezra's face, the blood he can still smell is not animal blood. "Is there a way to get DNA from what's left in the grooves?" I ask, eyeing the discolored channels.

Ari shrugs. "Maybe. But my guess would be there's too many different types of blood, and it's too old. It's also been exposed to the elements for so long."

"Um, guys?" Aspen suddenly says, voice trembling. "The fog is getting thicker."

I tear my gaze away from the altar and curse. The fog *is* getting denser. It's rolling into the alcove in great billowing white waves. It's entirely unnatural. I close my eyes and loosen my hold on my magic, letting it sweep through the fog. The cold seeps under my clothing, and the stench of sulfur invades my senses.

Drogues. Lots of them.

"We need to go," I say urgently, my breath fogging in front of my face.

Next to me, Aspen wraps her arms around her middle and shivers. I sense it a second before I see it. Faster than I've ever moved, I shove Aspen to the side right as a clawed arm reaches where she had just been standing. Aspen trips over the edge of the altar and she falls backward, landing on her ass. She screams when she sees what was gunning for her.

"Ari! Ezra!" I yell at the same time I let my magic lose from the tight knot I keep it in. "Get her out of here!"

From the corner of my eye, I catch a black and orange striped tiger lunging for Aspen. She doesn't cower away from it. Instead, she reaches out and grabs a handful of its fur.

"What are you going to do?" Ezra asks behind me.

"I'm going to hold these fuckers off and distract them from Aspen." I turn around and meet his golden gaze. "Get her back to the dorms." My voice is low and urgent.

"We will," he promises.

Ezra runs past me and grabs Aspen's wrist, pulling her to her feet. She glances at me over her shoulder with wide eyes, a protest on her tongue that turns into a scream when another drogue emerges from the fog.

I let my instincts take over, and a blast of my magic sweeps forward, a gray arc that slices through the air and pushes the spirit back, giving Ezra the space to drag Aspen away. With how thick the fog is, it only takes a few steps before I can't see them anymore. As soon as Aspen is out of my sight, my magic writhes inside of me, like it wants to follow her and make sure she's okay. I have to fight the urge to chase after them. I need to keep these spirits distracted.

Sending out another blast of my magic, I reverse the technique professor Schaffor taught me to keep it masked. Mentally, I rip off the blanket covering the core of magic inside me and let it fill the air. Hopefully this draws the spirits away from Aspen so Ezra and Ari can get her to safety.

With my magic spread wide in a softly glowing gray cloud, I can sense the insane number of restless spirits wandering through the cemetery. My mouth goes dry, and I swallow thickly. There are so many. At least a hundred of them. The majority are ambling my way, but the rest are too far away for me to get a good read on what they're doing.

I step out of the alcove, keeping my magic fanning before me so I don't run into anything. The fog is still rolling in thick waves, obscuring everything more than a foot around me. And it's so cold my teeth are chattering. It's been too long since I've used my magic in any sort of capacity, and I can feel it draining my strength quickly.

I sense a heaviness in front of me. A void that seems to suck all of the energy from the earth. It approaches faster than I can track, and I'm too slow to react. I jump backward in an attempt to escape its rushing attack, but jagged black claws slice through my thigh. Fire erupts in my leg, and I fall to the ground with a shout. Glowing red eyes stare down at me, and my heart lurches in my chest as it raises its clawed hand again.

It's not a spirit.

Aspen

Everything happened so fast, and I can barely wrap my mind around it all with the fear flooding my system. Just before Misha shoved me to the side, I'd caught a glimpse of something in the fog. Something tall and sinewy, with claws as long as my hand. And it was heading straight for me. I tripped over the corner of the altar and hit the ground, just barely missing the swipe of claws.

When a large tiger charged for me from behind the altar, some of that fear dissipated as a sense of calm overcame me. Instinctively, I knew it was Ari. I think even without knowing he's a tiger shifter, I would have known it was him. Something deep inside of me recognizes him for what he is, but I don't have time to wonder why that is.

As Ezra drags me out of the alcove and deeper into the fog, I realize Misha isn't following. Turning around, I open my mouth to yell for him, but another one of those spirits lunges for me. I scream and duck against Ezra, clutching his arm in a vise-like grip. A line of glowing gray magic slices forward and pushes the spirit back. By the time I look toward Misha again, he's already obscured by the fog.

"Wait!" I gasp, trying to pull Ezra to a stop. He doesn't let me slow him down, and Ari, following behind, uses his large body to herd me forward. "Wait! What about Misha?"

"He'll be fine," Ezra grunts. His golden eyes glow as he scans our surroundings. "He told me to get you back to the dorm, so that's exactly what I'm going to do."

I can't see anything in front of me. The fog is so thick I can barely see a foot ahead of us. The way the twin's tiger eyes glow, though, gives me hope they can pierce the mist better than mine. What if there's something up ahead waiting for us? I strain my ears, but sounds are dampened as if I'm underwater. The silence is even more eerie after all the chaos we just experienced.

Ezra glances down at his brother, and a moment later, Ari takes off, rushing forward in a swirl of mist.

"Where is he go—"

"Quiet," Ezra hisses, cutting me off.

I snap my mouth shut, heat blooming in my cheeks. We continue in silence, my harsh breathing the only sound. I'm sure with his shifter senses, Ezra can hear my heartbeat. In fact, anything nearby can probably hear it—it's beating so hard the echoes of it can be felt in my temples and fingertips. I desperately want to turn around and find Misha. What if something happens to him? But at the same time, I really don't want to stay in this fog shrouded cemetery for a moment longer.

Suddenly, Ezra's breath hitches, and he pushes his body against mine, shoving me against the side of a mausoleum with my hands pinned between us. I almost cry out in surprise, but swallow it down at the last minute. The cold of the marble seeps through my hoodie and bites at my skin. His heat surrounds me in a tantalizing way that makes me gasp for an entirely different reason.

It's the closest we've ever been. Usually, we keep our distance from each other. His permanent glower and the way he scowls whenever he sees me is the perfect barrier between us, and I have no desire to cross it. But right now, in the dark, it's harder to separate him and Ari, and I won't deny that I have a little crush on Ari. My body reacts instinctually, despite the situation we're in. I look at him, at the sharp angles of his face and his unsettling golden eyes. His blond hair is tousled, and I find myself wanting to reach up to smooth it back into place.

Ezra senses my attention on him, and he drops his gaze to my face. I try to look away, to pretend like I wasn't staring at him, but I can't. No matter how hard I try, my body refuses to listen to me. I'm drawn into his eyes. They swallow me whole, and I find myself falling, falling, falling, until I know nothing except him pressed against me.

His breath hitches again, but this time, I think it's for a different reason. He stares at me as if he is having a hard time looking away, too. The gold in his eyes darkens to a rich brown, and the way they swirl is breathtaking. When Ezra lowers his head the slightest inch, I lift my chin. A silent invitation I don't quite understand. But the erratic beating of my heart and the sudden flurry of butterflies in my stomach, seem to get it.

His throat bobs with a swallow, and he lowers his head even more. His face is so close to mine I can feel his breath fanning across my lips. Just as my eyelids start to flutter shut, he stiffens and whips his head to the side. A spirit ambles past, shuffling on battered limbs. It pauses next to us, and Ezra presses tighter against me, like he can push me into the marble to hide me. I stop breathing, waiting for the creature to turn its head and spot us. But it doesn't. It shakes itself like a dog before continuing on.

Ezra releases a breath and pulls away, shoulders slumping. "Fuck. That was close." He runs his hand through his hair, and glances at me from the corner of his eyes before quickly looking away. Taking my wrist again, he tugs me on. "Let's go."

I stumble after him on numb legs. The image of what almost happened keeps repeating in my head. I was seconds away from kissing Ezra. Ezra! The grouchy asshole who wants nothing to do with me. I'm glad he's paying attention and Ari is somewhere in the mist doing the same, because I cannot focus to save my life. Before, I was shaky because of the spirits chasing us and for Misha staying behind to fight them. Now, I'm shaky because I realize how badly I wanted to kiss Ezra, and that horrifies me.

I'm still in a daze when the fog disappears after walking for another couple of minutes. One second it's there, heavy and thick, and the next second it's gone. I stumble when we emerge, and turn to look back. If there was any question about the fog being unnatural, it's been answered. It stands before us like a brick wall. A solid dividing line between fog and no fog. I wrap my arms around myself to quell the chill. Ari presses against my side, and I drop a hand to his back, tangling my fingers in his fur.

"Come on," Ezra says.

We follow Ezra to the gazebo and out to the other side of the cemetery. I keep looking back, hoping to see Misha running to catch up to us. But he's never there. The fear of being in the fog with the spirits fades away, but it's quickly replaced by fear for his safety.

"What about Misha?" I ask, my voice trembling.

"He'll meet us back at the dorm." Ezra doesn't look at me. He keeps walking forward, setting a brisk pace.

Before I know it, the iron gate looms in front of us, and we're passing through, stepping back onto campus. There's no one around this late at night, and it's probably a good thing with Ari still prowling next to me on all fours. His ears flick back and forth, picking up sounds I can't hear even with my slightly enhanced hearing.

It's almost like being in another world. After the fog shrouded cemetery crawling with spirits, the calm, quiet of campus is surreal. No one here knows what just happened five minutes ago. All of the students and professors are going about their daily lives, sleeping, late night studying, grading papers. And I was just attacked.

When we reach the dorms, Ezra leads us to the second floor, to my room. My hand shakes when I place my palm against the wood, letting the wards zip over my skin and unlock the door. Ezra pushes inside and collapses onto the chair by the fireplace, while Ari stalks into the room, not wasting a second before turning his attention on me.

I stare at them, not moving away from the door. "You're just going to sit there? What about Misha?" My nerves tangle inside of me, a ball of yarn in my stomach so knotted I'm not sure it will ever come unwound.

"What else should we do?" Ezra asks, crossing his arms over his chest. "I already told you, Misha will be fine. He'll meet us here." He casts his gaze to Ari and grimaces before standing and heading to the fireplace to light a fire.

I glance between the twins. Can they talk to each other telepathically? It certainly seems like it. Back in the cemetery, Ari moved ahead of us after a look from Ezra. Then Ezra seemed to know about the spirit in front of us before it was close enough for him to sense. I tuck that little tidbit away to examine later when my anxiety isn't a poison circulating through my bloodstream.

"But—" I cut off as Ari saunters over to me, big paws padding on the floor. He uses his body to push me to the bed.

I sit on the edge and wait somewhat patiently as Ari's tiger looks me over. His nose twitches, long whiskers shivering with the movement. I'm assuming he's checking me for injuries, but I already know I don't have any.

My hands brace either side of his large head. "I'm fine," I say quietly, running my fingers through his fur.

Ari sits at my feet and rests his head in my lap. He makes a soft chuffing noise, his breath puffing warmly around me. I take a moment to wonder at the fact that a massive cat is cuddling up to me, and I have zero fear. If he were to open his mouth, I know there would be huge teeth, perfect for shredding flesh and breaking bones. But I also know he'd never bare those teeth at me. There's a comfort in his presence that settles some of my anxiety.

I don't know how long we sit in silence with only the sound of logs popping in the hearth. Running my fingers through Ari's fur calms me and helps to distract me from worrying about Misha. But it's still there in the back of my mind. It tries to take over and pull me under. Letting it get the best of me won't do any good, though. So I push it down and try to calm my racing heart.

Eventually, Ari lifts his head and turns his golden-eyed gaze on my door. A second later, Misha stumbles inside. I don't even have time to wonder how he got past the wards, because the first thing I notice are the bloody gashes on his thigh and the way he's limping unsteadily.

"Misha!" I jump to my feet, dislodging Ari, and dash forward.

Ezra gets to Misha before I do, and I watch in horror as Misha practically collapses into his arms. "To the bed," Ezra grunts, bearing most of Misha's weight.

I freeze in place, staring at the blood oozing from his wounds. The room around me tilts, the floor seeming like it's going to disappear and leave me free-falling through space. I close my eyes and swallow thickly, hearing only the ringing in my ears. But with my eyes closed, all I can see is the image of Misha stumbling into my room, bloody and in pain, so I snap them back open as Ezra settles him on my bed.

Ezra turns to his twin. "Go shift and get dressed," he orders gruffly.

Ari waits for me to open my dorm door, and then he dashes down the hall and disappears. When I turn back to the bed, I almost freeze again, but Ezra shoots me a glare over his shoulder, and it pushes me into gear. In my bathroom, I grab a bunch of first-aid supplies, trying to ignore the tightness in my chest when I think about Misha being injured. With shaking hands, I run back to the bed and drop to my knees next to Ezra who has already managed to get Misha's pants off and tossed to the floor.

"Scoot over," I say, voice trembling slightly.

Ezra eyes me with uncertainty, before giving me some room. "You're not going to pass out from the sight of blood, are you?"

"I'm half vampire. Blood doesn't scare me." My words don't hold the bite I wish they did, but I can't quite muster the sass with Misha bleeding in my bed. It's not the sight of the blood that makes me queasy, it's the fact the blood is coming from someone I care about.

Misha snorts, the sound more pained than humorous.

"You're not gonna suck my blood, are you?" His words slur together, his voice raspy like he's been screaming.

I glance at him with my heart in my throat. He doesn't think I'd do that, does he? But despite the pain I can clearly see in his eyes, there's a twinkle of humor there, too. I relax and give him a stern look. "Not unless you want me to puke all over you. Now hold still."

Misha's skin is hot under my fingertips as I clean the wounds as gently as I can. He still ends up hissing through his teeth and tensing his muscles, causing more blood to leak out. Once I get the wound clean enough to see it clearly, I bite my lip and sit back.

"These are really deep, Misha. I think you need stitches."

"Do you know how to stitch wounds?" he asks breathlessly.

I shake my head. "I could do small cuts, but nothing this big." Turning to Ezra, I raise my brow. "Do you or Ari know how to stitch?"

Ezra frowns and says quietly, "No."

I look at Misha again. His skin is pale, and a faint sheen of sweat covers his face. When I place my hand on his forehead, I can feel the heat radiating from him. Worry twists my stomach into knots. "You're already feverish," I mumble. "I think I need to call Adrian."

"We can't do that," Misha groans through gritted teeth. "What the hell would we tell him?"

I gently wipe away more blood that leaks from his wound. "I don't know, but if I don't call him, you're going to bleed to death."

"Tell him we were sparring," Ezra says suddenly. "I accidentally got Misha with my claws while in my tiger form."

The slashes on Misha's thigh could be caused by a big cat. Adrian has probably never seen an injury caused by tiger claws, so it wouldn't be hard to pass this off as being a sparring accident. I nod and pull my phone from my pocket. "Okay. Hold on, Misha."

Aspen

ARI RETURNS WHILE WE WAIT FOR ADRIAN. EVEN though he's back in his human form, he paces the length of the room like a caged animal. It makes me nervous, and I'm about to snap at him to tell him to stop. But I distract myself by fussing over Misha, making sure he's comfortable and keeping the towel under his leg clean to avoid getting blood on my comforter.

When Adrian knocks on my door, we all take a collective breath before I let him in. "Thank you," I say quickly, pulling him toward the bed.

Adrian's amber eyes—exactly like our mom's—take in the three guys in my room, one of them sprawled on my bed, half naked and bleeding, and he frowns. He casts a quick glance at me that screams disapproval. But as always, he keeps his thoughts to himself. For now at least. Adrian will wait until we're alone to give me a talk about being in a room with three guys.

"What happened?" he asks, sitting on the edge of the bed to get a better look at the injury.

I look at Ezra pointedly. If I try to tell Adrian what happened, he'll definitely catch me in the lie. I can't fool my brothers. Ezra sighs and pushes from the chair to stand by the bed.

"We were sparring," he says gruffly. "I accidentally got him with my claws."

Adrian looks at the wound again and frowns. My heart rate doubles, and I'm scared he's about to call us out. But instead, he lifts his hands and a violet glow spreads up his arms. Adrian gently places his hands on either side of Misha's thigh, and we all watch in amazement as the gashes stop bleeding then slowly knit themselves back together.

Adrian waits a moment longer, like he wants to make sure he heals everything properly before letting his magic settle inside himself again. "The one claw mark was pretty deep. It severed your nerves. I was able to heal them, but you might feel a little sore for a few days."

Misha flexes his foot, contracting his quads, and he lets out a little sigh of relief. "Thanks, man. I appreciate it."

Adrian stands and glances at Ezra. "Be more careful next time." Although his words are calm, there's something underlying them that makes me think he doesn't believe our story. When he turns to me and jerks his head in the direction of the hall, my stomach tumbles.

At first, Adrian says nothing. He just studies me with amber eyes that read me like an open book. "How are you?" he finally asks.

"I'm fine." I do my best to give him an encouraging smile while also not meeting his eyes.

"I don't believe you." He steps closer and places a hand on my shoulder. When I don't shrug it off, he continues. "Aspen, what's going on? I don't believe for a second that injury was caused by a sparring match with a tiger shifter."

I stare at the ground and bite the inside of my cheek. The words are right there on the tip of my tongue. I want to tell him. If my brothers know what's going on, if I could talk to them about the things that are happening to me, I'd feel so much better. But I can't, because they will never let it go.

"Aspen," Adrian says again. "Rho and I have been talking. You've never been good at hiding from us, and we're both concerned. There is something going on that you're not telling us."

Gee, am I that obvious? When I don't reply, he sighs.

"Look, if you're in trouble you need to tell us. We can't protect you if we don't know what's happening. But we do know you would never hang out with those kinds of guys. So please, Aspen, talk to me."

I take a breath and force myself to look him in the eyes, hoping I don't give myself away. "Really, I'm fine. I like Misha and Ari. They aren't what you think they are." And that sounds like the biggest line. Exactly the type of thing a girl would say when she's involved with someone she shouldn't be. "I know you're here if I need anything, and I appreciate that. But I don't need you right now."

Those amber eyes scan my face, and he shakes his head. "I'll let this go for now. But believe me, we're not done with this conversation. Please call me or Rho if you need anything."

"I will," I nod. "And thank you for helping Misha."

He gives me one final look before heading back to his dorm. I release a breath and rub my eyes. I hate how well my brothers know me. Keeping this from them is going to be impossible.

Back in my room, Misha's sitting against the headboard of my bed. His eyes are closed, but the strain around them is gone, and his complexion is more normal. When I step into the room, the conversation between them halts, like they don't want me to hear what they have to say. I stand uncertainly by the door, picking at the skin around my nails. What could they want to talk about that they wouldn't want me to hear? A million things fire in my mind, and each one makes my stomach drop a little.

They've decided I'm too much to deal with. Misha no longer wants to date me. Something bad happened tonight, and they don't want to tell me. They know Adrian knows we lied tonight, and now they're suspicious of him. They realized how dangerous this campus really is, and they've decided to leave me to handle it for myself. The list is never ending.

I stare at the ground, my picking intensifying to the point I draw blood. That small bite of pain is better than the burning in my eyes as every little insecurity rears its ugly head. This is what I do. I over analyze. I think the worst case scenario is real, and I let it consume me until I fall apart. I believe every negative thought I have about myself is true. My emotions and thoughts eat away the rational part of my thinking until no one but Rho can talk sense into me.

Misha notices my silence and interrupts my spiraling. "Aspen, come here."

I look up, my vision blurry through the tears I refuse to let fall. Misha holds his arms open for me, and I let myself be drawn in. The promise of his strength surrounding me is too tempting to ignore. As soon as I'm close enough, he grabs my wrist and tugs me onto the bed. He tucks me against his side, and wraps both arms around me in a squeezing embrace. The pressure of the hug is exactly what I need, and as relief spreads through me, I can't stop the tears that silently fall down my cheeks.

"What happened tonight?" Ari asks, sitting on the foot of the bed.

"I'm not sure," Misha says slowly. "I think my magic drew the drogues to us. But what attacked me wasn't a typical spirit. Actually, I don't think it was a spirit at all." He idly plays with a loose curl of my hair while he talks. "Did you guys encounter anything after you left?"

Ezra shakes his head. "Just a drogue that Ari warned us about in time. We were able to hide." His gaze flicks to me and away so quickly I'm not sure I'd have noticed it if I didn't know something had almost happened between us. "But, what do you mean you don't think what attacked you was a spirit? What else would it be?"

My head bobs with Misha's shrug. "It didn't feel like a regular spirit to me. I don't know how to explain it. It had more essence." He shakes his head and frowns. "I know that doesn't make sense to you guys, but it's all I got. It managed to get past my guard. I'm not used to using my magic, let alone fighting with it. But it's good to know I was able to distract them enough to let Aspen get away."

I sit up at his words, eyes widening. "Don't do that again," I whisper, angrily brushing tears from my cheeks. "I know you want to protect me, but ..." Another tear escapes. "Don't make me leave you behind. Don't make me leave *any* of you behind." That includes Ezra. Because while I may not like him, he's Ari's twin, and it would kill him if something happened to Ezra.

Misha gives me a small smile. "I appreciate hearing you say that, and I'm sure Ezra and Ari do as well, but there isn't much you can do against angry spirits. Even the twins are at a disadvantage. So I will always make sure you're safe, first and foremost."

I open my mouth to argue, but there's a steely glint in Misha's dark eyes that tells me I won't win. Instead, I ask the questions that have been circling in my mind tonight. "Why could I see the spirits this time? And what was with the altar?" That entire alcove gave me goosebumps. Something sinister definitely happened there, and the negative energy still permeates the space like a poisonous cloud of gas.

Misha releases a heavy sigh full of weariness. "They wanted to be seen this time. Whoever is behind this definitely wants you to know what's chasing after you." He shakes his head, a spark of anger glinting in his eyes. "As for the altar ..."

"I'll see if I can dig up any history books about LMU," Ari says, running a hand through his blond hair. "Like I said earlier, I'm not surprised to find a sacrificial altar on campus, but I am surprised to find it's been used in the not-so-distant past."

"Do you think you can find out about the recent sacrifices?" Ezra asks skeptically. "That seems like something someone would hide and not record."

Ari shrugs. "Probably not. But it's worth looking. Also, figuring out what exactly they were doing on LMU all those years ago might give us some sort of clue about what's happening today."

Ezra grunts. "Fine. If we're done here, I'd like to go back to my room and get some sleep." He doesn't wait for anyone to respond before stomping out of my dorm.

Ari glances at me and Misha. "He's right. It's late. We should all get some rest. You especially, Misha. Healing takes a lot out of a person. Do you need anything before I leave?"

Misha shakes his head, and as Ari walks to the door, I open my mouth to say something, but Misha's hand has traveled to my thigh. Suddenly every thought in my head disappears except the need to feel Misha touching me, to make sure he's really okay.

As soon as the door closes behind Ari, Misha grabs my chin and tips my face toward his. There's desperation in his eyes and urgency in the way he touches me. I think we both need the reassurance that everything is okay. He kisses me, hard and demanding, unlike the way he usually does. This time, it's like he's trying to remind himself that we're both alive, despite what happened tonight.

I meet him stroke for stroke, just as desperate as he is. Each brush of his tongue along mine pushes the image of him stumbling into my room, bloody and hurt, further away. Each flutter in my stomach from his touch drives away the cold that set in back at the cemetery. And each soft breath shared between us banishes the fear that snakes through my blood and leaves me shaky and nauseous.

Misha's hands glide over every inch of me, sliding under my shirt and up my stomach to cup my breasts through my bra. The heat of his palms draws a groan from me, and I arch my back in a silent plea for more. I shift so I can straddle his waist, careful of his thigh, even though it's been healed. There's very little clothing between us, so when Misha lifts his hips and presses against me, I can feel every inch of his hardness.

I gasp as heat floods my bloodstream and pools in my core. A slow ache builds between my thighs, and I grind down on Misha, seeking relief. He hisses through his teeth, fingers tightening on my hips in a delicious spark of pain. In a move my sex addled brain can't comprehend, Misha manages to get my leggings and panties down my thighs, and I shift back and forth to help him get them off my legs.

He keeps me in place with my knees on the bed on either side of him, but he slips lower until he's laying on his back and I'm kneeling on either side of his head. A flash of insecurity grips me by the spine, and I tense. He can't be asking me to do what I think he is, can he? I'll suffocate him!

But Misha doesn't seem to care, he grabs my hips and pulls me down until I'm sitting on his face. I try to fight him, but it takes one swipe of his tongue through my folds for me to give in. He growls lightly, and I feel the vibrations rumble through me, enhancing my pleasure. My fingers grip the headboard hard enough I'm surprised it doesn't groan under the pressure.

"Misha!" I gasp.

His answer comes in the form of his tongue sliding inside of me and his fingers grabbing my ass in a bruising grip. Misha devours me like he's never tasted anything so sweet. He turns me into a gasping puddle of shaky limbs. It doesn't take long for my hips to start rocking as I search for what I need. The pressure inside of me builds and builds. A rising inferno of pleasure that threatens to sweep me away.

Misha makes a noise and I freeze, glancing down in alarm. But instead of seeing him half-dead like I expected, his eyes are lidded and burning with a fire that makes my core clench. It was a moan, I realize. And I realize he's only holding onto me with one hand now. Peeking behind me, I find he's working his hand up and down his cock, the tip leaking with pre-cum.

Okay. That's hot. Heat floods me, and my hips start rocking again, a little faster this time.

"Misha," I groan. "I'm so close."

He redoubles his efforts, licking, sucking, and nibbling like his life depends on it. When his teeth graze my clit, I fall into the ocean of pleasure. My orgasm slams into me, and my body shudders as wave after wave crashes over me. I cry out, Misha's name on my lips, and he doesn't stop fucking me with his tongue until he's wrung every last drop of pleasure from me.

I fall to the side, panting and wanting to make sure Misha can still breathe. His eyes are closed and his back arches lightly off the bed as he finishes himself. I watch the lines of his body, the way his muscles tense and strain as he comes. The picture he paints is beautiful as he chases his orgasm, and suddenly I desperately want to see him completely naked.

When he falls back to the bed, he grins at me, his face glistening with my arousal. "Wait here," he says, his voice low and gravelly.

Misha tucks himself back into his boxer briefs on his way to the bathroom, quickly emerging with a washcloth in hand. I squirm uncomfortably as he cleans himself off, his intense gaze never leaving my body. It makes me self conscious being the center of his attention while completely naked. It shouldn't, seeing as I was just sitting on this man's face after all.

When he's done, he tosses the cloth to the side and climbs back into bed with me, pulling me into his arms. I go willingly, cuddling against him and resting my head on his chest, not even once thinking about how strange it is I so willingly welcome his touch.

Misha kisses the top of my head. "Sleep, Aspen. It's been a long night."

After everything that's happened tonight, I'm exhausted, but I'm not sure I can fall asleep. I'm scared of what I'll see when I close my eyes. Monsters in the cemetery. Misha bleeding in my bed. But with the echo of Misha's gentleness and the soft kiss on my head, I find myself slipping under. And instead of nightmares behind my eyelids, I see Misha's shining brown eyes and the orange and black stripes of a surprisingly soft tiger.

Aspen

THE NEXT FEW WEEKS PASS BY UNEVENTFULLY. No more ghost attacks. No more sensations of being followed. And despite the terrifying realization I'm probably being hunted, I've fallen into a nice routine.

I've slept like absolute shit, though. Every little creak and pop of the dorms sends me into a downward spiral of fear. I'm just waiting for the next shoe to drop and the constant threat looming behind me is wearing me down. Misha and the guys have quickly learned not to sneak up on me. The last time Ari did, I kneed him in the balls on instinct.

Despite our suspicions of Professor Malvanado, I'm still attending our meetings. We decided it was a good way to keep track of him, and possibly feed him misinformation. One of the guys always walks me to the meetings and waits outside to walk me to lab after. And if I'm ever alone on campus, or out late, they insist I call one of them to stay with me. I haven't been alone much since I learned of all of this wildness, so walking by myself is strange and somewhat unsettling.

"Pen!"

I turn around at the sound of Rho's voice and force a smile to my face. "Hey."

"How's it going? I haven't talked to you in weeks." He slings his arm around my shoulders and walks me toward the library.

"Yeah, I've been busy."

He studies me, almost tripping over a raised portion of the walkway because he's so distracted. "You okay? You're paler than usual. And you look tired. Are you getting enough sleep?"

No. I have to bite my lip to keep from laughing. I definitely haven't been getting enough sleep. "I'm pale because the sun doesn't shine here. Also, I'm part vampire."

Rho snorts. "And you're usually more tan than I am. I know Adrian talked to you the other day."

I stiffen and nod my head. "Yeah. And I told him everything was fine. It still is fine. You guys don't have to worry." It sounds like such a line, and I cringe inwardly. If the roles were reversed and Rho had just said that to me, I'd be jumping on him for the lie.

He laughs. "That's like asking the rain not to fall. Aspen, we'll always worry about you. And there is nothing you can do to stop that." He purses his lips as he looks at me. "You'd tell me if something was wrong, right?"

I nod and pray that I hide my wince well enough he doesn't catch it. There have been many times I've debated telling Rhory and Adrian about what's happening. But I know they wouldn't be able to let it go, and they'd insist I return home, telling our parents everything. Despite the danger I'm in, I don't want to leave LMU. I want to find out why I don't have magical powers. And it's looking like that reason goes deeper than anyone ever thought.

Plus, I'm enjoying spending time with Misha and the twins. Well, at least Misha and Ari. I could do without Ezra.

Luckily, Rho doesn't press further and he changes the subject. "Are you coming to the game tonight? It's our home opener. It'll be wild!" His icy blue eyes sparkle with excitement and his smile splits his face in two.

"I don't know. I honestly hadn't thought about it." I glance at him and catch the way his face falls. I would have missed it if I didn't know his tells as well as I do. His brows come together, just slightly, and little lines form at the corners of his eyes. His smile stays the same, but it looks forced. I sigh and bump into him. "I wouldn't miss it, Rho."

"Really?" He beams at me, and it makes it all worth it. "It will be the first time you've ever seen me play college level lacrosse."

How terrible am I that I've never watched my big brother play the sport he loves since high school? I just don't get sports. Why would anyone want to run around and chase a ball, run into each other, sweat, and get hurt for fun? But, I probably shouldn't have gone so long without coming to see a game.

"Aspen!"

This time, I turn around and find Ari jogging toward me with a smile. "Sorry I'm late. I got caught up in my last class." He stops in front of me and turns his attention to Rho.

Tension crackles like lightning between Ari and Rhory as they stare at each other. Ari's gaze narrows on Rho and he steps closer to me. I roll my eyes and huff.

"Ari, have you met my brother, Rhory? Rho this is Ari." I bump my shoulder against Rho, subtly letting him know to play nice.

Ari's slightly hostile expression softens. "Oh, hey! It's nice to meet you."

Rho's face doesn't shift. "Yeah. Nice to meet you. How do you know my sister again?"

"Rho, come on. He's a friend. Lighten up." I pinch the back of his arm, just above his elbow and he yelps, yanking his arm away.

"Ow! Fuck, Pen! Why do you do that?" He rubs the spot and glares at me.

"Because someone needs to put you in your place occasionally."

He gives me a baleful look before turning away.

"I have class, Rho. I'll see you tonight at the game." I wrap my arms around him and give him a hug.

"You better be there," he says sullenly before walking away with one last hostile glance at Ari.

"Seriously. Why are boys so obnoxious?" I shift the strap of my bag across my chest and turn to face Ari.

"I don't know what you're talking about," he says too innocently. "I was perfectly nice."

"Uh huh. Sure. Come on, or we'll be late."

"So were you going to tell us you're going to the game tonight? You shouldn't go alone."

"I just found out I was going. Besides, I thought there would be enough people there that it would be safe enough."

He hums thoughtfully. "Probably. But I'd rather be safe than sorry. We'll go with you. Besides, Misha loves lacrosse, and I'm pretty sure he has a poster of your brother hanging on his wall."

THERE'S a reason I've never been to any of Rho's college lacrosse games, and I'm immediately reminded of that reason as I step into the stadium.

People.

Way. Too. Many. People.

Instantly, my shoulders rise protectively, and I wrap my arms around my middle. The smaller I am, the less noticeable I am, right? It doesn't stop me from being jostled by unruly students celebrating the first home game of the season, and I find myself leaning closer to Misha and Ari. They're big, and they help keep some of the crowd at bay.

"Where do you want to sit?" Misha practically yells to be heard over the noise. "The student section is over there." He points to a large part of the stadium reserved for LMU students. I take one look at the roiling crowd of half drunk fans and blanch. Misha chuckles and tightens his arm around my waist. "The family section is probably quieter."

I follow the direction of his head nod and enthusiastically agree. "Oh, yes. Definitely. That's much better."

The family section is still crowded, but there's at least room to move without bumping into someone. And you don't have to yell quite as loud to be heard. I'm following Misha up the steps when I hear someone call my name.

"Aspen!"

I turn around and stop dead in my tracks. "Mom?" She's sitting in a row with all three of my dads, and when she meets my gaze, she pushes to her feet.

"Mom?" Misha mutters under his breath at the same time Ezra says, "Fuck this," and walks away.

I try to let go of Misha's hand, but he tightens his grip. My mom walks down the row to me and pulls me in for a hug. It's awkward, not only because I'm not huge on hugs, but also because Misha is still holding my hand. Mom notices, and her amber gaze bounces between me and Misha, then me and Ari.

"Who are your friends?" she asks. She's gone all out for the game. Besides wearing one of Rho's jerseys, her hair is braided into pigtails with black and red ribbons, and she has black under eye stickers with Rhory's number in red.

"Um, this is Misha and Ari," I say, just as my dads step up behind her.

Kai's gray eyes are unamused as he looks over the boys. He pulls his lower lip between his teeth with a fang, clearly sending them a message. Sterling folds his massive arms over his chest and glares. I try to make myself smaller and fervently wish for a hole to open in the ground to swallow me. This is one of the reasons I don't date very often.

Cade smiles at me and reaches over mom's shoulder to tug on a strand of my hair. "It's nice to run into you. We were going to surprise you after the game to take you and your brothers out for dinner." He looks around with a frown. "Speaking of. Where is Adrian?"

I grin. "This isn't really his scene. He's probably in his room studying."

Cade grins right back. "It's not exactly your scene either. Who convinced you to come?" His violet gaze travels to Ari then Misha, then down to mine and Misha's joined hands.

I quickly pry my hand away and shove them both in the front pocket of my hoodie. "Rho guilted me into it, and now he owes me a favor."

Mom tsks just as a whistle blows on the field. "Oh, it's starting. Do you want to sit with us?"

My mouth opens but nothing comes out. No, I absolutely do not want to sit with them while with two guys. Cade smiles at my hesitation and pulls mom back against his chest.

"You're fine, Aspen. Go sit wherever you want. We'll meet up after the game in your dorm?"

I swallow and nod, before turning around and fleeing. Without paying attention to where I'm going, I pick a random row and slide down it, sitting on the chilly metal bench. For once, I don't mind the cold. My face feels like a furnace, and I don't need a mirror to know my cheeks are flaming. I pull my pull hood over my head and attempt to hide in it. Misha doesn't let me though.

He tugs the hood down and grins at me. "So, that was your family?"

I grumble and pull the hood back up. This time he lets me hide. Ari sits on the other side of me, and I turn my attention to the field, letting both of the guys' body heat warm me.

I know nothing about lacrosse except Rhory's number is 34, and LMU's colors are red and black. I couldn't tell you what position Rho plays, the rules, or any of LMU's opponents. And as the game starts, I have to refrain from leaning over and asking Misha what's happening. I just clap when he does and hope I don't look like a total idiot.

Shortly after the game starts, Ezra returns. He sits next to Misha and leans around him to hand me a steaming cup. "Hot chocolate," he mutters, looking at the ground.

Taken aback, I slowly reach for the offering. "It's not poisoned is it?"

Misha barks a laugh. "Good question. Why are you being nice to her?"

"Fine. Give it back. I'll drink it." He throws out his hand like he's asking for the drink, and I clutch it tighter and turn away. "I just thought she'd like something warm. It's fucking freezing out here."

It is warm. The heat soaks through my gloves, and I bring the cup to my face to let the steam thaw my frozen nose. "Thank you, Ezra."

He shrugs uncomfortably, rubbing the back of his neck as he turns his glare to the field. I spend the next few minutes watching the players run around chasing a ball while I sip on my hot chocolate, propped up on either side by two guys who have come to mean something important to me.

Halfway through the game, Ari nudges my shoulder and grins. "You have no clue what's going on, do you?"

"I'm absolutely lost. Who's winning?" I look at the scoreboard, but honestly, how the hell do you read one of those things? What do all the abbreviations and numbers mean?

"We are. Sixteen to eleven. It's almost halftime, then there are two more quarters," he explains patiently. I must make a face of some sort because he laughs. "Don't worry. The quarters are only fifteen minutes long. The game will be over before you know it."

And then I have to meet with my parents. I pray they don't ask about Misha and Ari. Glancing down the stadium to where they're sitting, I can't help but smile. Of course Kai is plastered to mom's side. She laughs at something he whispers in her ear then playfully swats at him.

I've always admired the way my mom handles three guys. I know it hasn't been easy for them, and I know there have been hurdles to jump over, but I'm positive there has never been a moment where one of them has felt left out. Their joy and love for each other is contagious, and I hope one day to have a relationship as strong as theirs.

Ari catches me watching them and leans down to my ear to be

heard. "If I had to guess, I'd say your dad is the one with the black hair?"

I nod. "Malakai Thorne, yeah. But we never really made a huge fuss about who belongs to whom. All three of them are my dads." I glance at Ari and find him frowning slightly as he watches my family. "Is that weird to you? That my mom has three mates?" I try to not let the uncertainty show, but Ari must have heard the tremor in my voice.

"Not at all. If fate blesses you with more than one mate, I think that's something really special."

A weight I wasn't aware of lifts from my shoulders, immediately freeing and reassuring. "Thank you," I say so quietly I'm not sure he can even hear me.

He must though, because he gently takes my chin and forces me to look at him. "Were you worried I'd judge you for that?"

I swallow and nod as much as I can with him holding my chin. "It wouldn't be the first time." When I was younger, I used to beg my mom to only bring one of the guys to school events. She never listened, of course, because they all wanted to be part of my life. Having to listen to people talk about my mom being whore was just part of it.

Ari's golden eyes soften, and I swear his thumb strokes back and forth just a tiny bit. "I'll never judge you, Aspen. For any reason."

I open my mouth to thank him, but something happens in the game and Misha surges to his feet, accidentally bumping into me. The force sends me rocking into Ari, and my forehead cracks against his chin. The sting brings tears to my eyes immediately, and I grab my forehead with a groan.

"Ah, fuck," Ari mutters rubbing the red spot on his chin. He reaches for me again, cool fingers running over the sore spot on my head. "Are you okay?"

"Ouch," I whimper pathetically. When I lift my gaze, I find Ari's golden eyes staring intently at me. This is the closest I've ever been to him, and those eyes ... I swear they almost swirl, a myriad of golds and browns mixing together into a truly beautiful color.

A strand of his white-blond hair has fallen forward, and it looks so strange when he's always so put together. I don't even know what I'm doing when I reach up and brush the hair back into place. My fingertips graze his chilled skin, and as close as I am to him, it's impossible not to miss the way his pupils contract into vertical slits.

Oh. *Oh.* I shouldn't like that as much as I do. What the hell is wrong with me? Misha is right behind me, and here I am staring at his friend with butterflies fluttering away in my belly. But ... what exactly is Misha to me? We haven't talked about it. We just enjoy kissing and fooling around. Does that mean we're dating? I'm so bad at these things.

I swallow and quickly turn back around, clenching my fist and pressing it against my stomach to make the fluttering sensation stop. If I ignore what just happened, it will go away, right?

I focus on the game unfolding below, but I don't see what's happening. The knowledge that I'm currently sandwiched between Misha and Ari, the heat from their bodies warming me, makes it impossible to actually pay attention to the game, even if I knew what was happening.

Completely unaware of what just happened between me and Ari, Misha grabs my hand and squeezes. "This is it! Come on, Eagles!"

"What's happening?" I lean over and yell into Misha's ear. The crowd has surged to their feet, everyone screaming and clapping and stomping their feet. The noise is overwhelming, setting my teeth on edge.

"If they score now, we win," Misha shouts, not taking his attention from the field.

I search for Rho and find him just as he scores the final goal. The stadium goes crazy. Misha grabs me around my waist and lifts me off of my feet. His smile lights up his entire face, and I'm laughing when he brings his mouth to mine for a searing kiss.

THE HIGH OF THE GAME STILL THRUMS THROUGH MY veins, even as worry for Aspen curdles my stomach. I've been pacing the length of Ezra's room since we got back. I had to kick a path clear because Ezra is the biggest slob out of the three of us. After we dropped Aspen off at her dorm, we came here to discuss Ari's newest theory.

"So you're saying her mom has three mates, and each of the kids have a different dad?" Ezra drawls from his spot lounging on the bed.

"I don't know who's dad is who, except Aspen's dad is Malakai Thorne." Ari barely looks up from his laptop, researching Aspen's family.

"Malakai Thorne?" I whip my head in Ari's direction. "Like *the* Malakai Thorne? The vampire prince?"

"The one and only."

"I knew her dad was a vamp, but I had no idea he was someone so powerful," I mutter.

"So, couldn't that be the reason she doesn't have powers? What is her mom's ability?" Ezra asks.

"I can't find any information on her mom. But I know the other two are Cade Campbell and Sterling Harrison." Ari looks up from his screen and gives us a heavy look. "That's a hell of a lot of talent in one family."

So, Aspen's biological dad is a vampire. Her mom's power is

unknown. "What about her brothers?" I ask. "Harrison is a wolf, but Campbell is a mage, and obviously, so is Adrian."

"Rhory Grey is a shifter, according to admission paperwork." Ari sits back in the chair with a raised brow. "So I'm assuming Rhory's dad is Harrison and Adrian's is Campbell."

"That doesn't make sense, though," Ezra says, sitting up. "They all have the same mom?"

Ari nods. "Yeah. So despite having parents that are different races, both of their sons have powers. So why doesn't Aspen?"

"What the hell is up with this family?" Ezra mutters, laying back down on his bed.

We fall quiet, each getting lost in our own thoughts. Ari continues to plug away at his research, occasionally jotting down notes in his notebook. I have no idea how much time has passed when my phone buzzes. I pull it from my pocket and glance at the window to find the sun has already set.

> Aspen: My parents just dropped me off at my dorm and are heading out. Rho and Adrian are going back to their rooms now.

> Me: come to ezras room. 118

"She's on her way," I say, dropping my phone on the cushion next to me. "We can just ask her. Maybe we can find some answers."

"Fucking fantastic," Ezra mutters.

I lean forward, elbows resting on my knees. "Hey, chill the fuck out, Ezra. You don't have to like her, but you do have to act halfway decent. Besides, she may help us figure out what happened to Millie."

A soft knock on the door stops Ezra from responding, and Ari hops up from the desk and pulls it open. "Hey, pipsqueak. Come on in. Ezra's room is a disaster, but I'm sure Misha won't mind you sitting on his lap."

"Damn straight," I call out.

Aspen smiles at Ari before ducking her head, her cheeks turning an adorable shake of pink. She picks her way across the floor carefully before stopping in front of me. I reach out and grab her waist, tugging her onto my lap despite there being plenty of room on the couch next to me. She settles with a quiet giggle, moving her hips in a way that makes me grind my teeth.

I lean forward, pinch her thigh, and whisper in her ear, "You better stop moving like that, Dove."

Instantly, she freezes, her body going stiff against mine. The heat coming from her skin intensifies, and I chuckle darkly. This is more fun than I've ever had.

"So, Aspen," Ari says, clearing his throat. "Is it okay if we ask you some questions about your family? Not for anything weird," he adds quickly. "Just because we're hoping to get a better understanding of what's happening."

Aspen takes a deep breath then nods. "Okay. But I can't promise I'll answer everything."

"That's fair," Ari agrees. He pulls his notebook closer to him and grabs a pen. "You already told me your bio dad is Malakai Thorne. So you're half-vampire. Do you have *any* vampiric traits?"

"Not a lot. I'm a little stronger than the average human. And my senses are a little sharper. Nothing too extraordinary though."

Ari nods. "What about your mom?"

Aspen goes still, and she bites her bottom lip, staring at her folded hands in her lap. Instantly, I'm on alert. There's something there she doesn't want to share, and that something just might be the piece of information we need. I debate the best course of action to convince her to tell us without pressuring her. I don't want to scare her off.

"Everything we talk about stays with us," I say quietly, brushing her hair over her shoulder. The strands sift through my fingers like silk, and a floral scent greets my nose. Without thinking, I lean forward and bury my nose in her hair and inhale. Fuck. Why does that make my magic come alive in my veins?

"And every piece of information you give helps us to keep you safe." Ari's eyes practically glow as he says this, something shifting behind them that I can't read.

Aspen releases a breath. "Very few people know this. Only those who absolutely need to know. We've always kept it a closely guarded secret. It was drilled into mine and my brother's heads since we could talk, so it's not easy to share." She closes her eyes, and we all keep silent as she works through her thoughts. When she opens them again, she nods. "My mom is a harpy."

The breath whooshes from my lungs, and I see Ari jerk in surprise. Ezra shoots up from his pillows, golden eyes wide. "Bullshit," he breathes.

A harpy? I thought harpies were a myth? In the stories, harpies were violent creatures that destroyed entire races of civilization. There is no way they really exist, and no way in hell Aspen's mom is one of them. Right?

"It's true," she says quietly. I grab her hand to keep her from picking at her nails. Already, she's drawn blood. "My mom is a harpy, and my dads are her Shields. They were fated to be her protectors. The four of them restored the balance between good and evil before my brothers and I were born. There was a mage who was experimenting on magicals and humans, and his goal was to mutate magicals to create an army or something to take over the world. They stopped him." Her words are soft and hesitant, and her hand in mine trembles slightly. "They don't want people to know what she is. They always only wanted to live as quietly as possible."

And if the world knew harpies actually existed and one was currently living in Altair, I can imagine the uproar that would cause. Some people would call for her death, their fear of the stories of harpies leading the charge. Others would probably want to use her to their advantage. I can definitely understand them wanting to keep this quiet.

"We won't tell anyone, Aspen. We'll protect this as closely as you do." It's the only comfort I can give her. I look at the twins, and they both nod in agreement. Good. If they didn't, I wouldn't hesitate to beat the shit out of them until they did.

"A harpy?" Ezra asks, disbelief still painted on his face. "What the actual fuck?"

The image of Aspen's mom at the lacrosse game pops into my head. I try to reconcile the fact that the woman with the braided pigtails and LMU Eagles gear is a living myth. And her daughter is sitting in my fucking lap. Wild.

"Okay," Ari drawls. "That's a pretty big piece of information. Your dad is a vampire and your mom is a harpy. What about your brothers?"

Aspen relaxes as the topic veers away from her mom. "Rho is a wolf, his bio dad is Sterling. And Adrian, as you know, is a violet mage, like Cade."

Ari nods. "And you guys all have the same mom, right?"

"Yes."

"So, it doesn't make sense that your brothers would have powers but you don't." I rub my hand up and down her back, and she relaxes into my touch.

"There is almost no information available on harpies," Ari mutters almost to himself. "Who knows what's possible when a harpy mixes with other races." He turns his gaze to Aspen, eyes focusing. "What about the rest of your family?"

Once again, I lose track of time. Between discussing every detail we can of Aspen and her family, and her sitting on my lap, warm and soft, I'm surprised when Ezra yawns and calls it a night.

Aspen has long since laid her head on my shoulder, and I'm pretty sure she dozed off and on while we talked. Now, I gently shake her awake and help her stand. "Come on. I'll walk you back to your room. You have an early class tomorrow."

She blearily follows me as I lead her upstairs, her steps slow and unsteady. When we reach her room she pauses and looks up at me with sleepy eyes. "You guys really promise you won't tell anyone about my mom?"

Her cheeks are smooth and warm in my palms, and I rub my

thumb under her bottom lip. "We won't tell a soul. Don't worry about that. You have enough on your plate."

She nods, and before she turns away, I press a quick kiss to her lips.

"Goodnight, Aspen."

MORNING COMES WAY TOO EARLY. Still, I drag myself out of bed and to the cafe before heading to Aspen's room. The smile on her face when she opens her door and sees me with a donut and cup of coffee make it all worth it.

She's tired, I can tell. She didn't bother to do anything with her hair, just threw up into a bun on top of her head. There are dark circles under her eyes she tried to conceal with makeup. Even looking as exhausted as she does, she's still gorgeous.

"I'm sorry we kept you up so late last night." I tug up the hood of her hoodie and smile when I realize it's one of mine.

She snuggles into the hood and takes a bite of donut. "It's okay," she says after she swallows. "If we can figure out what's going on, it will be worth it."

"Have you had any more weird encounters or felt like you're being followed at all?"

"No, but one of you guys is always with me now. I'm rarely alone."

I nod and we make our way to Old Main for our lecture. "Just let us know if you ever feel unsafe. That's our main priority."

Sitting through the lecture is absolute torture. We chose seats in the back, and it didn't take Aspen long to rest her head on my shoulder and fall asleep. I force myself to stay awake and take good notes for her. Despite all the shit that's going on, we're both still here to get an education.

Every now and then, I glance down at her. Just the fact she feels safe enough with me to fall asleep means more to me than I ever thought it would. I trace the line of her jaw and lose myself in her for a moment. She's so fucking beautiful it hurts. I've had girlfriends in the past, but no one has ever made me feel so ... consumed. I want nothing more than to let this woman destroy me in every way possible.

The force of these feelings hits me, and not for the first time. I close my eyes and focus on my magic slumbering away in the pit of my soul. Whenever Aspen is around, it settles down, like a dog reassured its owner is home. If she's out of my sight, I have to put more attention into keeping it suppressed. But when I kiss her ... I smile just thinking about her lips on mine. When I kiss her, my magic becomes its own entity, and there is nothing I can do to stop it.

Is it possible? I shake my head. No. It's not possible. She's not a mage, and even if she had magic, she wouldn't be a mage. For some reason, that thought sits heavy in my stomach, a lead stone sinking all the way to my feet.

When the lecture finally ends after what feels like hours and hours, I shake Aspen awake and we head outside. It's one of the rare days that the sun is actually shining and campus is busier than usual as students enjoy the warmth.

"Thanks for letting me sleep," Aspen says, tilting her face to the sky.

"You can sleep on me anytime you want." I nudge her shoulder and chuckle when she blushes. "Wow, it's really nice to feel the sun."

"It is. I missed it." The longing in her voice makes my chest ache.

This might be a stupid thing to do with everything that's going on, but it's daytime and the sun is shining. I grab Aspen's hand and tug her toward the cemetery. It was obvious how much she loved it there, and the memory of what happened that night has ruined her joy for it. Maybe I can help her replace that memory with something else? Something better. Something that gives her back the peace she felt in that place.

Her steps slow as she realizes where we're going. "What ..."

"Trust me."

She studies me for a moment before smiling. "I do."

My stomach drops, and it takes me a moment to gather myself. This girl trusts me. I make a silent vow that I will never let her down. I don't know what I did to earn her trust, but I will not break it.

Grabbing her hand, I lead her through the cemetery gates and down the gravel path toward the gazebo. We walk leisurely, enjoying the sun and the sound of chirping birds. Aspen occasionally stops to look at a plant, but she always comes right back to my side, sliding her hand into mine.

We step under the gazebo, and Aspen walks to the other side. Her eyes fill with wonder as she looks around. It's like it's the first time she's seen it, even though we've been here before. But still, she hesitates to take the last step into the wild.

"I should have brought a blanket," I mutter, stepping out into the sunlight and tugging her with me.

She smiles at me and plops down onto the grass. "No need. Join me?"

Aspen

IT DIDN'T TAKE LONG FOR MY NERVES TO DISSIPATE. Being in the cemetery after everything that's been happening was unsettling at first. But with Misha by my side, I feel safe.

Trust me.

It was easy to tell him I do. And it's not because I enjoy kissing him or because he makes my heart flutter with just one look. There's just something deeper, something intrinsic, that puts me at ease with him. It's a safety net I can *feel,* even if I can't see it. I don't have to worry when he's with me. He'll protect me, and the surety of that takes the weight off of my shoulders.

I smile up at Misha and wait for him to sit next to me in the grass. When he does, I lay back and close my eyes, letting the sun bathe me in its warmth. My breath catches when Misha brushes my hair from my forehead, his finger trailing over my skin. I open my eyes and find him watching me. The intensity of his stare worms under my skin until I feel my cheeks heat. I close my eyes to save myself the discomfort.

"Tell me about yourself," I say quietly, not wanting to break the peaceful atmosphere that's settled around us.

"What do you want to know?"

Even with my eyes closed, I can hear the smile in his words. I shrug. "Anything. I feel like you guys know everything about me, but I don't really know anything about you."

He's silent for a moment then says, "You're right. Well for the basics, I'm from Crescent Falls. My parents are soul-bonded and I have an older brother, Brayden. I enjoy lacrosse and going to the batting cages. The twins and I have been friends since grade school, and at this point they're practically family. Umm, what else is there?"

"What are you studying? What do you want to do when you graduate?"

He's silent for so long that I open my eyes. His gaze has gone vacant as he stares off into the distance.

"I'm sorry. I shouldn't have asked that," I say quickly. "You don't have to answer."

Misha shakes his head and blinks, the light returning to his eyes. "No. I want to tell you, it's just not easy for me." He sighs heavily and lays next to me on the ground, closing his eyes. "I already told you that I'm a gray mage. As I'm sure you're aware, gray mages are not very common, and in the past, they haven't always been the most revered type of mage."

I nod, even though he's not looking. Gray mages have a reputation of being ... not evil, exactly, but not necessarily good. In the past, there have been gray mages that have taken their power too far, and used it for things that society frowns upon. Such as necromancy.

"Both of my parents and my brother are blue mages," Misha continues. "I have no clue how I ended up with this power, but it wasn't easy growing up with it. There was no one to teach me how to manage it. My parents and teachers did what they could, but gray magic is vastly different from the others. There was only so much they could do. I had to figure out the rest myself."

Misha falls silent, and I lean up on one elbow to look at him. His eyes are still closed, and he's rubbing his chest absentmindedly. Even with his eyes closed, I can tell the difference in his demeanor. Misha is always so confident and self-assured. He's happy-go-lucky, smiling and laughing. But right now, he looks smaller than usual, like he's trying to shrink into himself and hide.

"When I was twelve there was an incident." His words are so quiet I can barely hear them. "I lost control of my power, and I called a bunch of vengeful spirits from a nearby cemetery." He swallows, his throat clicking with the motion. "They drug me to a freshly dug grave and shoved me in. I fought as hard as I could, but there were too many of them. They tried to dig my heart out of my chest with their claws."

I can't suppress the gasp that escapes my lips. Misha's hand curls against his chest, and he digs his fingers in, grasping the fabric of his shirt in a fist. I sit up and grab his hand in both of mine, stopping him from scratching at himself. His hand is clammy, and his fingers tremble.

"I don't know how I did it, but I blasted them away from me. It gave me enough time to crawl out of the grave and run home. The spirits chased me the entire way. I couldn't let go of my magic, and somehow I was calling them to me. My dad had to knock me out to get me to release the magic so the spirits would go away." Misha finally opens his eyes, squinting at the brightness. "After that, I shoved it so deep inside of me it was almost impossible to sense it, and I never touched it again." He takes a deep breath and looks at me, his gaze searching like he expects to see disgust or derision on my face. "The reason I'm attending LMU is to learn how to better control it."

Oh. My heart breaks for him. To have to go through that alone, to not understand your own power, to not have anyone to turn to when you need help with your magic ... I can't imagine how terrifying that would be. I'm still holding his hand in mine, but his free hand now rubs his chest.

Not giving myself time to think about what I'm doing or talk myself out of it, I straddle Misha and slide my fingers under his t-shirt. He grabs my wrists immediately, stopping me from going any further.

"Aspen ..." His eyes are wide and uncertain.

I've never heard him sound so vulnerable before, his voice

shaky and urgent. I lean down and kiss his cheek, breathing my words onto his skin. "Trust me."

Misha stares at me. He stares at me for so long I'm sure he'll push me off of him. But then his grasp tightens before he lets go completely, arms falling to his sides. I slowly inch his shirt up his torso, letting my fingers graze his skin as I go. His stomach muscles tighten under my touch, and I enjoy the way it feels as I trail over the dips and valleys of his abs.

The higher I drag his shirt, the faster his breathing becomes and the wider his eyes get. I'm not sure if it's nerves or desire. Maybe it's a combination of the two. The first scar becomes visible, then another. By the time I get his shirt lifted all the way, my eyes are burning.

Misha's chest is covered in scarred claw marks. I count at least six big ones, and a myriad of smaller ones that criss-cross each other. It does indeed look like someone tried to dig his heart out of his chest. I can't fathom how a twelve year old boy lived through something so horrendous.

Misha won't meet my gaze, like he's embarrassed about the scarring. Despite how awful it looks, it's only awful because I know what happened. There is nothing unattractive about Misha, and that includes these scars. I hate that he feels so self-conscious of them, but I'm incredibly grateful he trusted me enough to show me.

I bend down and gently press my lips to the worst of the marks. Misha sucks in a sharp breath, but he doesn't try to stop me. So I keep brushing my lips over his skin, roadmapping each and every place where he was hurt. If only I could take away the horrible memories of these scars and replace them with something different, something beautiful. Something he could be proud of.

When I sit up, I trail my fingers over the raised marks and catch Misha's gaze. "Every part of you is beautiful, Misha. Even these scars."

Misha surges up and captures my face in his hands. I don't have time to react as he kisses me so thoroughly I see stars. He flips us so I'm laying on my back with my legs wrapped around him. His hips settle in the cradle of my thighs, and I gasp when I feel how hard he is. Misha takes advantage of that and slips his tongue between my lips, and I can't stop the moan that climbs up my throat.

"Fuck," he groans, hips thrusting against mine. "Aspen, if you want me to stop, you need to tell me now. If we keep going, I won't be able to."

Stop. Stop? Do I want to stop? No. No, I really don't want to. I shake my head and reach for him, grabbing a fistful of his locs and tugging him back down. "No. Don't stop, Misha."

He growls and slides his hands under my hoodie—his hoodie, actually—and fire follows in the wake of his fingers, heating me from the inside out. He pulls off both my hoodie and t-shirt, tossing them to the side, and the grass underneath me tickles my skin. With extreme gentleness, he slides the strap of my bra down, kissing my shoulder as he goes. Then he does the same with the other strap. The gentle teasing is too much. Every touch on my overheated skin is pure torture. I want *more.*

Arching my back, I beg Misha to keep going. "Please. Don't stop."

His dark eyes burn with an inner fire as he slides one hand behind my back and unclasps my bra. With the slowest movements possible, he drags it down my arms, the fabric scraping against my already sensitive nipples. He doesn't waste any time. Misha bends down and sucks one nipple into his mouth and rubs his thumb over the other, working them both into tight peaks.

I grasp his locs tightly and arch my back as pleasure slowly builds into an inferno. My core aches with need, and I rub my hips against his, eliciting a soft groan from him that sparks the fire even more. Misha releases my breasts and kisses a path down my stomach, his fingers digging into my hips in a way that hurts delightfully.

When he reaches the waistband of my leggings, he looks up at me. His eyes are impossibly dark, and even though I've always been self-conscious about this, I nod my head eagerly. Anything to keep him looking at me like … like he wants to eat me.

My leggings and panties join the rest of my clothing in a pile on the grass. Misha sits up tall, and his gaze burns as he takes his time looking at me splayed naked before him. I swallow, my throat suddenly dry. No one has ever looked at me quite like that. The last time we did this, it was dark in my room, and I wasn't so bared for him, despite sitting on his face. My legs twitch, a subconscious movement to try and close them, but he grabs my thighs and holds me open.

"Don't even think about hiding from me," he growls. "Every part of you is beautiful, Aspen."

The same words I just said to him but directed at me don't feel as true. I swallow and look away, but Misha grabs my chin.

"What do I need to do to make you believe me?" he breathes. "How do I show you that you are a fucking goddess?"

Oh gods. That intense stare, like he can see straight to my soul, will be the death of me. Those words with that look almost make me believe him. But I can't answer, because I don't know what I need to hear to erase years of self-consciousness and body image issues.

Misha's fingers bite into my thighs, and he shakes his head. "One day you'll believe me."

That's all he says before he forces my legs wider and lowers his mouth to my core. I tense, my breath freezing in my lungs as my anxiety rises higher. This has always been something that terrifies me. I'm too self-conscious to let someone do … this. But the way he looks up my body to meet my gaze while his tongue prods my entrance makes me forget all of those worries.

Misha destroys me. He obliterates every nervous thought until all I can do is beg for more. And he gives me more. His fingers and tongue work me higher and higher, my pleasure becoming too much to bear. I writhe on the ground, lifting my hips to meet his tongue, wordless pleas falling from my lips. Because I am so, so close.

I grab his head and push him down. Misha doesn't stop. Heat builds in my lower back and spreads outward as I tip over the edge. My legs shake and my toes curl. I cry his name as my back arches, and I fall apart into thousands of glittering pieces of stardust. Misha doesn't stop until my body's limp, and when he looks up at me and smiles, I reach for him. Misha climbs up my body and kisses me, letting me taste myself on his tongue.

I still haven't caught my breath, but there is no way I'm letting him end things here. Reaching between us, I work the button of his pants, but he grabs my wrist to stop me from doing more.

"We don't have to—" He stops abruptly and hisses between his teeth when I press my palm against his very hard erection.

"You sure about that?" I breathe, pressing harder.

His hips grind against my palm and then he moves faster than I've ever seen him. His pants join my clothing on the grass, and I take my time studying his body the way he did mine. When he leans over me, I stop him with a hand on his chest.

"I want to see you," I breathe. "All of you." I can feel his scars through the material of his t-shirt, and I trace them by touch alone. Misha hesitates, but when I sit up and grip the bottom of his shirt, he lets me pull it over his head. I rest my hands on the sides of his neck and kiss him. "I meant what I said," I say against his mouth. "You're beautiful, Misha. All of you."

He grabs my wrist and gently runs a finger over the small scar on my forearm. "Implant?"

I nod and Misha kisses me again, lowering me to the ground. He reaches between us and aligns himself at my entrance. It's been a little while since I've done this, but I'm so wet and ready for him, when he slides inside all I can do is gasp in pleasure. Misha holds himself still, letting me adjust, and he bites his bottom lip like it's the hardest thing he's ever done.

"Oh, fuck." He bows his head, breathing heavily, and mutters, "It's so much better than my dreams."

I blink in surprise, but he doesn't give me time to think about that statement. Misha moves his hips and every thought in my head just floats away on a wave of pleasure. The pace starts slow but gradually builds, faster and faster, until all I can do is cling to Misha and try to keep myself from falling apart too soon.

With each thrust of his hips, something inside of me grows. A seedling that slowly sprouts and unfurls its leaves, spreading through my blood and bones and soul. It's a sensation of rightness. A connection with this man that I've never experienced before and never thought I'd experience in my life. It leaves me feeling unmoored and shaky, but Misha is the tether that keeps me grounded.

The wave of pleasure that erupts inside me takes me by surprise. It crests, and I cry out, shaking and gasping as my orgasm rolls through me. When it ebbs, I'm left with an unexpected surge of sadness. Like my body knows I will never get to experience this again for the first time with him. I squeeze my eyes shut against the burning of building tears as Misha's hips finally stutter to a stop with his release.

Misha freezes suddenly, lifting himself off of me. "Shit. Aspen, what's wrong? Did I hurt you?" His thumb brushes away the tear that leaked from the corner of my eye unbidden.

I shake my head and give Misha a shaky smile. "No. I'm sorry. I don't know why ... You did nothing wrong. That was ... I ... I don't have words ..." I snap my mouth shut with a click of my teeth. Damn it. Why can't I explain to him what's going on? "That was perfect."

He relaxes and leans down to kiss me. "It was perfect, wasn't it?" Misha wraps his arms around me and rolls us so my head is resting on his chest.

I settle against him, gently tracing the lines of his scars. We lay in the sunshine, and I let the pull of whatever this is draw me closer and closer to Misha. I don't think I could fight it, even if I wanted to. And I don't want to.

Misha

"I can't believe it's already Thanksgiving," Ari says as we walk to class.

"Yeah. And it's been relatively peaceful," I add.

He frowns. "Too peaceful, in my opinion. We had two major incidents, then radio silence. What's up with that?"

"And we've hit a wall with our research. I hate to say it, but I almost want something to happen. Maybe it will give us a clue we can use to keep digging." The thought makes my stomach curdle. I don't want Aspen in danger, but this quiet is like an anvil over our heads just waiting to drop.

My phone buzzes, and I pull it out to find a text from Aspen.

Aspen: Have fun in class. Pay attention.

I huff a laugh and reply.

Me: Not likely. To either one of those comments. I'll be too busy thinking about you.

"Gross," Ari says, shuddering dramatically. "I forgot how lovey dovey you get when you're in a relationship."

"Psh. You're just jealous."

Something flashes in Ari's expression, but it happens so fast, I'm not sure I actually saw it. But it looked suspiciously like hurt.

We've reached Old Main so I have no time to ask him what it was about. After agreeing to meet in the cafe for a late breakfast after class, we head in different directions. This elective was an incredibly poor choice. I thought Chemical Properties of Magic would help me with understanding the basic nature of my magic, but so far it's been pointless. It probably doesn't help that I haven't paid much attention to anything the professor says.

Point proven when I sit in my seat and pull out my phone to text Aspen.

> Me: What do you want to do on our first day of break?

Instead of tuning into the lecture, I stare at my phone and wait for the little three dots to appear. It's embarrassing how excited I get when they do.

> Aspen: I haven't had much time to just read for fun. I kind of want to curl up with a book and do absolutely nothing.

Immediately my brain starts working on a plan. A lot of students go home for Thanksgiving break, so the library should be pretty quiet. I can pack a bag with blankets and snacks and we can hang out in one of the reading lounges all day. Smiling, I send Aspen a quick text.

> Me: I think I can make that work. In fact, I already have a plan.

The three bubbles appear, then disappear. I wait, but they don't appear again. It's still early, and she doesn't have any classes today, so she probably fell back to sleep. Sighing, I slouch in my seat and try to tune into the lecture, but my mind just ends up wandering.

I can't stop going over everything we know so far about

Millie's death and the attack on Aspen. Admittedly, it's not much. It seems like what happened to both of them was more paranormal than anything. And if so, what's causing it? Is there someone behind it or is it just a natural thing that occurred? If someone is behind it, who and why? Thinking about all of this just frustrates me. I want to help the twin's answer their questions regarding Millie's death. I want to keep Aspen safe. But I don't know enough about what's happening to do either.

My phone buzzes, and I glance at it to find a text from Ezra in our group chat.

> Ezra: something happened. Come to my room after class. Aspen's here.

I sit up so fast I knock my book to the floor, but I'm too focused on responding to Ezra to notice.

> Me: What happened? Is she okay?

Before I realize what I'm doing, I'm packing my bag and rushing from the lecture hall. I round the corner, heading for the stairs, and bump into Ari. His bag is open and hanging from one shoulder while he tries to shove his notes inside. There's a harried expression on his face, brows pinched in worry and golden eyes wild with concern.

We barely acknowledge each other before we run down the stairs and out the side door of Old Main. The wind smacks me in the face, sucking the air from my chest in its brutal iciness, but I ignore the way it makes my lungs ache and run across campus as fast as I can. I need to make sure Aspen is okay. I need to see her with my own eyes.

By the time we reach the dorms, Ari and I are both gasping for air. Each breath burns in the bitter cold, but I welcome it. It gives me something to focus on instead of the spiraling fear that wants to take over. When we get to Ezra's room, I throw open the door and rush inside.

Aspen is sitting on the couch with her knees pulled to her chest. Dried tear tracks stain her cheeks, and her lashes are wetly clumped together. Vaguely, I realize she's in pajamas, and her hair is a mess.

"Aspen," I gasp, trying to catch my breath. She visibly relaxes when I drop onto the couch next to her and pull her into my arms. "Are you okay? What happened?"

"I don't ... I don't know," she hiccups, clutching my coat.

"She showed up here, banging on my door and yelling at me to let her in," Ezra says, pacing the length of the room in the path I made the last time I was here. "She was terrified, and had a scratch on her arm that was bleeding pretty badly. I bandaged it up, but she was crying too hard to tell me anything."

"Which arm?" I ask, pulling away.

She holds out her right arm, and I slide up the sleeve of her shirt to reveal a white bandage wrapped around her forearm. A faint pink line blooms across the fabric, and I gently lift the edge to peer under and curse.

"Fuck. Aspen, tell me what happened." She can probably feel the tremble in my fingers as I take her face in my hands and force her to look at me. "Now."

Aspen pales even further at my ferocity, but pulls in a shaky breath. "I was laying in bed, and I saw something out of the corner of my eye. When I looked, there was nothing there. I just thought it was my mind playing tricks on me. But then it happened again in a different part of my room. When I looked, there was nothing there. It happened a couple more times, and I started to freak out." She grabs her injured arm and winces. "I reached for my phone on the bedside table, and there was something there. Something on the floor between the bed and the table. I didn't get a good look at it, but it was like it was hidden in shadow. It reached out and raked a claw down my arm. I ran here because I knew you and Ari were at class."

I close my eyes and take her arm, placing the palm of my hand over the wound. With immense focus, I pull a tiny bit of my magic from the pit I shoved it into and let it brush over Aspen's arm. She gasps, and my attention is torn in two separate directions. Part of me is trying to sense the amount of evil coming from Aspen's wound, the other is staring wide-eyed at the misty strand of magic now winding up her arm.

I attempt to tug it back, but nothing happens. I pull harder and get a sense of irritation from my magic. By the time the strand has reached her chest, I'm sweating. What do I do? How do I stop it? But then Aspen giggles, and I notice the misty strand brushing against her cheek.

"It's cold," she says with a smile. She brings her uninjured hand to her cheek, and brushes her fingers through the mist. It winds around her fingers until a small ball of it sits in the palm of her hand like a miniature rain cloud. She looks at me with a smile. "I didn't know you could do this with your magic."

I stare open mouthed and wide eyed. "I ... I ...I'm not ... That's not ..." My words fall away, and the silence in the room builds. It's surprising no one can hear my heart beating a frantic rhythm in my chest. My magic is touching Aspen. It's right there, and I can't control it.

"What do you mean?" Aspen asks quietly.

"I tried to stop it, but it just keeps going." I grit my teeth and try again, but nothing happens. "It's like it took on a life of its own."

Aspen tilts her head to the side and frowns as she studies the gray cloud in her palm. She pokes the little ball and it puffs up before deflating again, and Aspen laughs. I try again to pull it back into myself, and this time it works. The cloud on Aspen's hand dissipates, and she lets her arm fall. Relief rushes through me, and I sag where I'm sitting on the couch.

"Misha?" she whispers, gray eyes searching my face.

I clear my throat and take her injured arm. "We need to keep an eye on this," I say roughly, changing the subject. "I can't tell what caused it, but some vengeful spirits have poisonous claws."

"What?" She jerks back, tucking her arm against her chest. "What does that mean?"

"It means, if you start feeling sick, we need to go see Adrian." I reach out and place the back of my hand on her forehead. She doesn't feel warm, but that doesn't necessarily mean anything. "Maybe we should have him heal you just in case."

Aspen shakes her head vigorously. "No! We can't. He'll question what happened, and then we'll have to tell him. If my brothers know, they'll tell my parents. All hell will break loose then."

"All hell is going to break loose at some point anyway," Ezra mutters.

"I don't want my brothers to know," Aspen says firmly. Her gaze travels between me and the twins, and I've never seen her look so fierce before.

My lips twitch, but I nod. "Okay. But if you start showing any signs of being poisoned, we're going to him. That's not up for debate."

She hesitates, but eventually nods reluctantly.

"You should have Adrian reinforce the wards on your door," Ari says. "And add some to your window and fireplace as well. Any place a spirit can get inside."

"And how do I ask him to do that without telling him what's going on? He'll be suspicious."

Ari shrugs. "Tell him you think there's a ghost in your room. Nothing nefarious, just a spirit that's causing a ruckus. It shouldn't be too suspicious. This campus is old, and there are plenty of stories of hauntings and strange things that have happened here."

"That could work," she says slowly.

"Are you sure you're feeling okay?" I ask, taking her injured arm again. Peering under the bandage, I don't see anything that would indicate she's been poisoned, but I can't help being paranoid. "You really won't let your brother heal you? It would make me feel a lot better."

She sighs and shifts on the couch so she can lay her head on my shoulder. "I'm not telling Adrian."

Ari approaches and kneels on the ground in front of Aspen. He holds out his hands and asks, "May I?"

Aspen doesn't hesitate to place her injured arm in his hands. Ari brings it to his nose and inhales. He closes his golden eyes and moves his nose further up her arm, sniffing the entire time. I watch him closely, so it's obvious to me how his jaw clenches each time he breathes in her scent.

"I don't smell anything strange. Our tigers are sensitive to things like that, and Aspen just smells like herself." He releases her arm and backs away. "I think you're probably okay. But you need to tell us if you start to feel any different."

She nods and releases a breath, rubbing her cheeks that are suddenly a darker shade of pink. "I will. I promise."

"Do you want to go find Adrian? Have him reinforce the wards then hang out in your room for the rest of the day? We can watch cheesy movies and eat junk food and just relax."

Aspen smiles at me and nods. "That sounds nice."

Nice is an understatement. Ari joins us, and after Adrian lays down some wards in Aspen's room, the three of us pile on her bed and just enjoy ourselves. At first, I was a little jealous of Ari lying on the other side of Aspen. I haven't missed the way he occasionally looks at her, or the way she reacts when he does. So when he lays down, I have to bite my tongue to prevent myself from saying something. It doesn't take long for the jealousy to abate though. Especially after I come to a realization.

"This movie is ridiculous," Aspen huffs. "She obviously likes both of them, why is she trying to choose just one?"

Her comment smacks me in the face harder than a ton of bricks. Aspen grew up watching her mom with three guys. That's the norm for her. It shouldn't be surprising she's comfortable being with more than one person.

I glance at Ari and study him while he's absorbed in the movie. Aspen is sitting sideways on her bed, her upper body leaning against my chest and her legs thrown over Ari's waist. His hands rest on her calves, and I watch as his thumb gently rubs back and forth. I don't think he even realizes he's doing it.

Could I share her with him? The thought doesn't immediately make me want to punch him, so I really examine it. I've known Ari almost my entire life. I know what kind of guy he is. While he sometimes gets lost in his studies, he's always there if I need him. He's loyal and true to his word. And I know he's never treated a woman badly, despite the fact he's only ever had few casual relationships.

If I were to share Aspen with him, I know she'd be treated well. And it would be even more protection for her during these uncertain times. But in the end, I don't think I could say no to her if she wanted it. If Aspen wanted to date both of us, I'd do anything for her, as long as it makes her happy.

With that realization, I catch Ari's attention and smile at him. He has no idea what I'm so happy about, but he smiles back, even though his brows furrow in confusion. I settle against the headboard and wrap my arms around Aspen's waist. Yeah. I think I could get used to this. But what about them? A thought springs into my head, and I don't even think before I act on it. There's only one way to find out.

I lower my head and gently nibble on Aspen's ear lobe. She stiffens, and I feel her suck in a breath. Not giving her anytime to react, I drag my tongue up the column of her throat and she shudders in my arms. As inconspicuous as possible, I slip my hand under her shirt and trail my fingers over the soft skin of her belly. Her hand comes up and grasps my wrist tightly, but she doesn't try to stop me from sliding my hand lower, teasing her skin the entire way.

Her chest rises and falls more rapidly, and she flicks her gaze in Ari's direction. He's still staring at the screen, seemingly oblivious to what's happening. But I know him. I know his tiger senses are picking up on every little movement and every little gasp. And I know him clenching his jaw like that means he's trying to not say something.

My fingers slide under the waistband of her leggings and panties. I glide lower and lower, until one finger slides between her folds. She gasps louder this time, and her hips jerk. Ari finally gives up on pretending to ignore what's happening, and he turns to face us, his golden eyes flashing.

"Misha," Aspen hisses between her teeth.

"Yes?" I purr.

"Ari ..."

I raise one brow and grin at him. "What about Ari?"

"He's right here."

"Oh, right. How rude of me. Aspen, why don't you kiss him?"

Aspen whips her head around to look at me completely flabbergasted. "Wh- wh- what?"

I lean down and whisper in her ear. "You heard me, Dove. Kiss him. If you want to." She doesn't move, just keeps staring at me almost like she's a little afraid. "I've seen the way you guys look at each other. So if you want to kiss him, do it."

I flick my finger over her clit and she moans. The sound that I've heard so many times that causes me to come undone, has the same effect on Ari. His eyes flare, his pupils contract into slits, and he leans forward. Instead of kissing her, he stops inches from her mouth, waiting for her to make the move. She holds herself stiff at first, hesitant about closing the distance between them.

"Only if you want to, Aspen," I whisper in her ear.

My words are the spell that breaks her free. She leans forward and presses her lips to Ari's. He wraps a hand around the back of her neck and deepens the kiss as I keep working my fingers around her clit. A soft moan climbs up her throat, and I can see how much the sound undoes Ari. He turns almost feral in his attempts to kiss her as deeply as possible.

"I'm lucky, and I already know what you taste like, Aspen. Should we be fair and give Ari the chance, too?" I pump my fingers in and out, and Aspen lifts her hips in time.

She breaks away from the kiss, cheeks flushed and eyes glassy with pleasure. She looks stunning. I give her a small smile and pull my fingers from her pants, licking them clean. "It's okay with me, as long as it's okay with you."

She glances at Ari and the desire burning in that golden gaze is obvious. Aspen nods, and quietly says, "Okay."

Ari gives her a crooked smile and wastes no time repositioning so he can pull her leggings and panties down. I use my legs to spread Aspen's wide and gently pinch her thigh when she tries to shut them.

"Remember what I said. No hiding. You're perfect just as you are." I slide my hands up her stomach and under her bra, cupping her breasts in my hands. "Let Ari have his fill."

I've seen Ari look at other women before, but I've never seen his eyes quite so intense as they are now. It makes my stomach clench, but not necessarily in a bad way. The thought of watching my girl find her pleasure from someone else, from Ari specifically, is surprisingly hot.

Ari grips her thighs and lowers his head. The sound Aspen makes when he licks up her core makes my cock twitch in my sweatpants. I roll her nipples between my fingers, tugging gently and making her squirm even more. Fuck. I could come just with her rubbing against me like this.

I watch her body flush and writhe as Ari licks and sucks. His grip on her thighs is tight enough to leave indents in her flesh. Those fucking curves of hers are so godsdamn tempting. I tip her head back and claim her mouth. She moans and gasps into my mouth, and I greedily swallow every sound she makes.

Aspen pulls away and throws her head back against my chest. "Oh gods. Oh gods. Oh gods." Her fingers tangle in Ari's hair and her thighs tighten around his head. "I'm going to- to-" Her words stutter to a stop as her body shudders and she cries out in pleasure.

Ari brings her through the orgasm, and when he lifts his head my balls tighten. Seeing her glistening arousal on his chin while Aspen lays limply on top of me, it's fucking hot as hell. Ari wipes his mouth and slowly climbs up her body, gently kissing her.

"Thank you," he whispers before tugging the blanket at the bottom of her bed to cover her.

I settle Aspen between us, and she looks back and forth between me and Ari, a blush crawling up her neck and into her cheeks. Before she can say anything, I raise my hand and give Ari a grin. He smirks back and gives me a high five. That makes the tension Aspen was feeling disappear, and she giggles.

We snuggle back on the bed to continue watching the movie. A few minutes later, she turns to me.

"Thank you," she whispers with a kiss on my cheek.

Aspen

"Rho, shut up!"

He does no such thing. "Penny has a boyfriend!"

My head falls forward, landing in my hands. "Rho," I whine.

"Boyfriend? Who is it?" Cade says, his voice coming through the speaker phone.

Kai growls, "I don't approve."

"You don't even know him," Sterling says. "But, you're probably right."

"*Mom*," I beg. "Make them stop."

"Oh honey. I wish I could. But I learned long ago there was no point in trying to control them. They'll do whatever the hell they want."

I turn my glare on Rhory and point at him. "You are so dead."

Rhory laughs and slings his arm around my shoulder. "Hey now. They asked if anything new was going on. It's been dreadfully boring here. It was the first thing to pop into my head."

"Well pop it right back out next time." My jaw hurts from gritting my teeth together so hard.

"So, who's the lucky guy?" mom asks, a smile evident in her voice.

In the background, I hear Kai say, "He's dead, that's who he is."

"It's no one," I say quickly. "Just ignore Rho. He's talking nonsense."

"Bullshit," Rho barks. "You spend all of your time with him. I haven't seen you in weeks. The only reason you came to my room today was because I told you I was calling home."

I lunge for Rho, my hands outstretched to wrap around his neck, but he launches from the couch with a laugh.

"I hope you're keeping up with your studies," mom says, ignoring the bickering happening between me and Rho. "Have you made any progress on your magic?"

That cools my anger like a bucket of ice water, and I collapse onto the couch. "No," I say quietly, picking at a thread on my sweater.

There's a beat of silence on the phone before Cade says, "That's okay. As long as you're working hard and still getting good grades."

I nod mechanically, even though they can't see me. My meetings with Professor Malvanado have been useless, and it probably doesn't help that I don't trust the man. All of the discussions I've had with Misha and the twins have led us nowhere. There's been no sign or indication I have magic or am supposed to have magic. I think I'm just human.

But that doesn't explain why I've been experiencing weird things. The attacks on me from vengeful spirits. The times I've felt like I was being watched or followed. The strange similarities between me and the twin's sister, Millie. None of it makes sense.

Adrian has been sitting quietly through the entire thing between me and Rho. He must sense the change in my demeanor, though, and quickly chimes in, changing the subject. "The Solstice Ball is in a few weeks. Are you guys going to come up for dinner again like you usually do?"

"Of course we are," mom says cheerily. "I wanted to talk to you about that. The day after the ball, your dads and I are going on a trip, so we won't be home for Christmas. I thought we could exchange gifts then."

"Where are you going?" Rho asks with a pout. "And why can't we come?"

"Because I haven't been on a trip with just your dads since Adrian was born. And we're going to the beach. No kids allowed." There's a commotion in the background and mom squeals. "Stop that Cade."

"Okay, ew. I'm hanging up now. Love you guys! Bye!" Rho ends the call before anyone else can say anything. "Why are they so gross?"

"Because they're in love," I say. "You'll be like that one day. Maybe. If you take your head out of your ass."

"Psh." Rhos flops down on the couch next to me. "So, are you going to the ball with your boy?"

I shake my head. "Nope. He's going home for break. I'm going with the twins."

Rho whips his head in my direction, eyes popping cartoonishly. "Excuse me?"

"Just as friends. Jeez. Calm down."

Speaking of. I pull my phone from my pocket and send a text to Sterling.

Me: Do you think you could buy me a dress for the ball? I don't have anything.

Daddy S: Of course. Anything you're looking for in particular?

Me: No. I trust your shopping skills better than anyone else.

Daddy S: Okay. One ball gown coming up!

Me: Thank you! Love you!

Daddy S: Love you too, Aspen.

I settle back against the couch and close my eyes. In just a couple of hours I'm meeting Ari at my room before my last class of the day. Things have been ... tense, between us. After that night in my room over Thanksgiving break, nothing else has happened. I've waited for him to make a move, but he hasn't. Of course, in my head that means he doesn't want me. Which of course means I did something wrong that night. So whenever I see him, I get all self-conscious and weird.

"Here," Rho says, handing me a piece of chocolate. "You seem like you need a pick-me-up."

I huff a laugh and take the candy, popping it into my mouth. "That's an understatement." Frowning, I look at him. "What kind of chocolate is this? It tastes weird."

He waggles his eyebrows and grins. "What kind of chocolate do you think it is?"

If I hadn't just swallowed, I'd have spit it out. "Rhory! Was that weed?" I stand up and clutch my stomach.

"Relax. There's barely any in that kind." He waves me off and starts scrolling on his phone.

I slap his phone from his hand, letting it clatter to the ground. "Rhory! I don't do that kind of stuff. You know how paranoid I get about these things. Why would you do that? And I have class in two hours!" I put my hands on my hips and glare at him.

"Pen, seriously there's not enough in that one piece to do anything other than take the edge off. You'll be fine."

I stare at him for a moment before plopping onto the couch. "I'm not leaving here. You can deal with the aftermath this causes. Asshole."

He grins and shrugs. "Fine. Because there won't be an aftermath."

"Have anything stronger?" Adrian asks.

"Like you have to ask." Rho points to his dresser. "In the top drawer."

The three of us fall quiet, Rho and Adrian scrolling their phones, and me analyzing everything going on in my body. Is the room tilting? Was that twinge in my stomach anything? Is my vision going blurry? I put my fingers on the pulse point of my neck and count the beats of my heart. One, two, three, four. What's a normal heart rate? Was that my stomach rumbling? Am I getting the munchies?

"Rho—"

"No. It hasn't been long enough for you to notice anything," he says without looking up from his phone.

I sigh and let my head fall against the back of the couch. Closing my eyes, I try to clear my mind of the paranoid thoughts floating through it, but as soon as I manage to do that, I think of that night with Ari and Misha.

Why did Misha insist on that happening? He said he noticed the way Ari and I looked at each other. What did he mean by that? I don't look at Ari in any particular way, and I don't think he looks at me any differently. Except ... There have been a few times his golden gaze seems to pierce me straight to my soul, and in those moments my stomach does flutter. It's kind of like when Misha looks at me. The same sensation of fuzzy warmth in my belly. The same overwhelming surge of rightness. But that doesn't mean anything. Right? I groan and rub my eyes. None of this matters. Ari doesn't seem interested anyway.

My phone buzzes, and I check the text. It's from Ari.

> Ari: I'll be there in a few minutes.

"Shit," I mutter, looking at the time. How has it already been almost two hours? I jump to my feet and pause as the room wavers slightly. "I have class." Ignoring my brother's goodbyes and the weird feeling in my head, I quickly make my way to my room.

Ari's leaning against the door and he pushes off when he sees me coming. "You ready?"

"Yep." I duck my head, avoiding his gaze. "Let me get my bag real quick."

In my room, I snag my bookbag and throw on my coat, and

when I turn back to the door, Ari's standing just inside my room. My brain isn't thinking properly, so when I look at him, I don't keep my eyes down. Instead, I let them travel up his chest to his face. Ari really is beautiful, with his animalistic eyes, blond hair that's always styled to perfection, and broad shoulders. I could stare at him all day. What would he look like with his hair mussed from my fingers?

Normally, I'm pretty good about not letting my intrusive thoughts win, but right now, thanks to Rho, I'm having a hard time fighting them. *Kiss him. Just kiss him already.* The thoughts are so convincing, and looking at his lips doesn't help at all. I remember how they felt against mine. Soft yet demanding. He kisses differently than Misha. While Misha kisses like he's trying to memorize every second, Ari kisses like he's trying to swallow my soul. And right now, I want my soul devoured.

I take a few steps toward him, and he turns to head out the door, so I grab his arm to stop him.

"Wha—"

Standing on my tiptoes, I press my lips against his, cutting off the rest of what he was going to say. Ari holds himself still at first, but when I wrap my arms around his neck, he pulls me against him and deepens the kiss. It's exactly how I remembered from that night. Ari devours me, and I give him everything I am. He kicks the door shut and spins us, pinning me against the wall. There is no space between us. His body is pressed so tightly against mine I can feel every hard inch of him.

I slide my hands into his hair, grasping the strands and tugging at the same time I rock my hips against his. Ari groans, the sound low and deep in his chest. It rumbles against my own, and I feel each vibration down to my core. His hands slip under my sweater and my stomach tightens at the sensation of his fingers running along my waist.

I'm burning for him. There isn't an inch of space between us, but I'm still not close enough. I want to feel all of his skin against mine. I want to know what kinds of noises I can drag out of him with my hands and tongue. Does he look as sexy and free as Misha does when he finds his release?

Ari pulls away, breathing heavily, and rests his head on my shoulder. "Aspen," he breathes. "We need to stop. You have class."

I shake my head, running my fingers down the ridges of his back. "I can skip."

His laugh is a mixture of amusement and pained wanting. "No. I won't let you skip class." He takes a step back, then another.

The space between us feels like a canyon stretching miles and miles. It's not surprising when my anxiety rears its ugly head. *He doesn't like me. That's why he stopped us. I forced him to kiss me, and he doesn't want that.* I swallow and take a breath, calming my racing heart. I can't meet his gaze as I pull the hood of my coat up to hide my face.

"Okay," I say quietly before opening the door and stepping into the hallway.

I shouldn't assume anything when it comes to these boys. Ari might not want to kiss me. Misha might not want to date me. We haven't had any kind of talk to figure out what we are. For all I know, they could have girlfriends back home.

A sharp ache follows that thought. Thinking of Misha and Ari with another girl is unbearable. Anger and jealousy spreads and grows like a creeping vine taking over the garden. I have no right to that jealousy, and I don't want to let it grow even more. So instead of dwelling on it, I ignore it. Like I do with all of my problems.

We're both silent as he walks me to class. The racing thoughts in my head won't stop no matter how hard I try to ignore them. *Why did I do that?* I'm not the type to make the first move. I'm too shy and too self-conscious to put myself out there. So why did I do it today? I silently curse Rho. I'll kill him the next time I see him. Tricking me into taking an edible.

Ari stops outside of my lecture. "Ezra will be here when your class is over. He'll bring you to the library."

I nod and step into the lecture hall, too embarrassed to look at Ari let alone say anything. Taking my usual seat at the end of the middle row, I pull out my books, and try to get into the headspace for class. It's impossible though. I can still feel Ari's fingers against my skin. I can still taste his mouth against mine. And the incessant self-destructive thoughts of Ari not liking me and not wanting to kiss me won't shut up.

Class is halfway through when I first notice it. A dark shadowy spot in a corner of the front of the lecture hall. I rub my eyes and look closer, but there's nothing there. Shaking my head, I tune back into the lecture, only to see the same shadowy blob, slightly humanoid in shape, standing behind the professor. I glance around, but no one else seems to notice it.

I rub my eyes again. Am I that tired? No. Of course it's not that. Fucking Rhory Grey. I'm so high I'm seeing things. I'll murder him. I squeeze my eyes shut, and when I reopen them, the blob is gone. I'm just settling back into the lecture when I notice a shadowy figure gliding through the rows of seats. No one bats an eye at it, but a few people shiver as it moves past them.

What the hell? I blink, and the figure disappears, only for another to pop into existence two rows in front of me. That one disappears in the blink of an eye as well, and when it reappears, it's standing at the end of the row I'm sitting in. A shiver crawls down my spine, and I roll my head side to side to ease the unsettled feeling. Slowly, I look behind me, and I have to bite my cheek to refrain from screaming. There are three shadowy figures behind me, standing in various rows.

I whip my head back around and dig through my bag for my phone. My fingers shake as I pull up Ezra's contact and send a message.

Me: Where are you?

Ezra: OMW. Why?

Me: Hurry. Please.

I take a deep breath and keep my gaze on my books in front of me. My leg bounces up and down and my heart patters so fast in my chest it's almost painful. Unable to sit still, I shove my books in my bag and pull out my phone again. *Don't look. Don't look around you, Aspen. There is nothing there. You're fine. You're fine. You're fi—*

Something brushes through my hair, fingers tangling in my curls, and a cold chill spreads over the back of my neck. I jump, somehow managing to contain my scream. But I can't sit here any longer. I shove to my feet and dart down the row. In my peripheral vision, I see a dark, shadowy shape following me. Picking up my pace, I run down the steps and push through the door, running smack into a hard body.

The golden eyes and messy blond hair immediately register in my panic. I grab onto Ezra's shirt and cling to him, breathing heavily despite not having run that fast or far.

"What's wrong?" he asks, immediately on guard.

"Some kind of spirit. A lot of them." Motion to my left draws my attention, and I muffle a scream in Ezra's chest. "There's another one."

Ezra frowns and looks around. "I don't see anything," he mumbles.

My eyes bulge. "What do you mean? There's one right there." I point a shaky finger down the hall to the black amorphous blob. "There were at least four in the lecture hall."

Ezra pulls his phone from his pocket and puts it to his ear before taking my arm and dragging me down the hall. "Where are you? We're on our way there. Yeah she left early. Something happened. No, she's fine. We'll be there soon." He slips his phone back into his pocket as we step outside into the frigid winter evening. "Misha and Ari are in the library."

The wind blasts me in the face, making my eyes water. But all that does is make the ghostly blobs appear blurry, because there are more of them outside. They line the covered walkway to the library and float about outside of it. I squeeze my eyes shut and press my forehead against Ezra's arm, letting him guide me.

"Are they out here, too?" he asks.

I nod, and Ezra wraps his arm around my shoulders, tucking my head against his chest. Shock almost makes me pull away from him. He's never willingly touched me like this. But he's also never not protected me, even when he makes his dislike of me so well known. So I press my face against his hoodie and squeeze my eyes shut, letting him lead me.

We make our way to the library like this, hurrying as fast as we can. When the warmth of the inside wraps around me, I peek my eyes open, but I don't relax. Especially when I see another of the spirits.

"Aspen!" Misha rushes forward and pulls me into his arms.

The fear that's been hounding me since I saw the first spirit dissipates with his presence. He'll keep me safe. I know without a doubt he will. With his arms around me, my heart finally slows down.

"Are you okay? What happened?" Misha asks, rubbing my back.

"Let's not talk about it here," Ezra says pointedly. "Do you have a table somewhere?"

Misha

WE LEAD ASPEN AND EZRA TO OUR TABLE ON THE second floor. It's become a habit of ours to take the most private study area we can find, usually the one in the back corner with the worn down couches. Aspen keeps her eyes closed, and I notice that when she peeks them open, she quickly shuts them again, burying her face in my sweatshirt.

I sit on the couch and pull her into my lap, grabbing her face in my hands. "What happened? What's going on?"

"There are spirits everywhere," she whispers. Aspen cautiously looks around, her eyes wide and her face pale. When she looks back at me, tears shimmer along her lashes. "What's happening?"

"What do you mean spirits? I don't see anything." A tear slips free, and I wipe it away with my thumb. "What do they look like?"

"Black, smokey blobs. Almost humanoid. They just hover there. I saw some in my lecture and the entire way here. There aren't as many in the library, but there are still a few."

I relax a little at her description. "They don't do anything? They just kind of float there?"

Aspen nods. "Yes. Except the ones in my lecture. They kind of swarmed around me. One of them touched my hair. What are they, Misha?"

"It sounds like lemures," I explain. "Most of the time, they're harmless. Lemures are restless spirits. It's pretty typical for there to be at least one lemure hanging around a lot of people. There are probably more here since there's a cemetery nearby, and this campus is old."

"Most of the time they're harmless?" she whispers shakily.

"They can become vengeful spirits if provoked. Lemures are people who were harmed in their past life in one way or another and never afforded a proper burial. Most of them are content to wander aimlessly. But if they become provoked, it's easy for them to drag up their anger and resentment and use that against humans."

"Are there supposed to be so many? And why can I see them all of a sudden and no one else can?"

I frown. "There probably shouldn't be as many as you're describing. Unless something awful happened on campus in the past, and a bunch of people died and weren't given proper burials."

"That's something we could look into," Ari says. "I honestly wouldn't be surprised if something like that happened and was covered up."

I nod. "Yeah. That's a good idea. And as to why you can see them ..." I tip her head up and stare into her eyes. They're glossy from unshed tears, but they're also a little red, her pupils bigger than usual. It could be because she's crying, but ... "Did you smoke anything today?"

She shakes her head. "I don't smoke." Then her eyes go wide, and her mouth pops open. "Rho gave me an edible. I didn't know that's what it was, or I wouldn't have eaten it. I don't like to do drugs. It always makes my anxiety worse."

"That's probably what it is then. Something about the weed has opened your senses to be able to see the lemures. My guess is, they sensed this, and that's why they swarmed around you. Normally, they just leave people alone." I cup her cheek and give her a kiss on the forehead. "You're okay, Aspen. Once it's out of your system, everything will go back to normal."

She rests her head on my shoulder, her entire body seeming to deflate.

"Wait," Ari says. "You're high?" He clenches his fists at his side, and the look he gives Aspen is a mixture of hurt and disbelief. He huffs and shakes his head before muttering under his breath and stomping away.

"Ari, wait!" Aspen sits forward, reaching a hand out like she'd grab Ari to stop him. But he's already disappeared into a row of shelves. Aspen's hand falls to her lap and she sighs.

"What's wrong?" I ask. "What was that about?"

Aspen shakes her head. "Nothing," she says quietly. "It's nothing."

It's obvious it isn't nothing. Even when she was afraid of what she was seeing, she didn't look this upset. Her entire demeanor changed in the blink of an eye. I take her chin and tip her head up. "Aspen, what's wrong?"

"I messed up," she whispers before dropping her head to my chest.

"How did you mess up, Dove?"

Her gray eyes are unfathomably sad when she looks up at me. "I kissed him."

Ezra snorts and walks away, causing Aspen's shoulders to curve inward even more.

"Aspen, you know I don't mind, right?" I tuck a strand of her hair behind her ear, letting my hands rest along her neck when I'm done. "Why do you think I had Ari go down on you over break?"

"I know you don't mind." Her brow furrows, and she frowns. "I mean, I don't know *why* you don't mind, but I know you don't. That's not what I meant. I don't think Ari wants me to kiss him."

Understanding dawns, and I can't help but smile. "First of all, trust me. Ari wants you. He holds himself to incredibly high standards, and he would never take advantage of a girl who was under the influence. He's probably upset about that, thinking he took advantage of you."

"But I was the one who initiated it. He didn't take advantage of me at all."

"I know. But that's not how he'll see it. Ari will think you only kissed him because you were high, and when he kissed you back that means he took advantage of the situation. You just need to talk to him. Tell him you would have kissed him whether you were high or not. If that's what you want?"

Aspen bites her bottom lip and lowers her gaze. "I do. What does that say about me that I want both of you?"

I hate the way she sounds ashamed of herself for admitting out loud what she wants. I can only imagine what she heard growing up about her mom being with three guys. I tilt her face up and smile at her. "It doesn't say anything about you, so don't even let that thought cross your mind." I grip her chin and give her a gentle shake. "And this brings me to my second point. I don't mind that you like Ari. I don't mind that you want to be with both of us. In fact, it's kind of a relief. I know what kind person Ari is, and I know he'll treat you the way you deserve to be treated. Things are uncertain right now, and knowing Ari is a second pair of eyes to look out for you makes me feel better." I smile at the way her eyes light up with hope. "I want you to know that I would do anything to make you happy. Sharing you with my best friend isn't such a sacrifice."

Aspen's lips wobble. "Why are you so amazing?" she breathes.

I laugh softly and lean down to kiss her. It's not hard to be amazing for her. Once again, I examine what it is about her that makes this so different from every other girl. And once again, I can't pinpoint what it is. It's just a feeling. A suspicion that I can't squash. Something deep inside of me that tells me this girl is *mine*.

"Why are you staring at me like that?" Aspen asks.

I realize I'm looking at her like I'm studying an insect under a microscope. Shaking my head, I smile. "Just lost in thought. Do you want to work on our lab project for a little bit?"

She looks toward the direction Ari disappeared to before nodding. "Sure."

"UGH," Aspen groans, letting her head fall forward to the desk. "I thought for sure that would work."

I quickly wipe the liquid that spilled from the top of the beaker. "Back to the drawing board."

While Aspen pulls her notebook in front of her to look over it again, I take the contents of the beaker and test tubes and dump it in the large container of bleach in the back of the room where it will sit until Professor Anderson disposes of it. I grab a new beaker, and as I walk back to our table, I look around the room to find the rest of the class struggling just as much as Aspen and I are.

"Calcium didn't work," Aspen mutters, crossing out something in her notebook. "And sodium didn't either." She taps her pen on the page, biting her bottom lip as she thinks.

I love watching her work, when she's deep in thought and the wheels in her brain are turning. She forgets about her insecurities, and I feel like I get to see the real Aspen.

"Oh!" she exclaims, sitting up straighter and turning to face me. Her eyes sparkle with excitement, and I smile. "What about potassium? It helps move nutrients into cells and removes waste out of cells. It's also a neuromuscular transmitter, so it works with neurons. This might be exactly what we need!" She looks at me and finds me staring at her with a goofy grin. "What?" she asks.

"You're cute when you get excited. But I agree. That might work."

Aspen gets up and heads to the cabinets for the potassium while I get the saline ready. Professor Anderson tasked us with finding a solution that would remove a poison that causes blood cells to attack neurons. Aspen's idea is brilliant.

We prepare our solution and drop some into the test tube of infected blood. She looks at me with a hopeful smile. "After you," she says, waving to the microscope.

I quickly drop some of the blood onto a slide and place it on the stage. After adjusting the lenses, I peer through. Keeping a straight face, I slide the microscope to Aspen and let her see for herself. I watch her reaction closely, because I know seeing her excitement will be everything. And I'm not disappointed.

Aspen straightens with a gasp. "We did it!" she exclaims with a broad smile that lights up her entire face.

If we weren't in class, I'd grab her and kiss her silly, her excitement is that contagious. Her statement gets our professor's attention, and she comes over to peer through the microscope.

"Well done. You found one of the two solutions. You may clean up, and head out when you're done."

Aspen smiles up at me, and I can't stop myself from pulling her in for a hug and kissing the top of her head. "Great job, Dove."

In my room after lab, Aspen suddenly gasps and sits up from the couch. I'm immediately on guard, searching for any threats, but I don't see anything.

"What is it?" I ask.

"Do you think Professor Anderson would let us borrow a microscope?" she asks, brows pulled down into vee.

"I don't see why not. Why?"

"What if we look at a sample of my blood? Maybe there's something we could find biologically."

I tilt my head to the side and think this through. "You haven't had any blood work done before?"

She shrugs. "When I was younger probably. I don't know. You're right. It's probably pointless." Her shoulders droop, and she slumps on the couch.

I toss aside the book I was studying and turn her to face me. "I didn't say it would be pointless, Aspen. It just seems like something the doctors would have already done. But I think it's worth a shot. At this point, I'm willing to try anything to find answers for you. Maybe Professor Anderson will have a theory."

I pull my laptop from my bag and send an email to Professor Anderson. When I'm done I flop on the other side of the couch and hold my arms open. Aspen puts her books down and lays on top of me.

"Thank you," she says.

"No need to thank me, Dove."

She props herself up to look at me. "Why do you call me Dove?"

I open my mouth, the answer on the tip of my tongue, but then I think better of it. If I tell her I saw her in my dreams before I ever met her, she'd probably freak out. So instead, I say, "Your eyes are gray, like a dove." It's not technically a lie. That's why I started calling her Dove in my dreams.

"Oh," she says simply.

"What? Is that not a good enough answer?" I grin and pinch her side.

Aspen squeals and tries to squirm away from me, but I grab her tighter. In her attempts at escaping, her thigh rubs against my half hard dick, and I groan. She goes still, eyes meeting mine as her cheeks flush with heat.

"You started this," I say hoarsely. "You better finish it."

She gasps. "*I* started it?"

I nod. "You did. You were squirming around."

"I was squirming because you were pinching me."

"Doesn't matter. You have to finish it now." I take her hand and push it between us, placing it on my erection and rolling my hips. *Fuck.* The way her fingers contract has my blood heating in seconds. "Shit. Now you really can't quit."

She gives me a shy smile and kneels between my legs. Her fingers move so slowly as she unbuttons my jeans, and each click of the teeth of the zipper sounds tremendously loud in the silence. My stomach clenches in anticipation of her touch, but she makes me wait. Aspen curls her fingers around the waistband of my pants and then stops. Her gaze travels to mine and something wicked swirls in the gray depths.

I'm just about to beg her when my door opens. We both whip our heads in that direction, and Aspen goes stiff.

"Shit," Ari mutters, turning away. "I'm sorry."

"Ari, wait!" Aspen cries.

He freezes with his back to us, hand outstretched for the doorknob. Aspen opens her mouth, then closes it. She chews on her cheek in uncertainty, and I know if I don't do something, she'll let this opportunity slide past. I sit up and gently dump Aspen from my lap. Her gaze stays glued to Ari. Shoving my desire back down, I quickly button my pants and walk out of my room. As I pass Ari, I give him a look. *Don't fuck this up.*

Aspen

Misha steps out of his room, giving Ari a look as he goes. I stand up, fidgeting with my hands while I wait for Ari to turn around. What should I say to him? I didn't mean to blurt out his name. It just fell from my lips unbidden when I saw him turning around to leave. Thinking of him walking away was unbearable. Since the incident in my room when I kissed him while high, he's been distant from me, only being around me when necessary. And I think I miss him.

Ari doesn't turn around. It's like he's waiting for me to say something, so I say the first thing that pops into my head. "Will you go to the ball with me?" I wince. It should be him asking me that, right? But since Misha won't be here, I had planned on going with the twins, but maybe making it more official will ease some of the tension between us?

He finally turns around and studies me with those all-seeing golden eyes. The space between us goes taut and he takes a step forward before jerking to a stop. Ari's jaw clenches making the muscles jump in his cheeks. He looks uncertain, and panic rushes through my veins leaving me clammy.

"Look," I blurt in an attempt to let go of all of my self-consciousness. "I don't know how to do these things. I'm shy and awkward, and I tend to just clam up and ignore everything. But I can't do that now. I kissed you because I wanted to. The edible just gave me the courage to actually do it." I twist my fingers together until they hurt. Looking at the ground, because I'm too scared to see his reaction, I continue. "Misha can see how much I like you, and he's willing to share if you are. I mean ... If you even want—"

I don't see him approach since I'm looking at my feet and consumed with embarrassment. When Ari takes my face in his hands and tips my head up, I gasp. He kisses me deeply, grabbing the back of my head and tangling his fingers in my hair. The kiss is so consuming I'm scared my knees will give out and I'll fall to the ground.

"It's never been a question of what I want," Ari breathes when he pulls away. He doesn't go far though. Our breaths mingle, and it takes me a second to reel back in from that kiss to understand what he said. "You call to me in a way no one else ever has. I haven't been able to get your taste out of my mouth, and I find myself craving it all the time."

"Then why ..." I let my question trail off, unsure how to word it without sounding weird.

"I didn't know what you wanted. Even after that night with Misha, I didn't know if it was just him or if you wanted both of us. I didn't want to pressure you by asking. You have so much going on right now, it seemed like something I should just ignore as best I could."

I stare up at him, at his beautiful eyes and strong jaw. His words register a beat later and I give him a hesitant smile. "I guess this is a prime example of how communication is key." My smile falls a second later as doubt creeps in like it inevitably always does. "But, are you sure you're okay with sharing? I mean, it's nothing new for me because I grew up with three dads. But I know not everyone would be okay with this."

Ari cups my cheek, and I lean into the touch, letting my eyelids flutter shut. "It's not something I've ever thought about or imagined happening. But I can't think of a better person to share with than my best friend. Besides, I think you're kind of worth it."

"Kind of?" I tease. I open my eyes in time to see him smile and close the distance between us.

"Okay. Maybe more than kind of," he breathes against my mouth.

I push onto my tiptoes and wrap my arms around his neck. His hands immediately grasp my waist and he tugs me hard against him so I can feel every inch of his body. I can't help but marvel at the fact that I'm kissing Ari and just seconds before I was kissing Misha. Is this how my mom feels?

Ari picks me up effortlessly, and I wrap my legs around him, and he carries me to Misha's bed.

"Do you think Misha will care that we're in his bed?" I gasp between kisses as Ari gently lays me down.

"Only if you don't invite me to join," Misha says petulantly from the doorway.

Ari and I both jump and turn to see Misha standing with his arms crossed over his chest and a spectacular pout on his face. My cheeks heat instantly, and I try to squirm away from Ari on instinct. He stops me with a hand on my belly and grins at Misha.

"Well, what are you waiting for?" Ari says and takes my wrists, pinning them above my head as he slides off of me to the side.

Misha chuckles and pounces, landing on top of me while being careful to keep his weight from crushing me. He gives me a gentle kiss and smiles. "Happy?"

I nod and the smile on my face grows until I giggle.

Misha's grin turns wicked. "Let's show Aspen how happy we can make her, Ari." Misha slides off and kneels on the other side of me by my head and unbuttons his jeans. "I believe this is where we left off before we were interrupted."

I reach out and help him free his cock before wrapping my hand around him. He groans and his hips thrust forward almost as if he has no control over his actions. I work my hand up and down, squeezing at the tip until a bead of pre-cum drips from his slit. Pushing myself up, I flick my tongue over his tip, tasting the salty drop of moisture, shuddering slightly, and not from pleasure.

Misha pulls away and looks at me. "Are you okay?"

I nod, and my skin heats. "I don't ... I don't like ..." Sighing, I push through the discomfort. "I have issues with different food textures. It's why I'm such a picky eater. Swallowing makes me gag. I don't like the texture."

Misha relaxes and cups my cheek. "That's fine, Dove. Don't worry about that." In a flash, his eyes go from sweet and caring to devilish and desperate. He threads his fingers through my hair at the same time he runs the tip of his cock over my lips.

Still laying on my back, I open for him and let him guide his length into my mouth, humming in satisfaction at the way he groans. But my attention is drawn away briefly as Ari drags up the hem of my shirt, exposing my black lacy bra. He bends down and closes his lips around my nipple through the fabric, gently biting until I moan around Misha's cock.

I pull away and gasp for breath, back arching in pleasure. "Please," I beg.

"Please what?" Misha asks darkly, stroking himself leisurely.

There's no way I can vocalize what I want. Thinking about it makes my face burn hotly. But as soon as I opened my mouth and begged, they both stopped. Now, they're waiting with smirks and wicked glints in their eyes, like they know exactly how hard it is for me to say this and are taking great pleasure in my discomfort. Frustrated, I take matters into my own hands.

I pull Ari up and kiss him. As soon as his body goes pliant against mine, lost in the kiss, I flip him over. I know he lets me flip him. There is no way I could do that if he didn't want me to. But now that I'm on top, I can control this. I slide my hands under Ari's shirt and slowly lift it until he sits up enough to pull it over his head. It's the first time I've seen him without a shirt. His pale skin stretches tight over his lean muscles. He's not as bulky as Misha, but no less defined.

I trace my fingers over his abs, watching as goosebumps erupt over his skin from my touch. It gives me a jolt to realize I have this effect on him. Even though I can feel just how aroused he is, there's something different about seeing him shiver from just my fingertips.

I lean down and kiss him again, letting him steal my oxygen and devour me. His hands trace up my arms and around my back so he can unclasp my bra. It slides down my arms, and he tosses it aside so he can cup my breasts in his hands and pinch my nipples between his thumb and fingers.

Pleasure shoots down my spine, and I rock my hips against his, eliciting a groan from deep in his chest. It's almost a rumble, like his tiger's growling happily inside of him. It vibrates through me, increasing the fire burning in my gut.

"Ari," I whisper against his lips.

He groans again, lifting his hips into mine. "Take off her pants, Misha."

I almost forgot Misha was here. Almost. It's not really possible to ignore the heat of his gaze as he watches me and Ari together. I get a little thrill thinking of the way he continues to touch himself as I lose myself in Ari. Then his lips are on my back, kissing a path down my spine. His fingers grip the waist of my leggings and panties and he yanks them off. I gasp and fall on top of Ari.

"You too," I breathe heavily. "Both of you." I kneel over Ari as he shimmies out of his pants, and I watch Misha slowly pull his own off. He hesitates when he grabs the hem of his shirt. "Shirt too, Misha. Let me see all of you."

When he finally drops his shirt to the floor, I reach out and gently trace the scars criss crossing his chest. Leaning over, I press soft kisses to the marks until Misha curses and tugs my chin to claim my mouth. I lose myself in his kiss, softer than Ari's but no less soul crushing.

I'm still kneeling over Ari, and I gasp when his fingers dance up the inside of my thighs, teasing and stroking higher and higher until he finally slips a finger through my folds. My hips rock, pleading with him to touch a little higher, and he thankfully does. His finger circles my clit, and I moan into Misha's mouth.

Misha grins and slides a hand down my chest, stopping to pinch my nipple almost painfully, before moving lower. When his hand bumps Ari's, he directs Ari's fingers to my opening, and they both push a finger inside of me. The stretch is perfect, giving me exactly what I need for now. My head falls back, and a sound falls from my lips that I'd be embarrassed of if I wasn't so distracted by the absolute pleasure they're driving me toward.

"Fuck, Aspen," Misha groans, kissing and nipping along my throat. "Do you like that? Do you like both of us inside of you at the same time?"

The dark promise of his words, the subtle hint of everything they can offer me, makes me clench around their fingers. Suddenly, it's not enough. I move my hips, seeking more, but it's still not enough.

"More," I gasp. "I need more." My gaze drops to Ari, his golden eyes burning so brightly they sear down to my soul. "Please, Ari."

He grins and slowly removes his finger, bringing it to my mouth. "What do you want from me, Aspen?"

I suck his finger into my mouth, cleaning my arousal off of his skin. "I want you inside me," I breathe when he pulls his finger away.

His eyes flash at my words. His pupils compress into vertical black slashes before changing back to normal. "Fuck," he growls, more animal than man, and yanks Misha's hand away. He grabs his cock and runs it through my folds, collecting my wetness.

We both moan, and when he angles himself at my entrance, I slowly sink onto him. He's not as big as Misha, but he feels just as amazing. Each inch I lower, the more my legs shake, barely able to hold myself up. When he's finally seated all the way inside, I pause and give myself a moment to adjust.

Ari's hands grip my hips tightly, and he stares at me with an emotion I can't wrap my head around at the moment. Whatever it is, though, it makes my breath catch. The space between us grows taut, and time seems to stop entirely as we stare at each other. No one else exists at the moment except the two of us. A warmth in my middle ignites, not too different from when I slept with Misha. I gasp at the sensation that feels so strange but so right, not able to focus on the sudden thought worming its way through the back of my mind in the intense pleasure.

Ari growls, a low sound that vibrates all the way through me, and then he flips us. It's like something inside of him snaps, and he drives his hips forward, thrusting inside of me in quick, hard motions. All I can do is grasp his shoulders, my nails digging into his skin, and hold on.

Pain prickles my scalp as Misha grabs a handful of my hair and angles my head. I open my mouth when he rubs the tip of his cock along my lips, and I greedily swallow him down. I'm at their mercy. I can do nothing but take what they give me, and I do my best to give it all back. It's hard, though, especially as my pleasure grows and my brain seems to short circuit. Forming a coherent thought is nearly impossible as Ari fucks me with everything he has, and Misha chokes me on his cock until tears spring to my eyes.

The first tingles of pleasure begin to crest, and I whimper around Misha's length, straining for the last bit I need to tip over the edge. They answer my wordless plea at the same time. Misha pinches my nipple, and Ari flicks a finger over my clit. My back arches, and I scream as my orgasm tears through me with wave after wave of mind blowing bliss.

When the last flickers of pleasure fade, I barely have time to catch my breath before Misha is pulling out of my mouth and spilling his cum all over my chest. Above me, Ari groans, his body stiffens then shudders, his release filling me.

I'm left gasping for breath, my limbs shaky, and my body feeling lighter than ever, like I could float away. Fingers brush down my cheek and my eyes flutter open to see both of the guys staring at me with similar expressions of wonder and happiness.

Ari leans down and kisses me deeply before standing and walking to the bathroom. Misha lays on the bed next to me and pulls me into his arms.

"Are you okay?" he asks quietly.

"Okay?" I ask blearily. My mind is fuzzy, filled with the remnants of pleasure that make it difficult to focus.

"Aspen," he says, gently taking my chin and turning me to face him.

It's hard to keep my eyes open. For some reason, I just want to curl up and go to sleep. "Misha," I manage to mumble past lips that don't seem to want to work anymore.

Misha brushes sweaty hair from my forehead. "Can you tell me if you're okay, Dove?" He chuckles as I hum contentedly and smile, cuddling closer to him. "I'll take that as a yes."

I hear the bathroom door open and the sound of feet padding across the floor. Then a warm washcloth is pressed between my legs. I gasp, eyes opening.

"It's okay," Ari says, quietly, kissing my temple. "I'm just taking care of you."

Warmth spreads through me. Besides Misha, no one has ever done that for me before. I close my eyes and relax again, letting Ari wipe Misha's release from my chest next. I sigh when Ari climbs into bed on the other side of me and wraps his arm around my waist.

"Sleep, Aspen," he says against the shell of my ear. "We'll be right here."

Aspen

MISHA HASN'T EVEN BEEN GONE FOR HALF A DAY AND I miss him already. He left this morning for winter break to spend time with his family. Before he left, he woke me up with coffee and a donut, and a sweet goodbye kiss. He's already texted me twice, but it hasn't helped the ache that's settled in my chest in his absence.

I don't know how I've gotten so attached to him in just four months, but I have. His presence is a comfort that I've gotten used to. His smile and his laugh are things that I look forward to to brighten my day and chase away my fears. I know I can count on him for anything, at any time. He's proven that to me over and over again.

I shake off the lingering melancholy as I make my way toward the little cafe on campus. There's still a couple of hours before I'm supposed to be meeting Ari there for lunch, but I don't want to be alone right now in my room with my feelings. The warmth of the cafe surrounds me as I step in from the bitter chill outside. I grab a coffee and look for a place to sit. I'm surprised to find Ezra sitting at a cozy booth in the corner.

I hesitate for a moment before going to sit across from him. While my relationships with Ari and Misha have grown, I still feel miles away from Ezra. He's never warmed up to me, despite the amount of time we've spent together. Even though he tends to be colder than it is outside right now, I still feel comfortable with him. After all, he's been there for me more than once when something bad has happened to me on campus.

"Hey," I say quietly, sliding into the seat across from him.

Ezra glances up from his phone, eyes glittering like frozen citrines, and grunts before tuning his attention back to his phone. I take that as a hello and pull a book from my bag. I haven't been able to read for fun as much as I've wanted, and I'm looking forward to getting as many books read as I can during break.

With Ezra's quiet presence across from me, I find myself relaxing and falling into the pages of the story. I let go of the constant worry I have whenever I'm alone, knowing he's here if anything were to happen. Not that I expect it to in the middle of the day with people around. Campus isn't quite as busy as it normally is. Many students returned home or went on vacation for the two week break. But there are still a decent amount of students and staff left behind.

I've made it through a good chunk of the book by the time Ari arrives. I don't notice his arrival, too absorbed in the story, but he plucks the book from my hands without any warning.

"Hey!" I exclaim, grabbing for the book uselessly. "I was reading that."

He grins. "I said your name three times, and you ignored me each time." He tucks the book into his bag, making me gasp in outrage. "I'll give it back after you give me some attention."

I glare at him and cross my arms over my chest. "Jerk," I mutter.

Ari winks at me and slides onto the bench beside me. His arm brushes mine, and I suddenly remember what happened between us last night. Between the *three* of us. My face floods with heat, and I quickly lose the glare, eyes widening instead.

Ari's smile grows and he leans toward me. "Hi, Aspen," he says quietly, before kissing me.

I expect a quick peck, we're in public and his brother is sitting right across from us. But he proves me wrong when he slides his tongue between my lips, urging me to open for him. I do, on instinct alone, even as my brain sluggishly tries to tell me to pull away. It's a lost cause, though. All I can do is meet his tongue thrust for thrust and melt.

Ezra clears his throat, and I finally find the strength to pull away, cheeks burning even hotter now. "Um, hi," I breathe, tucking my hair behind my ears.

"If you're going to do that, at least go somewhere I can't see it," Ezra grumbles, eyes glued to his phone. Then his head pops up and he stares at us with shocked eyes. "What the fuck?" he exclaims, like he's just realized what actually happened. "Misha hasn't even been gone a whole day, and you're already shoving your tongue down his girlfriend's throat? Are you fucking insane, Ari?"

Ari just chuckles. "Have you eaten yet, Ezra?"

"No?" he says, more a question than a statement. His golden gaze bounces between the two of us, trying to figure out what's going on.

Ari nods before going to the counter to order, leaving me with his twin. Instead of going back to his phone, Ezra leans forward and narrows his eyes.

"What are you doing?" he practically growls at me.

"What do you mean, what am I doing?"

"I've put up with you because I'm hoping you'll lead us to answers about Millie. But I won't stand for you coming between Ari and Misha. It's been the three of us for years, and I won't let you jeopardize that."

I barely refrain from flinching at his words. He's only putting up with me in the hopes I'll lead him to information about his sister? I knew he didn't really like me, but I didn't realize he hated me quite that much. And I don't want to look too closely at the way those words hurt. It doesn't matter if Ezra hates me. I tell myself that, but it doesn't ease the sting of what he said.

I lift my chin and cross my arms over my chest. "Put down your pitchfork. I'm not coming between Ari and Misha."

He raises a brow. "Oh yeah? Sure as hell looks like it."

"You don't know what you're talking about," I mutter, glancing at the counter and silently urging Ari to hurry.

"Just because your mom fucks three different guys doesn't mean you have any right to whore your way into our group and destroy friendships." His words are low and reverberate with a growl deep in his chest.

I rear back, heart lodging in my throat. Anger flares inside of me, along with hurt and something like shame that slithers through my stomach. The combination of emotions leaves me queasy. I open my mouth to give Ezra a piece of my mind, but I can think of nothing to say. My mind has gone completely blank, every thought erasing at the hurtful words he spat at me. I want to rage at him. To stand up for myself and tell him to back off. But I can't help but fall into the emotions of the little girl I used to be.

I can't help but hear all the times that word was thrown at me. *Whore.* Of course, they were calling my mom a whore, but that made it no less painful. It didn't make me feel any less ashamed. And now that I'm old enough to really understand my mom and her relationship with my dads, the shame that rears its ugly head sends me into a spiral. I'm ashamed to feel ashamed.

Ari returns with a tray of food before I can formulate anything to say to Ezra. Instead, I drop my gaze to the table, hands clenched tightly in my lap to hide how badly they're shaking. A grilled cheese with tomato slides into my vision, and I swallow the nausea that tries to climb up my throat.

Ezra sits back in his seat and takes the food Ari offers him, acting like nothing happened, like he didn't just tear me down with a few simple words. Ari doesn't appear to notice anything amiss, until he realizes I'm not touching my sandwich.

"Did you want something else?" he asks with a frown.

"Hmm? Oh, no. This is fine." I grab the grilled cheese and rip a small piece off, slowly popping it into my mouth. I chew and swallow without tasting it.

Whore.

My throat burns, and so do my eyes. I take a breath and shove the word far away, hopefully where I won't be able to hear it echoing anymore.

"Aspen?" Ari asks, his brows pulled down into a worried vee.

Before I can respond, someone calls my name.

"Pen!"

Relief floods me so fast and so hard I'm not sure I don't whimper with relief. I turn around and see Rho heading our way. His smile slips when he sees my face, and he stops at our booth and studies me for a moment before turning his glare on the twins.

"Hey, Rho," I say quickly, hoping to distract him enough to prevent him from saying something to them. "What are you doing?"

He shrugs. "Getting some food then heading back to my room. Just being lazy today before mom and company comes tomorrow." His gaze bounces between the three of us.

Ezra isn't doing a good job of hiding the hate in his gaze when he looks at me. Each time he does, I hear his words. Each time I hear them, a small piece of me shrivels and breaks away, like a leaf on a dying plant. I can't sit here anymore. I can't hide the hurt much longer, and I don't want to talk to Ari about it.

"Pen?" Rho asks quietly.

I push to my feet and grab my bag. "I'll join you."

The look on Ari's face tells me I didn't do a good enough job of hiding the tremble in my voice. "Aspen, wait."

I shake my head and grab Rho's arm. "I'll talk to you later," I mutter, before walking out the door with my brother.

Rho doesnt talk on the way back to his dorm, but he does shoot me the occasional questioning glance. However, as much as I had hoped, his silence doesn't last. As soon as the door to his room closes behind us, he turns on me.

"What's up, Pen?"

I shrug. "Nothing." Moving past him, I flop onto his couch and close my eyes, hoping to hide the truth from him. It doesn't work.

"Nice try, sis. But that's not going to work on me." He sits next to me, crossing his arms over his chest. "Start talking."

"Really, Rho. It's nothing. You know me. I overreact to everything, and I'm overly emotional." I glance at my phone, hoping to see a text from Misha. There isn't one. And it must show when my stomach drops and the weight on my shoulders increases.

"Aspen," Rho says gently. The fact he uses my full name and not the nickname I hate means he's being serious. "Please talk to me. I can't help if you don't let me in."

"There is nothing you can do to help." I exhale and decide to put myself out there for embarrassment in the hopes of distracting him. "Misha left this morning to go home for break. I miss him. That's all."

Rhory studies me with narrowed eyes. "While I'm sure that's true, that's not all that's bothering you. You can't hide things from me, Pen. I know you too well. And based off the vibe in the cafe I picked up on, it has something to do with that Ezra kid."

Why can't my brother be the stereotypical jock? This isn't the first time I've wished he was more braun than brains. Unfortunately, he's incredibly perceptive which is part of the reason he's so good at lacrosse. He's also so in tune with me, sometimes I think we might as well be twins, despite the year difference between us.

"It really is nothing. I promise," I say, exasperation thick in my voice. This is the last thing I want to discuss with him. Not only will he lecture me about letting people get under my skin, but he'll probably make an effort to harass Ezra as well. "Can we just drop it?"

Rhory purses his lips, and, for a second, I think he won't let it go. But luckily he does, even if he doesn't sound happy about it.

"Fine. But you know I'm here if you need anything. And if I ever find out that bastard has done something to you …"

I nod. "Yeah, yeah. I know."

Rho grins and grabs the remote for his T.V. "Wanna watch My Mom is Dating a Vampire?"

Eara

"I THINK WE NEED TO BE PROACTIVE," ARI SAYS, sprawled on his bed. "Things have been too quiet, and we're at standstill. We're getting nowhere."

I grunt an agreement from my spot on his couch. The ball is tonight, and while we bide our time until we have to get ready, we've been discussing what we know about Millie's death in the hopes of finding something we missed. So far, we're coming up empty handed.

"What are your thoughts?" I ask, keeping my eyes closed. I've been exceptionally grumpy the past two days, and it's taken too much effort to remain civil with Ari.

"I can't stop thinking about how Millie had to meet with Malvanado, the same as Aspen." Ari sighs and sits up on the edge of his bed. His blond hair is uncharacteristically mussed, a sure sign of his stress.

I nod. "What are you thinking?"

"We need to get into his office."

Slowly, I sit up, a grin spreading across my face. "Now we're talking."

Ari rolls his eyes. "Tonight may be our best opportunity. All of the staff on campus will be distracted with the ball. You're better at picking locks than me, so you can be the one to break in. I can keep watch on Malvanado and make sure he doesn't try to go to his office while you're there."

"What about Aspen?" I ask, and immediately regret it. That girl is going to be the death of me. She is always in my thoughts, no matter how hard I try to not think about her. It sends me in a rage whenever her name comes to mind or an image of her eyes floats to the surface. The tension in my neck and shoulders has been off the charts lately. Why can't I just ignore her?

If I'm being honest with myself, the reason I've been so pissy the past two days is because of what I said to her at the cafe. It was totally uncalled for, but I can't stop myself from lashing out at her. If I don't, I'm scared I'll find myself caring. And I don't want that. For so many fucking reasons. The biggest being that she's with my best friend. And I'm not going to think about how she kissed Ari yesterday. That only makes my anger burn hotter. I hate that I care. I hate that I'm jealous of Misha and Ari. I just fucking hate all of it.

"I figure she can go with you. Two sets of eyes are better than one." Ari frowns at me and purses his lips. "Don't be a dick to her, though. I don't know what you said to her the other day, but don't do it again."

I have to actively unclench my jaw as a sharp pain radiates outward from how hard I'm grinding my teeth. "I'm not going to pick sides when you fuck up things with Misha," I growl, my tiger pacing anxiously in my chest.

Ari laughs. "Who said I'm going to fuck things up with Misha?"

I give my twin a pointed look. "No one has to say anything. Kissing his girlfriend is a pretty big middle finger thrown right at him."

Ari leans forward, resting his elbows on his knees. "He knows, Ezra. In fact, he was the one who insisted on Aspen kissing me first."

I stare at him, blinking as his words slowly register. Well, isn't that fucking great. Not only did I call her a whore for no reason apparently, I also get to watch my twin and best friend get wrapped around her fucking finger.

"This better not get in the way of what we're here to do," I say darkly. The irrational anger simmering just beneath the surface is getting harder to control. I don't know why I'm so on edge around her, or why the thought of both of them with her makes me want to slowly choke the life out of them.

Ari sighs. "It won't, Ezra. Relax."

"Are you sure it's a good idea to have Aspen come with me? Isn't it too dangerous for her?" I really don't want to have to watch out for her while I'm searching Malvanado's office for information.

"It'll be fine. Besides, Malvanado might notice us watching him if she's with me. If he has any kind of interest in her, I want to keep her out of his sight."

I grudgingly agree. It makes sense, but it doesn't mean I have to be happy about it.

"How much time do you think you need?" Ari asks.

I shrug. "The more the better. If I have to pick any locks it will take even longer. Try to at least make sure I have fifteen minutes."

Ari nods. "Will do. I'll text you if he starts to head toward his office so you guys can get out of there." He stands from his bed and stretches. "I'm going to shower. We're meeting Aspen at 7:30 in the lounge on her floor. Don't be late."

FOR THE HUNDREDTH TIME, I stick my finger in the neck of my white button up and tug. The stupid thing is already driving me nuts, and I've only been wearing it for twenty minutes. Growling softly to myself, I tug on the tie to loosen it, then undo the first two buttons, breathing a sigh of relief.

"Stop fidgeting," Ari says, exasperation tingeing his words. He glances at my now disheveled appearance, and shakes his head. "Dramatic much? It's just for one night. You'll live."

"I can't help it. It's like being choked to death."

Ari looks like the epitome of a rich billionaire. He's wearing the same crisp, slim black tux with a white button up as I am. His blond hair is styled like usual, slicked back with every strand in place, but with the fit, it makes him look more sophisticated. The only difference in our clothes is the pale blue bowtie he's wearing. Of course, I attempted to style my hair, but in the end I just put some gel in it and mussed it up, at least sweeping it to one side to expose the shaved side of my head.

I hear voices coming from the lounge on the second floor before we get there. My back stiffens and a frown tugs down my lips. I recognize her brother's voice. The annoying one that plays lacrosse. If I had known he'd be here, I would have just met Ari and Aspen at the ball. Something about that guy makes me want to shove his face into the wall. Repeatedly.

We round the corner, and I find myself stopping in my tracks. Aspen's entire family is here, but I barely notice them. My gaze is drawn to Aspen, and I can't look away. She's ... stunning. The gown she's wearing hugs every curve, highlighting her hourglass figure and making her hips and chest absolutely mouthwatering. Midway down her thighs, the skirt flares out in layers of flowing tulle. The low cut bodice is dark blue, fading into a stormy blue-gray on the skirts, with the very bottom a bright, pristine white. Golden gems encrust the top and skirts in swirling patterns. And sheer dark blue sleeves flutter off of her shoulders to her elbows.

My mouth goes dry as my gaze travels over her. With her black hair curled in loose ringlets and the sides pulled back to expose her elegant neck and throat, she looks like a fucking goddess. If my feet hadn't been rooted to the floor, I would have turned around and fled. Like a fucking chicken. There is no way I can spend any time alone with her tonight. Not with her looking so ... tempting.

As Aspen's soft laughter pulls me from my daze, I blink to find her smiling up at Ari like he hung the fucking moon in the sky. My stomach clenches, and I swallow back the green writhing thing that climbs up my throat. To distract myself, I glance around the room to find her brothers dressed in nice tuxedos, and her mom and dads smiling at Aspen and Ari.

I've never been good with this type of thing, and it's probably best if I keep my mouth shut and stay out of the way. Crossing my arms over my chest, I lean against the wall, and watch from the outside as Aspen introduces Ari to her parents.

"A shifter?" her dad with the long silver hair says. "What kind?" His ice blue eyes glow with animal intensity. That one is Sterling Harrison. I can see the resemblance between him and the lacrosse brother.

"Tiger," Ari replies with ease. "Both me and my twin." He hooks a thumb over his shoulder in my direction.

I refrain from shrinking against the wall as their attention turns to me. It doesn't stay long though.

"I thought you were dating a mage?" the one with black hair says. He grins wickedly at Ari, fangs glinting in the light. Malakai Thorne, vampire prince. And Aspen's bio dad.

"He's home for break," Aspen says, brushing her curls over her shoulder.

I notice she doesn't elaborate on the fact she's also dating Ari. But Malakai Thorne narrows his gray eyes on Ari all the same.

"She spends as much time with Ari as she does with Misha," her brother pipes up, bumping Aspen with his shoulder and grins.

"Shut up, Rho!" Aspen hisses through her teeth.

Aspen's last dad, the one with violet eyes, smiles. "It's nice to meet you, Ari."

I cast a glance at her mom, the harpy. She doesn't look like anything special. I mean, she's gorgeous, but she doesn't look like a harpy. I don't know what a harpy would like, but I never expected a short woman with curly brown hair and amber eyes. Eyes that tear up as she looks at her children.

"You guys look so good," she breathes, covering her mouth with her hands. "Sterling, you did great picking out Aspen's dress. She looks beautiful."

Once again, my gaze is drawn to Aspen, and I couldn't agree more with her mom. In my chest, my tiger prowls restlessly. It's like this whenever Aspen is in my presence, but it's even worse right now with her standing there looking like … that.

Before I know it, she's saying goodbye to her parents and Ari is putting his hand on her waist, directing her out the door. I start to slip away, but stop in my tracks at the sound of a low growl.

"Watch your hands," the vampire says, fangs bared.

Ari raises his arms in surrender and nods his head in apology.

"Kai," her mom hisses. "Leave them alone."

I wait for Ari and Aspen to pass me, keeping my eyes on her dad before following them. As I walk away, I hear someone chuckle, and I think it's the mage.

"No wonder she never brought dates home. She was too scared you'd eat them, Kai."

"Rhory, Adrian, keep an eye on her," Malakai says darkly. "I don't trust them."

"Oh, quit," her mom says.

I don't hear the rest of the conversation as I get too far away for even my shifter senses to pick up.

"Your dad seems nice," Ari says drily.

Aspen sighs. "He's all talk. All I'd have to do is tell him to stop and he would. I have him wrapped around my finger."

"You probably have all three of them wrapped around your finger."

"You're not wrong."

Walking behind them, I can't see her face, but I can hear the smile in her voice. Her dads won't be the only ones wrapped around her finger. I guarantee Misha and Ari already are. And if I'm not careful, I'll find myself there, too.

STEPPING into the grand ballroom is like stepping into another world. Green garland wraps around the wooden beams spaced evenly through the room, twinkling lights hidden amongst the pines. Blue and silver ribbons drape over archways and doors. And the ceiling has been spelled to look like the night sky with gently falling snowflakes. Silver candelabras hold blue candles with silver flames that dance merrily in a stray breeze. A DJ is set up on a raised stage at one end of the space, and students already mill about, talking and dancing.

I'm not one to marvel at scenery, but Aspen's face when she enters the ballroom is something I could look at forever. Her gray eyes go wide and her mouth drops open on a silent breath of air. She positively glows as she takes in the space.

"Okay," Ari says, leading her across the room to a darkened corner. "We'll wait until there are more people here, more of a distraction, before you guys head to Malvanado's office."

Aspen nods, just as the DJ plays a slow song. She glances at Ari with a shy smile.

He smiles back at her, taking her hand. "Want to dance while we wait?"

I don't linger to watch them stare at each other with gooey, lovestruck expressions. The thought makes my tiger bare his teeth in frustration. I head to the table set up along the edge of the room with various hors d'oeuvres and bite-sized desserts. I snag a glass of pale pink bubbling liquid and take a sip, barely refraining from gagging. Of course any alcohol they served on campus would be so weak it couldn't even get a fly drunk.

I find a shadowy spot along the wall and lean against it, watching everyone on the dance floor have fun. My gaze keeps traveling to Aspen, no matter how hard I try to stop it. Her smile is contagious, and I find my lips tugging up when she laughs at something Ari says. But as soon as I think of Ari, the reason why she's laughing, my smile falls. Fuck this. I grab another disgusting drink and down it in one swallow, grimacing. I desperately need something stronger.

About thirty minutes later, the ball is in full swing. Ari and Aspen find me in the shadows. Aspen's face is flushed a rosy hue, making her even more beautiful. It's hard to keep my eyes off her.

"I think we're good," Ari says, glancing around. "Malvanado is over by the DJ. I'll keep him in my sights. If he heads your way, I'll text you."

I nod, and grab Aspen's wrist. "Okay. Let's get this over with."

Aspen

I follow Ezra out of the ballroom. The air is cooler in the hallways without the mass of bodies dancing and having fun. I release a breath as it hits my skin, cooling the sweat beading along my hairline. I've never been big on events like this. Too many people, too hot, and too loud. And being the center of someone's attention while you dance has always been uncomfortable for me. I always end up worrying about where I should put my hands, who I should look at, and what to talk about.

But with Ari, it came naturally. There were no fears about stepping closer to him, resting my head on his shoulder, and tangling my fingers in his hair. There were no awkward silences or pressure to fill the quiet between us. And any conversation we did have flowed easily. I enjoyed being in his arms, having his fingers trail over my shoulders and down my back.

But now isn't the time to think about that. I keep my attention on my surroundings as I follow Ezra through Old Main. Butterflies flutter nervously in my stomach when I think about what we're doing. Breaking into a professor's office and going through his things. If we get caught, we could get expelled or worse, arrested. This is quite possibly the stupidest thing I've ever done.

Professor Malvando's office is on the third floor. It's quiet up here, and it's strange to be here with no one else around. With the lights off, the spookiness of Old Main is increased tenfold. The skulls sitting in the niches along the walls stare at us with their pitch black eyes, and I can't stop myself from shuddering as I imagine things watching me from the shadows.

Ezra leads us to Malvanado's door, and he drops to his knees, pulling something out of his jacket pocket. My mouth falls open when I realize it's a lockpick set. He hands me his phone with the flashlight on and gets to work on the door.

"Do you pick locks often?" I whisper, keeping my attention on the hallway around us while shining the light for him to see.

He grunts. "Sometimes it was the only way to get food for me and Ari."

His words make me realize I don't know about the twin's history. Why would Ezra need to pick locks to get food for them? I don't have time to wonder about it though. Ezra stands and slips the picks back into his pocket.

"Come on," he whispers, pushing open the door.

"How do we know there aren't wards to alert Malvando we're here?" I ask, hesitating in the hallway.

"These picks are spelled to break any wards without alerting the owner," Ezra replies, stepping into the room. "Cost me a fucking fortune," he mutters.

I glance around the office that has become familiar to me, and a chill crawls down my spine. I really hope Ari's doing a good job of keeping his eyes on Malvando. What would he do to us if he found us in his office?

"I'll take the desk," Ezra says. "You can check the bookshelf."

I nod and step up to the shelf. I'm not really sure what I'm looking for, but I scan the titles on the spines, seeing nothing that jumps out at me. An old worn journal is stuck between two newer textbooks. I pull it down and flip it open, peering at the pages. It looks like an old grade book. Nothing remarkable.

My fingers trail over the books as I continue my search. When I pass over a dark green leather tome, a spark jolts me back—like when you touch a doorknob during the winter and the static electricity passes between you and the knob. The book looks older than all the rest on the shelf. The letters on the spine are so faded I can't make out what it says, so I slowly reach out and pull it down.

The cover is slightly bumpy and the corners and edges crumble a little from age. It's warm in my hands. Unnaturally warm. It's like there's a fire burning between the pages, heat emitting out from the cover. Before I'm able to flip it open, Ezra curses.

"Fuck," he growls, grabbing my hand and tugging me down behind the desk. It's uncomfortable crouching in my dress, the fabric too tight around my hips to let me move easily. "There's someone in the hallway."

He shoves me under the desk and crawls in behind me. We quickly turn off the flashlights on our phones, plunging the space into darkness. Ezra must have picked up the sound with his tiger senses, because even with my slightly heightened hearing, I can't make out anything. All I can hear is my heart pounding in my chest and my breath stuttering in my lungs.

The space under the desk isn't that big, and Ezra's body crowds against mine. I can feel the heat pouring off him. As a shifter, his body temperature runs higher than non-shifters. And as I'm part vampire, my body temperature always runs just slightly cooler. It's almost impossible to ignore how close Ezra is to me, with that heat radiating from him and soaking into my skin. His face is inches from mine, his eyes glowing softly, and I can see every swirl in their golden depths.

I suck in a breath and immediately regret it. He smells good. Really good. Like sandalwood and fresh cotton and something that is strictly Ezra. At the soft sound, his gaze drops to my mouth, and we're so close I can clearly see the way his pupils contract into vertical slits. I'm reminded of the time in the cemetery, when we almost kissed, and my heart flutters.

But then I hear it. Footsteps in the hallway. We both freeze when the knob turns, and the door is pushed open. I look at Ezra with wide eyes, silently asking him what we're supposed to do. He gives me a subtle shake of his head.

"Hm," the person says. "I could have sworn I locked all the doors after I swept."

I hold my breath, straining my ears to catch every sound. The door closes and the lock turns, then the footsteps retreat. I heave a breath, shoulders dropping as the tension in me evaporates.

"The janitor," Ezra mutters, before climbout out from under the desk.

He reaches down for my hand, and I take it without thinking, letting him pull me to my feet. We're inches from each other again, this time he's holding my hand. His fingers tighten before he drops it, stepping back.

"Did you find anything?" he asks, his hushed voice rougher than usual.

I hold the book, still not sure what it is exactly. It's no longer pulsing with warmth, though. "Only this. What about you?"

He shakes his head, then jumps slightly when his phone vibrates. "Yeah?" he asks, holding it up to his ear.

I hear Ari's panicked voice on the other end. "I lost him. I looked away for a second, and when I looked back, he was gone. I don't see him anywhere down here. You guys need to get out of there."

"Fuck," Ezra curses, shoving his phone into his pocket. He takes the book and tucks it into his jacket before grabbing my hand.

At the office door, he listens for a moment, checking to make sure there's no one in the hallway, before leading us out. I walk on my tiptoes, trying to keep my heels from clicking too loudly on the tile floor. As it is, I'm breathing so heavily it probably echoes all the way to the other end of the hall.

We've just slipped into the stairwell, when Ezra freezes. The door at the bottom of the stairs opens, and then someone's climbing up. Ezra pulls me back into the hallway and hurriedly looks around. Seeing a shadowy alcove, he shoves me into it, pressing himself against me so our chests are touching. I watch his throat work on a swallow, his head turned to the side as he listens for approaching footsteps.

"Ezra," I whisper, staring at him. We're not hidden. The alcove is darker than the hallway, but we're still visible.

He keeps his head turned, but he raises his hand and places it on the wall next to my head. I'm about to say his name again, when he suddenly turns to face me. I don't have a chance to react when he lowers his head and presses his mouth to mine. My body freezes, all of my senses narrowing to the place where our bodies touch. Then his other hand is cupping my jaw, sliding to the back of my neck and tangling in my hair.

Ezra is kissing me. I want to push him away, to tell him to fuck off. I'm not the whore he thinks I am. But the anger is short lived. Ezra's tongue sweeps into my mouth and steals every coherent thought in my head.

I barely notice the stairwell door opening and footsteps approaching before halting at our not-so-hidden hiding place. Ezra kisses me like he's trying to claim my soul. His body presses mine harder to the brick wall, and I can feel every hard angle of him. My arms lift on their own, and I wrap them around his neck, holding him tighter.

"You're not supposed to be up here," Professor Malvando says gruffly. "Break it up, and head back downstairs."

The sound of his footsteps receding barely registers in my mind. A moan climbs up my throat unbidden, and Ezra swallows it down, angling my head and kissing me even deeper. I'm burning. If this doesn't stop I'm going to combust. My head is fuzzy, pleasure filled and confused. Torn between wanting more and wanting to push him away. I want to drop my hands to his pants and free the hard length that presses against my thigh. I want his lips on my throat, my shoulders, my nipples. I want to rip his hands off of me and claw at his face until he bleeds. But the longer he kisses me, the harder it gets to hang onto the anger. The more I just *want*.

Suddenly, Ezra pulls away. I gasp for air, and a cool breeze passes between us sending a shiver across my skin at the sudden loss of him. Ezra's eyes are dark but his jaw is clenched so hard I can hear his teeth grinding. The tendons in his neck stand taut, and he angrily runs his hands through his mussed hair.

"He's gone," he says gruffly. "Let's go."

Oh. Right. There was a reason he did that. It's not because he wanted me. Of course not. Ezra fucking hates me. He was making sure we were hidden. I press my hands to my overheated cheeks and follow him, blinking as I try to ground myself. We don't say a word to each other as we walk down the stairs, and the silence stretches between us like a rubberband pulled too tight.

Ari's waiting outside of the ballroom, bouncing on his toes nervously when we emerge from the stairwell. The music still plays, the dull thumping bass making my head ache in time to the beat. Relief washes over Ari's features when he sees us.

"You didn't get caught?" he asks. "I swear, I don't know what happened."

Ezra only grunts and pulls the book from his jacket before handing it to Ari. "This is all we got." He waits for Ari to take it, then he turns and heads for the main doors.

I watch Ezra leave without a word or backward glance. I can't comprehend the emotions inside of me. Why are my eyes suddenly burning? Why does my heart hurt like he ripped it from my chest and stomped on it? Where is the anger that I so desperately cling to when he's around? My cheeks heat in embarrassment. I fucking kissed him back like he was the very thing I needed to survive. And it meant *nothing* to him. Why do I care?

"Aspen?" Ari says, taking my hand. "Are you okay?"

"Fine." My voice is soft and choked as I try to hold back the infuriating tears. "Let's go. I don't want to stay any longer."

THE NEXT FEW days pass in a blur of hazy numbness. It's been awhile since I've shut down like this, but it's really no surprise it happens now. Sometimes I get too overwhelmed and everything becomes too much. Each sound, touch, and thought bombards me like ice pellets relentlessly falling from the sky. When this happens, I shut down. My mind dissociates in an attempt to re-regulate. If I don't, I'll crack, and all the ugly parts of me will seep out.

I spend the time in my room, the lights off and curtains closed. I barely get out of my bed. The Wandering Fey softly plays on repeat, just enough of a distraction to keep myself from thinking, but not enough to overstimulate me. My phone is off because I don't want to talk to anyone, and whenever someone knocks on my door, I ignore it. I know it's Ari. And I know he's worried, but I just need time to put myself back together.

On the third day, my door opens and I groan. Rho lasted longer than I thought he would. I'm kind of surprised he wasn't here on the first day insisting I talk to him.

"Hey, Pen," he says quietly. "I brought you some food and water. I figured you probably haven't been eating."

"Thanks," I mumble, not even bothering to open my eyes.

He sighs, and the bed dips as he sits on the edge. "Can you at least drink the water? Please?"

I groan as I sit up, leaning against the headboard, but I grab the bottle of water and take a sip.

"Ari's been worried about you. I don't really like the guy, but I have to give him props for coming to me and asking me to check on you." He gives me a wry smile. "I told him you'd be fine and that you just needed some time. He didn't like that answer. I thought he was going to try and bust down your door, so I decided it would be better if I came in and talked to you."

I rub my eyes, trying to force myself to feel more alert. It doesn't help a lot, but some of the haze dissipates. "Thanks," I whisper, taking another drink of water.

"I know what you're going to say, but I'm going to ask

anyway because I'm your brother, and it's my job." He pokes me in the side to get my attention, and I reluctantly turn to face him, my eyes glued to his chest instead of his face. "Do you want to talk about it? About whatever has put you in this funk?"

"It's a lot of things," I mumble. A lot of things piled up and up and up until I couldn't carry the weight of them anymore. "And, no. I don't want to talk about them."

He nods in understanding. "As long as you know I'm here if you want to. You can always tell me anything, Pen."

"I know. Thank you," I whisper, blinking as my eyes burn. Ugh. I hate when I get like this, and every little thing makes me want to cry.

Rho looks at me like he understands. I know he doesn't really get it. Most people don't. Unless they have ever experienced the way everything feels wrong. The way even your skin doesn't feel the way it should. The way everything feels like it's against you, trying to tear you down and make you crumble into pieces. But at least Rho has never told me to suck it up or ignore it. He at least understands that I can't help it. Once it starts, there is no stopping it. He may not truly get it, but he supports me no matter what.

"I'm going to shower. Thanks for the food." I slide out of bed and past Rho.

He stands and grabs my wrist. "Can I give you a hug?"

I turn my gaze inward, cataloging how I feel. Imagining Rho wrapping me in his arms. A shiver walks down my spine, and my skin feels like I want to rip it from my bones. Shaking my head, I give him a small, apologetic smile. "Not right now."

He nods and heads toward the door. "Make sure you eat. And let me know if you need anything."

When the door closes behind him, my shoulders slump. Already, I'm exhausted. Just that little bit of interaction took so much of my energy. Thankfully, my bathroom buddy is home for the break, so I don't have to worry about running into her, and I'm able to shower for as long as I want.

While the hot water cascades over me, I let myself dip into my thoughts, slowly. The thing that pushed me over the edge was kissing Ezra the night of the ball. That kiss, along with Misha being gone and everything going on with the mysterious ghost stuff became too much for me.

Ezra. I shake my head and close my eyes, letting the water run over my face. While I feel safe around him, and he's proven to me he'll protect me, I've only ever felt frustration with him. He's cold and harsh. The words he spits my way are usually hurtful. Most of the time, his attention on me is negative. So why did it hurt so much when I realized that kiss was only to distract Malvando, to keep our identities hidden?

I won't lie that I find him attractive. At least in terms of appearance. He looks almost identical to Ari, afterall. But his personality is the polar opposite of his twin. In that moment though, shrouded in darkness with his overbearing presence looming over me and invading every one of my senses, it was hard to remember why I don't like Ezra. And when he kissed me like he was trying to claim me, the way my body burned and craved more, it muddled every coherent thought I have about him.

Even now, the phantom touch of his lips, his hips pressed against mine, that spark inside of me flickers to life. It wants to ignite. It wants Ezra to fan the flames until I'm burning, burning, burning.

When I finally step out of the shower, I don't have the energy to do anything with my hair. I brush it and throw it in a ponytail, not caring that it's still wet. Grabbing a donut from the food Rho brought me, I turn on my phone, and text Ari.

Aspen

The next day, I walk by myself to the library. I snuggle into the warmth of my coat, and hurry my steps. The wind bites through the fabric and threatens to rip the hood off of my head. It's bitterly cold outside, and tears spring to my eyes from the frigid temps. There aren't many people on campus, and the ones who are, are similarly dressed, hurrying on their way with their heads down.

I told Ari yesterday that I'd meet him in our usual study spot in the library after lunch. He tried to convince me to meet with him yesterday, but I still wasn't quite ready for that. After some persuasion, he reluctantly agreed. I only hope Ezra isn't there. I don't think I'm ready to face him.

As I step into the library, the warmth surrounds me, and I groan, wiping the stray tears from my eyes. The usual peace I feel in the library settles deep inside of me, and I'm glad to be able to experience it again. I was scared I had lost that comfort after everything that has happened to me here. But there's something about being surrounded by books that will always provide me a sense of welcoming.

I hurry up the steps and find Ari already sitting on the couch in our back corner study area. He sets his book down and pushes to his feet when he sees me.

"Aspen." He rushes toward me and pulls me into his arms.

I melt against him. The usual discomfort at being touched

mysteriously missing when I'm in his arms. For what feels like the first time in days, I take a full breath.

Ari pulls away, just enough to take my face in his palms and study me. Those golden eyes scan my face, taking in everything. Finally, he smiles and says, "Have you eaten?"

I nod. "Yeah. I ate with Rhory and Adrian."

"Good." He takes my hands and draws me to the couch where he sits and settles me next to him. "What are you going to read today?"

He mentions nothing about the past few days and how I disappeared. I'll have to thank Rho for that, probably. He most likely told Ari what happened and to not bring it up. One of the few times I don't mind Rhory meddling in my life.

I pull my phone from my pocket with one hand and hold out my other. "Can I borrow your earbuds? I can't find mine. I want to listen to an audiobook."

He passes them over, and I quickly sync them to my phone. As I put the buds in my ears and pull up the book, Ari kisses the top of my head. I snuggle against him and close my eyes, losing myself in the lilting voice of the narrator. The book I picked is a sweet MM romance with nothing spooky or too emotional. I can't handle any of that right now. And as I listen to the words, with Ari's warmth surrounding me, I feel myself slowly piecing back together.

I've made it a quarter of the way through the book when someone presses a kiss to my forehead. I open my eyes and barely contain a shout. Ripping the earbuds from my ears, I sit up and throw myself into Misha's arms.

"Misha!"

He catches me, falling backward onto the floor with a laugh. I collapse against him and tuck my face into his neck, breathing in his scent. With his arms around me, and Ari sitting on the couch behind us, the world seems to have righted itself.

"I missed you," I breathe against his skin.

"I missed you too, Dove." He sits up, taking me with him.

I can't help but stare at him with a silly grin. It seems like it was forever ago he left, even though it was only a few days. "I thought you were supposed to come back in a few more days?"

He nods, his smile slipping for a moment. "I was. But Ari called me, and I decided to come back sooner."

Oh. Well. That's great. Because of me he didn't get to spend as much time with his family. I'm tempted to say something to Ari, but I bite my tongue. They were worried. I get that. They don't really know me that well to know this is just something that happens occasionally.

Misha takes my chin in his fingers and lifts my head so I'm looking at him instead of his chest. "Hey. It's okay. I was looking for a good excuse to come back early anyway. Being away from you ..." he purses his lips as he thinks of what to say. "I didn't like the way my ma—" He cuts off, shaking his head. "I didn't like it. Being with you is exactly where I want to be."

I exhale and lay my head on his shoulder, loving the way his fingers brush up and down my back. Unfortunately, I don't get enough time to enjoy the moment. Someone behind Misha clears his throat, and my body tenses. I refuse to look at Ezra. As I've thought through what happened between us, I decided the best thing for me is to pretend it never happened, and to ignore Ezra as much as I can.

"Well, isn't this cozy," Ezra drawls, and I don't fail to hear the slight notes of disgust in his voice.

Remembering the words he spit at me at the cafe, I get up from the floor and sit back down on Ari's lap. Let Ezra see me being *cozy* with his brother while Misha is standing right there. Misha sits next to us and pulls my legs across his thighs. When he slips off my boots and digs his thumb into the arch of my foot, I let my eyes close and rest my head on Ari's shoulder. It feels amazing.

"Tell me what happened while I was gone," Misha says as he continues my massage.

Ari fills him in on the night of the ball and how Ezra and I broke into Malvando's office. "What was the book you found anyway?" he asks me.

I shrug. "No clue. I haven't looked at it." But I bend down and pull it from my bag, handing it Misha.

Not only was I trying to not think about that night and everything that happened, I was honestly just too scared to look at it alone. It hasn't warmed in my hands the few times I've touched it, but I know I didn't imagine it that night.

Ezra sits in the chair opposite our couch, and leans forward. "Well?" he asks Misha.

Misha frowns. "It's old, that's for sure." He flips the cover open and his mouth drops. "Sacrifices for Spiritual Bindings." Misha slowly raises his gaze to Ezra. "What the fuck?"

My blood runs cold, and I shiver in Ari's arms. That's the book I pulled off the shelf in Malvando's office?

Ezra turns to me with a frown. "Why'd you grab that book?" he asks gruffly.

I shrug uncomfortably, not really sure I want to tell them what made me take the book. "I was running my fingers over the spines, and when I touched that one it was like I was shocked by static electricity. When I pulled it from the shelf, it was warm in my hands."

Misha frowns and hands me the book. "Is it still warm? Do you feel anything now?"

I shake my head before I even grab it. "No. I haven't felt anything since that first time."

I slide to the floor and set the book on the low table. My fingers tremble slightly as I run them over the dark green cover. It helps knowing all three guys are with me. This is the first time all of us have been together since Misha and Ari and I hooked up. The fear isn't overwhelming with them here. But when I grasp the corner of the leather, a sense of foreboding settles over me. A shiver works over my body, and I get the weird sensation of time slowing to a crawl.

I flip to the first page, the paper yellowing and brittle, the ink faded to wispy gray. Without thinking, I trace the first line of the text, reading quietly. "Spiritual bindings have been used …" As my finger runs over the page, the letters shimmer and wobble. I yank my hand back and gasp as the ink that's been printed onto the pages follows my hand, drawing from the paper and soaking into my skin. I stare at my hand in horror as the ink swirls and eddies before settling and disappearing. But the words that had been on that page now echo in my mind, like they belong there. Like the knowledge from them has been part of me this entire time.

"Wh- wh-" I can't form the question. My body shakes and my gaze is glued to my palm like I can still see the swirling ink that had been there seconds ago.

"Holy shit," Misha breathes, taking my wrist and turning my hand this way and that. He looks at the book, at the missing lines of text.

"What the fuck was that?" Ezra growls, placing his hands on the table and glaring at the pages like they'll give him the answer he demands.

Ari's hand lands on my shoulder and squeezes. I look back at him, seeing a clarifying light glow in his golden eyes. When he opens his mouth to speak, I hold my breath, knowing I'm not going to like what he has to say.

He looks at me with wonder and shock, cupping my cheek in his hand. "Aspen," he breathes. "You're an ink eater."

End. For Now.

Acknowledgments

This book was hard to write for many reasons. One of which being Aspen is very much me. While I'm still discovering who I am, it's been cathartic to write Aspen and put my own anxieties, insecurities, and quirks onto paper. I just hope people treat her kindly.

This book wouldn't have happened without the constant encouragement from Lou, my forever cheerleader. Thank you!

I also want to thank my beta readers, Meg and Leslie, for the criticism to help get this book where it is today.

As always, thanks to my hubby for always giving me the time and space to write.

And finally, to my readers. I keep doing the writing because you keep doing the reading!

About the Author

 Whitney L. Spradling is a neurospicy, full-time Occupational Therapist and autism mama, who has had a dream to write and publish a novel since she was a little girl. She lives outside of Cincinnati with her husband, son, and two cats.

She is a strange mixture of Disney adult, elder emo, and board game nerd with a love of tattoos, k-pop, skulls, moths, bees, Gengar, and otters.

When she is not writing, she can be found in her craft room making custom tumblers, watching C- or K-Dramas, or curled up with a good book and a cup of coffee.

More by Midnight Tide Publishing

See the full catalog at:

www.midnighttidepublishing.com

***

Heat Of Seas by DeAnna Hill

SOME ARE LED BY DESIRE.

After the mysterious death of the kingdom's queen ushers in a deadly plague, Carnaxa, Princess of Antalis, is promised to a rival kingdom. As ancient prophecies unfold, not only is Carnaxa in danger, but the fate of her kingdom as well.

Meanwhile, Anara, a gift of sorts and nothing more, was taken from her homeland. She didn't realize giving her heart away would keep her emotionally shackled, mirroring the physical chains she wore.

OTHERS ARE LED BY DUTY.

Captain Thylas has guarded Carnaxa since the day he washed ashore. When he's asked to accompany her to marry another, he finds himself torn between serving his kingdom and the desires of his heart.

Ereon, the Prince of Shaston, was raised in blood and battle. Faced with an uncompromising demand, he must choose between his birthright and his destiny.

WHEN DESIRE AND DUTY CLASH, LEGENDS ARE MADE.

Of Hearts and Hunters by Cynthia Brubaker

He's a Vampyr.

I'm a Korama.

And I love him.

Tough-as-nails Verity 'Veri' Eadaoin has never trusted Vampyrs. They've killed everyone she loves. She finally gets an opportunity for revenge after a deadly Vampyr raid against her pack. Her new mission: retaliate against the Vampyr Queen by killing her newly-minted Prince. Simple enough. But Verity is unprepared for her encounter with the unsuspecting Vampyr.

Still reeling from his murder in Saguenay, Darren Pierce-Crané is freshly-turned and reluctant. He's barely begun to adjust to his unlife when there's a wolf at his door. Darren barters for his survival, resulting in a precarious pact with Verity. This deal uncovers sinister secrets that could spell the undoing of the entire city.

War is on the horizon, and time is of the essence. Verity and Darren will have to decide what is most important to them: their faction or each other.